When Eden Falls

This book is a work of fiction. All names, characters, places, organisations, and events portrayed in this novel are a product of the author's imagination and used fictitiously.

ISBN (Paperback) - 978-1-7393578-1-8
ISBN (eBook) - 978-1-7393578-0-1

2023 First Edition

Cover design – Dissect Designs
Copyright © 2023

WHEN EDEN FALLS

ALANA FAYE WILSON

Authors Note:

When Eden Falls is recommended for readers 18 years and above.

This story includes violence, blood, death with references to suicide, as well as scenes of a sexual nature, including attempted force.

Some scenes maybe found disturbing.

*Only the darkest skies
can reveal the depths of the universe.
Never give up!*

PART ONE

The Myth

Chapter One

It was a myth, but the question was, how much of this ancient myth was fundamentally true?

It was said the human race originated from a distant planet called Earth. Three thousand years ago, our species fled the planet Earth to find salvation from the demons who killed everything and spared nothing. Images of savage beasts with multiple eyes and deadly fangs filled our ancient texts, with claims they emerged as a punishment from the Gods for mankind's century long mistake. Towns and cities were brought down, food supply became non-existent. The people were left with no choice but to leave to search for a new home.

They searched the cosmos for centuries, finally discovering a habitable planet in a red dwarf star system. For those who survived the endless search in the darkness, years of suffering followed. Years full of disease and hunger, where primal instinct became a necessity. Only the fittest survived. Only the warriors who called themselves the Nux triumphed against the odds and were able to create a new world. My world—Allura.

To a species whose average life expectancy was sixty-eight years of age, three thousand years was an eternity. The context of any story could've been distorted in that time. I had often wondered if the myth only existed to justify why we honoured the ancient Nux temples scattered throughout our two continents. On Allura, everywhere you travelled the temples were identical. Circular sanctuaries made from black Alluran stone, with high pitched roofs and heavily inscribed walls. Even though the Alluran people were now segregated into five nations, we all worshipped the Nux; the warriors who delivered us salvation when humanity faced its darkest years.

I sat at the helm of the Alluran Solarfleet ship, The Orka, staring at the small figurine of a Nux warrior sitting in the centre of the control panels. For as long as I had flown with Rooke Maddox, this tiny figurine was always kept visible on the bridge. His black boots and gold painted armour glistened in the artificial light. A golden sword scaled down his back with an archer's bow slung over his shoulder. His facial features barely distinguishable from years of wear and tear. When and where Rooke had originally got it from, I didn't know, but its presence was meant to give the crew the courage and motivation to continue our task, to succeed, to thrive.

I was reaching for that inspiration now. Deep down I felt unnerved, restlessly apprehensive. This mission was like no other. Never before had a Solarfleet crew been permitted to exit the safety of the Alluran solar system. No crew had ever been assigned to a task without a definitive directive.

The Alluran Solarfleet was primarily used to transport employees and mining produce to and from the several mined moons and asteroids orbiting our sun. Vessels like The Orka were used for research missions to study the potential for said mineral mining, whilst others scouted the edges of the solar system, checking for approaching comets or other potentially catastrophic entities. But no ship had ever ventured outside of the safety zone...

That was, until now.

Six months ago, one of our scouting ships went missing. One month later, their distress signal was picked up. And somehow, five months following that discovery, here I was, piloting The Orka across the depths of space, tracing that very same distress signal. Where we were going, we had no idea. We only knew the signal had stopped moving and we were getting closer.

"Looks like we've cleared the asteroid field."

The tenor voice startled me out of my trance. I looked across the control computers and met a pair of young, friendly brown eyes. Troy MacIntosh, my co-pilot.

I glanced towards the driving window, only darkness and billions of twinkling stars met my gaze. "There didn't seem to be many."

"There wasn't." Troy tapped on a screen in front of him. "We seem to be approaching the signal fast now. I estimate only another fourteen hours and we'll be on top of it."

I walked around the dozens of screens towards him. "Judging by how the signal disappears every eight to twelve hours, I'm starting to believe it's on a planet or moon." We both surveyed the charting data in front of us. "Where the hell are we, Troy?"

He shook his head. "I don't know. The more I think about it, the more this feels like a disturbing horror story."

I grimaced. "Don't start scaring the crap out of me. I'm already questioning my decision to join Rooke on this mission." My current nightmares weren't helping either.

The sound of footsteps scurrying along the metallic floor echoed through the bridge doorway. We both looked up as Cora entered holding a thick, hard covered book. Wearing the standard blue-grey jumpsuit, her curly golden hair neatly pulled back, her light green eyes shone with excitement. Stopping between Troy and myself, she placed the old book on the flat surface before us. "I think I know where we are." Her pretty face beamed, glancing between us.

"What are you talking about?" I asked, genuinely baffled.

"We've just passed through a barrier of sparsely segregated asteroids, yes?"

"Yes."

"And over the last couple of days we've passed two gas giants. One being a bright planet with a dividing ring, the other with red and orange stripes."

"Yes." I looked at Troy, who was frowning at Cora.

She smiled, opening the book up to a marked page. An illustration of a red, white, and orange planet, with a brown-red swirling spot in the southern hemisphere, dominated the faded paper. "I've looked closely at the images The Orka took whilst scanning the area, and they are the exact replica of this planet. The other was further away, but it clearly resembles this planet." She

5

turned the page, displaying a yellow planet with a thin but wide ring.

Peering at the pages, both Troy and I were still baffled. Cora jumped on the spot. Her young eyes filling with overzealous excitement. "This solar system was charted thousands of years ago. This is the ancient Sol system."

I straightened up and loosed a breath. "Cora, are you sure? They could be two very similar looking planets."

"The characteristics are exact. And meeting the asteroid ring was too much of a coincidence to deny this logic." She pointed to another page showing the layout of the planets orbiting a yellow dwarf star. A ring of asteroids sat in between planetary orbits of Mars and Jupiter. "We are currently flying through the orbital line of Mars. I have no doubt about it, we are heading towards Earth."

I rubbed the back of my neck, unnerved by the discovery. "And you're certain?"

Cora huffed. "Yes!"

"Does Rooke know?"

She shook her head. "I wanted to pass it by you first."

I rolled my eyes. "I am not the commanding officer."

Cora shrugged her shoulders. "Close enough. Besides, he's asleep. Never wake a sleeping baby and all that." She grinned, catching Troy's eye as he laughed.

"He's a twenty-eight-year-old man," I said. "He's not a baby."

"Yeah, yeah. He just likes his sleep."

A gruff voice rumbled from the corridor. "I can hear you, you know?"

Watching Cora squeeze her eyes together with a grimace, I chuckled. She leant into me and whispered, "I'll leave you to tell him the news." She fled to the doorway, only to be met by Rooke's commanding form as he emerged from the kitchen area opposite. Holding a metal bowl in one hand and a spoon in the other, he scooped in a mouthful of porridge before saying, "Tell me what?"

Cora gaped at him. "How did you hear that?"

"I hear everything." He flashed her a teasing glance. "Even when I'm asleep."

Cora tsked, shooting an awkward look at Troy, before scurrying out the door. Rooke watched her go, taking another spoonful of breakfast.

I eyed him as he wandered fully onto the bridge. He was on the tall side of average; lean but strong. His white skin was mildly tanned, and his dark hair was short and tidy, joining up with a neat line of stubble around his jaw. His eyes were a dark shade of green. They looked almost black in some lights, and I would know. I had lost myself in those mesmerising eyes more times than I would ever willingly admit. Although, unbeknown to Rooke, himself. Thankfully.

He met my gaze and sniffed, swallowing down his mouthful. "Did I hear that correctly?"

"Which part?" Troy joked.

"The part," Rooke shot Troy a playfully disapproving look, "about our location."

I nodded. "Apparently. What are your thoughts?"

"Believe it or not, I had come to the same conclusion yesterday."

"What? Why didn't you tell me?"

Rooke downed the last traces of porridge directly from his bowl and placed it on the side, spoon on top. Wiping the corner of his mouth with his fingers, he said, "I was going to. I wasn't entirely convinced at first. It was a farfetched possibility. But hearing the resident astrogeologist voice the same opinion, I feel certain about it now."

"So, we're going to Earth?"

"Theoretically, yes." Rooke searched my face. A frown formed on his brow. "You look petrified, Eden."

"Aren't you?"

Rooke shrugged permissively, glancing at the multitude of data screens around us.

"I thought Earth was a myth," I said softly, walking over to the driving screen.

"Clearly, it isn't."

"But…what are the chances that a scouting ship goes

missing, only to be potentially found on mythical Earth? It seems too…too convenient."

Rooke appeared next to me. He was half a head taller and far broader. Together, we gazed out the driving window, pensively watching the endless darkness.

"So, what's the mission objective?" I asked tentatively.

"The same as it's always been. We find the missing ship. If the crew are alive, we escort them back home."

"And if they're not alive?"

Rooke took a deep breath. "Then we find out what killed them."

As simple as that.

Chapter Two

I woke with a start.

It had been the same dream for the past two months. The same haunting memory was plaguing me and leaving me with a painstaking ache in my chest. There was always a funeral, always a coffin—I remember it so vividly. But it was never my brother laying inside. It was Rooke.

I rubbed my face with my hands, trying to fight the daunting confusion from consuming me. My brother, Jacob, had been gone nine years, nearly ten. It had taken me half that time to accept he'd died, and years to understand his heart was a ticking time bomb ready to strike at any moment. We hadn't realised he had a heart condition. It was only after he died the coroner discovered his abnormally bulbous heart was diseased.

Rooke had been playing hockey with Jacob when he'd collapsed, dying in his arms just a few minutes later. I still remembered Rooke coming to the house with a police officer. I still remembered how I'd lost all sense of control as I was told the devastating news, and my sobbing became uncontainable. To my surprise, it had been Rooke's arms comforting me. It was Rooke who sat with me for hours, holding me whilst my mother dealt with the loss in her own way. I'd been fifteen at the time.

Before the events of that agonising night, Rooke had simply been an annoyance to me. Since I was eleven, he had been my older brother's best friend, and at the time I hated him. For a paranoid girl who was going through the awkward stage of development, he used to taunt and poke fun at me, and my brother endlessly encouraged him.

I grew up resenting him, slowly finding the courage to retaliate and bite back at his comments. Our interactions usually turned into a ping pong match of banter-ish bickering, resulting in me sulking and Rooke grinning when he realised he'd finally won. And he always won.

I smiled at those memories, at how trivial they seemed now. But our relationship had changed entirely the day Jacob died. We'd helped each other through the initial grief, then kept in touch, even when life took us in different directions. It had been Rooke who encouraged me to follow in his footsteps and become a pilot for Solarfleet. It hadn't taken much persuading.

I pondered the thought, the memories it surfaced, and it still amazed me how my brother's infuriating, teenage friend, who had bullied me with malice, had won my esteem and respect, and was now a friend—my closest friend. But as the years had trickled by, I'd discovered something deeper about myself. Something about how far my esteem for Rooke went. It had struck me a couple of years ago, when he was considering leaving Solarfleet…

I was in love with him. I'd follow him to the ends of the universe without a second thought. Well, my current situation clearly proved that.

But I could never confess the truth. How could I? He was an attractive man, oozing with confidence and charisma. His girlfriends were stunning, the type of women you'd see in old movies or beauty campaigns. He'd never look at me in the same way he did them. To him, I was his best friend's little sister, a sister he had adopted and taken under his wing. And I would never allow myself to jeopardise the strong foundation of our platonic and working relationships.

What we had worked.

So, I kept my secret locked up inside, trying to disregard it on a daily basis.

But this recurring dream…it was messing with my head. No matter how hard I tried to bat it away, I couldn't help thinking something bad was going to happen—that Rooke would be taken from me. There was nothing normal about this mission. It screamed danger and uncertainty from the start. And now that there was a chance we were heading to mythical Earth—my paranoia tripled. I was petrified.

With that thought in mind, I discounted how tired I was. I showered and dressed, immediately heading for the bridge.

Rooke sat alone in front of the wide, curving driving screen. He looked up as I approached. "We're nearly there." He inclined his head towards the window before looking down at his handheld computer. I peered into the darkness outside, and sure enough, there in the distance, a spherical object was coming into view. Although it was just a tiny glimmer of light, it was larger and far more defined than any other specks on the vast horizon.

I sat down next to him. "Do you still believe we're approaching Earth?"

"Yep." He sounded confident. "Cora sent me a mountain of information on Earth and the ancient Sol system. It's pretty conclusive."

"And that doesn't worry you?"

Rooke searched my face and sat up straighter. "This mission has always been a mystery. I don't know what to expect, nobody does. So, the fact we have information on our destination must be seen as a benefit."

"Yes, okay, but…"

"But what, Miss Pessimist?" He smirked.

"But," I huffed away his teasing, "if the Earth part of the ancient myth is true, so could the horror story about why the human race left. Weren't there demons roaming the land?"

"It's been three thousand years. And truths and stories get morphed. I wouldn't be surprised if our ancestors fled because the land no longer held any nutritional value. If my memory serves me correctly, my science teacher always preached in disgust how the ancients' antics damaged the biodiversity of the natural ecosystems. I won't be surprised if we find a barren land full of nothing."

11

I lounged back in my chair, a deep resounding sigh escaping me. I wasn't convinced.

"Don't worry," Rooke's voice chirped. "I'm not taking any risks. We're taking plenty of weapons down for protection."

"You sound like we have an army. There are only seven of us."

"Eden, stop worrying." He lent forward and squeezed my hand. The green in his eyes twinkled with reassurance. "If I knew you were going to be this finicky, I would've left you on Allura."

I stuck my tongue out at him. "You wouldn't have dared."

Pulling his hand away, Rooke chuckled, then glanced towards the doorway. "Speaking of seven, where's number eight?"

"If you mean Troy, he's saying his farewells to Cora."

"Farewells?" Rooke rolled his eyes. "I'm planning on us being away for a day not a month."

I pouted my lips to one side and shrugged. "They're in love."

"Having a quickie in cupboards and behind locked doors is not love."

"I didn't realise you were such an expert."

Rooke threw me a glare, which made me laugh. "Oh, come on, Rooke. They clearly like each other. It's been going on for months now…"

"Too long, in my opinion." Rooke huffed. "Just because I've graciously turned a blind eye to it, does not mean I encourage it. Nux, if Solarfleet found out, they'd likely reprimand *me* for allowing it to continue under my command."

"Solarfleet do allow relationships."

"Not quickies in cupboards whilst on duty." He tapped the radio mic on the dashboard in front of him. Well aware he was broadcasting to the whole ship, he announced, "Troy, I don't care what position you and Cora are currently in, I need you on the bridge. Now."

I shook my head. "You are so mean."

Rooke was grinning mischievously. He shrugged. "If they wanted to be discrete, they should've done so from the start."

*

Two hours later, a blue and white planet filled the view of the outward windows. I sat at the driving screen, carefully guiding The Orka into orbit. Troy sat beside me, reeling off numbers to aid my task. The task itself was easy, but it had become far more demanding due to the number of old satellites floating across my path. Trying to concentrate, it was hard not to wonder where these satellites had come from. If they were from thousands of years ago, wouldn't the Kessler effect have happened already?

Not taking my eyes off the screen, I asked, "Has anyone checked if those satellites are live?"

"They're obsolete," Rooke's voice rumbled directly behind me. He stood, watching with his arms across his chest. "Most look damaged."

Placing the ship at the correct angle, I locked the controls. We were in high orbit, floating around a world that shone with vibrant colours, different to those of Allura. I was in awe. It was beautiful, like nothing I had ever seen before. Earth.

"There's life down there," said a firm voice from the control panels behind us. I looked back at the ship's scientific advisor, Kobe Chang. His tall, slim body was hunched over the screens. His almond shaped eyes frantically scanning the data in front of him.

"A lot?" Rooke asked, striding to his side.

"Yes," Kobe replied. "I can't determine what form from this altitude. The planet could be covered in algae for all we know."

"So, we don't know what we're walking into?" I said sceptically.

Rooke shot me a nonappreciative look before analysing the information Kobe was referring to. "We're still going down."

Within an hour, we had packed and boarded the smaller, streamline ship attached to the side of The Orka. Parvos bore a sleek set of wings for atmosphere control, and a complex, durable, atmospheric thruster system for flight and take off. The flight deck was at the front of the vessel, sitting up high behind the pointed nose, where the upper section of the outer wall and curving roof space were transparent. The dashboard spanned the width of the small cockpit, leaving only enough room for the two pilot chairs.

I sat in the confined area, initiating the engine start up, rechecking the atmospheric information Kobe had given me. The hubbub of activity and conversation resounded throughout the metallic ship, and I heard delicate footsteps approach. Glancing over my shoulder, I smiled at Zamya, our medical officer, as she emerged in the restricted area.

"I need to check your temperature," she indicated for me to offer access to my ear, "just in case it drastically changes whilst on the surface."

"Do you think it will be very different from Allura?"

She zapped my earhole with a gun like contraption. I watched her read and document the result in a handheld computer, pausing to push a strand of silky, black hair behind her ear.

"It looks as though the air will be a tolerable pressure and breathable, but it's the bacteria that concerns me. I've told Rooke we should remain in our suits. I don't want anyone picking up something I can't treat."

"Wise decision."

"Apparently, I'm full of them today." She overemphasised the arch of her pristine eyebrows. "I asked Rooke if I could sedate Cora. Her excitement is doing my head in. He critically said no."

I chuckled. "Cora's excited. This is every geologist's dream."

"It should be every biologist's dream, but this biologist is full of nauseating anxiety and dread."

I assessed the look on Zamya's petite face. The warm brown skin of her forehead appeared sweaty. Her usual hard expression replaced with one of worry and suspense. I tapped her arm. "It's normal to feel anxious. Cora is just an exception."

"A lunatic, if you ask me."

Rooke appeared behind her. "I hope you're not asking Eden for permission to sedate Cora."

I rolled my eyes. "As if she would."

"I would," Zamya said abruptly, "if it was completely necessary." She pointed at Rooke. "Don't tempt me, commander."

Rooke smirked and ushered her petite frame out of the way. "We're ready to leave. Go belt up."

She left while Rooke took his seat to my right. We both clicked our safety harnesses on, placed our radio earpieces over our preferred ear, covering them with our inflight helmets. The dark glass of our visors dispersed the overpowering glare of the sun and bright atmosphere below.

Once the rest of the crew were secure, Troy's voice came through our earpieces. "De-docking sequence has been successful. You're ready for departure."

"Copy that," I confirmed.

"We'll keep you posted on our position and situation," Rooke said to him. "I plan to be back for dinner."

Troy chuckled. "I'll make sure it's ready and waiting."

"Do you know, Troy," Rooke chimed, "you'll make a wonderful housewife one day."

"Is that a proposal, sir?"

"Nah, you're not my type. Too hairy."

Troy laughed.

"In all seriousness, though," Rooke continued in a more solemn tone, "if we lose contact, you know the procedure."

"Yep. Thirty-two days."

"And then you head home."

There was a pause. One I felt an emotional tug towards. The responsibility to abide by that rule was a harrowing thought to anyone, let alone the twenty-two-year-old we were leaving behind.

"Yes," Troy finally replied. "Following no contact for thirty-two days, I'll head back to Allura without you."

Rooke nodded pensively. I couldn't help glancing at him. He *was* nervous, just capable of hiding it well. He snapped out of his short-lived stupor and said, looking my way, "Right. Let's get this over and done with."

Within thirty minutes we had made atmosphere entry and I was flying Parvos over a vast blue ocean. The sun was high in a sky of sapphire blue. The signal getting closer.

A vast fringe of land appeared on the horizon, and as it grew nearer, lush textures of green reaching into the sky came into view, spreading for miles and miles. I'd never seen green trees before. The ones we had back home were yellow or orange, with thick swirling trunks that didn't reach anywhere as high as the ones I was viewing.

I glanced across at Rooke and said, "A barren land full of nothing, yeah?"

Rooke's eyes were wide, analysing the glorious sight. He was speechless, shaking his head in awe.

Allura was beautiful, full of gold tinted water and cascades of orange and yellow foliage falling from hillsides and caverns, but it was a poor second to this. Here on Earth, the land was covered in vibrant colours. The sea water was continually changing from sapphire blues to turquoise. The land shone like honey gold along the coastline, transforming into a richer red further inland. The trees were a mix of emerald and lime greens, casting elongated shadows of dark jades and indigos across acres of forest and meadow. The span of both land and ocean were immense, causing a wave of insignificance to fall over me.

"This is insane," Rooke murmured. The first sound he'd uttered since entry. "Why would anyone leave a land this beautiful?"

"They must have had their reasons." Which worried me.

Rooke pointed north-eastwards. "The signal is coming from that direction."

I realigned the ship, lowering our altitude and initiating the thrusters to slow down. We flew over the edge of the land, skimming the coastline. Less than twenty miles along, a large silver shape emerged from behind a dense rockface. We flew past, assessing the scene from above.

Partially submerged under a mound of fallen boulders was the Solarfleet scouting ship, Challenger. The front of the ship had disintegrated into the rockface where jagged metal panels bent backwards at haphazard angles. The rest of the silver body showed signs of breach damage along the lower areas of the hull.

I steadily circled the area, confidently taking us lower with each pass. "I'd be surprised if anyone survived a crash like that."

"That's an atmospheric ship," Rooke mentioned. "I don't understand why they crashed. The ground next to the sea edge is flat and wide enough to land on."

"That ship is old. I doubt it's been in atmosphere for years. And they could've misjudged. The air is humid. It could've caused issues with their descent. Humidity isn't something we're used to."

"You don't seem to be having trouble."

"Don't jinx it, Rooke."

He grinned. "Always the sceptic."

As I took another pass over the wreckage, Rooke sat forward and pointed to an open area of land further north. "Can you take us down over there?"

"You're planning on landing already?" I glanced at him, shocked at his premature decision. Standard procedure for any research mission was to scan the area from the air for at least an hour before landing, to give us a better perspective of what to expect on the surface.

"We've found the wreckage. Let's go investigate."

"Are you sure?"

"This isn't a standard mission."

Reluctantly, I nodded, lining the ship up for landing. The honey-gold strip of land, set in between the sea and a steep line of vertical rockfaces was more than twenty miles long and at least half a mile wide. Theoretically, landing should be easy.

With the humidity, the descent was unexpectedly rapid. I felt the ship attempt to slip from my control. Holding my breath, I waited for the landing gear to extend fully. It clicked into place just in time for the wheels to strike the ground. Thankfully, the landing was smooth and resilient. As I pulled the ship to a halt, my heart was thumping against my chest. I slumped back into my chair, finding it hard to release my hold on the driving levers.

Nux, that was close.

Rooke's chuckle echoed in my ear. I glared over at him,

unappreciative of his response. He was grinning at me devilishly. No sign of relief or worry whatsoever. "I knew you could do it." Taking his helmet off, he stood up and tapped my shoulder. "You're the best pilot I know."

As he walked out of the cockpit, I called after him, "And you can be a condescending bastard, Rooke Maddox."

He looked back and winked before flashing me a teasing smile. It was a good thing I liked him.

After contacting Troy on The Orka to confirm we had landed, I found the crew in the rear-section of the ship, fidgeting into their atmospheric suits. The blue reflective material was light but inflexible. Although streamlined and easy to manoeuvre in, they weren't the easiest garment to pull on.

Rooke approached offering me a suit. "Kobe's confirmed the air is nontoxic. Signs of life are primarily in the water with some on land, but not in the direct vicinity." I eyed him warily. He was trying to convince me his swift tactics were plausible.

Zamya caught my eye. She was still brooding over the situation. It was apparent I wasn't the only crew member he needed to convince.

Once we were all suited up, our slimline helmets attached, and our oxygen supply compressed, the only way we could communicate was through the radio integrated into our helmets. I watched our two military crew members, Oz and Sym, open the airlock to the rear loading door. They walked down the landing ramp, their large guns raised to attention, scouring the area for any form of hostility. The scientific crew members always referred to these two as The Muscle. I'd known them both for two years.

From behind, the two soldiers looked indistinguishable. Both men were at least six-foot-two with strong shoulders and thick, powerful bodies. Oz was the eldest of the crew. Being thirty-three and from the nation of Qubbos, he had seen his fair share of military action. On Allura, Qubbos' relations with its neighbour, Eonia, had been tense for centuries. Purely over the ownership of a spit of land dividing them. This had resulted in a fleeting war seven years ago. A truce was put into place, but tensions remained.

Armies still patrolled either side of the border, and the occasional fight broke out. Oz had been one of those soldiers. The scar that ran down the left side of his jaw, across his ear and neck, was evidence enough of his past commitment. He looked menacing with his multitude of tattoos and shaven hair. His bright, narrow eyes were always surveying, calculating. His presence intimidated me on a good day.

Sym, on the other hand, was a friendly giant. He was the same age as me, twenty-five, and had only ever served as a soldier in Solarfleet, employed purely for crew protection. He was constantly humming or smiling, showing off his perfect white teeth. There was nothing malicious about him. Rooke continuously teased him about his choice of hairstyle, which currently was an afro mohawk with shaven zigzags around the sides, but it suited him. Not that you could see it now. I could only work out who was who because Oz insisted on going first.

I followed Rooke down the ramp, the sunlight bright and warm. As I touched my booted feet to the honey-gold, grained surface at the bottom, I noticed it twinkled, resembling billions of stars. Some particles danced across the surface when caught by the breeze, swirling up into mini tornadoes. Cora bent down next to me and brushed the texture between her gloved fingers. Looking up, she was full to the brim with excitement. "It's like fairy dust."

"I highly doubt we'll find fairies."

She scooped a sample into a glass pot and stood up. "You never know. This could be where dreams are made."

Or nightmares.

My eyes scanned the area. Anxiety still gnawing at my instincts. But I couldn't deny it, this place had an enchanting aura about it. The blue sea glistened as gentle waves crashed against the ground less than half a mile in the distance. Opposite, the steep tanned cliffs looked as though they were topped with short blades of green grass, and deep pink flowers were visible in amongst the rocks where the rockface dipped towards the ground.

Rooke was leading the group towards that area. The boulders had formed a cascade of steps and it looked climbable. I remotely

19

closed the ramp up securing the ship and rushed after him. "What's the plan, Rooke?"

He pointed ahead. "If we ascend the cliff, the wreckage is only a two mile walk southeast." Fully focused, he marched on, and I clutched my laser rifle a little tighter.

When we arrived at the wreckage, the damage was far worse than first assumed. Looking down from the clifftop above, scorch marks littered the roof of the long, bulbous shaped ship. Melted and deformed metal dominated the port side.

The scouting ship was as large as The Orka, and they tended to hold an immense amount of fuel. Their slow scouting journey around the perimeter of the Alluran solar system took more than half a year to complete, and as the sun was only a speck in the distance, solar power was useless. It was the only feasible reason for how they'd lasted the five-month journey here. The excess fuel must have caused the fire.

Carefully, we climbed down the craggy rockface onto the top of the ship, avoiding the sharp fragments of metal scattered along the obliterated front edge. Our boots clonked along the metallic body. If any of the crew were alive, they didn't come out to greet us.

We descended the ship via the back body flap. The long, tilted piece of metal was closer to the ground due to the impact of the crash. The two-metre drop was easy enough, but I helped Cora down anyway. She was now laden with more glass pots clipped to her belt. All filled with soil, rocks, plants, and anything else that had taken her fancy. She was clearly in her element.

The sound of Oz and Rooke cursing through the radio brought my attention to where they had disappeared to. I found them standing on the starboard side of the ship next to an extended ramp. The side airlock was open, the ship was exposed, but it was the disturbing trail of dark red smeared down the ramp that caught everyone's attention.

Zamya hovered at the base, while Rooke and Oz boarded the ramp vigilantly. Rooke glanced back at the rest of us. "Sym, Kobe, stay out here. Keep your eyes peeled."

Both men turned their backs to the ship, guns in check, scouring the area with sharp eyes.

I followed Rooke and Oz onto the ship, Cora and Zamya at my back. All of us tried to avoid stepping in the trail of what looked like blood.

The ship was dark. The airlock doors stuck open at an odd angle, and panels of the interior metal walls were missing. I glanced at my feet. The dark smear on the floor became thicker as we walked further into the mid-section of the wide hull.

Rooke and Oz stopped a few steps ahead, peering at the ground. I realised they were questioning how or why fragments of the floor were missing, similar to those on the walls. I removed my torch from my belt and lit up the floor surrounding me. The panels looked as though they'd been chewed. But how? They were metal. What could eradicate metal in such a way?

Still questioning the thought, I flashed my torch light around the vast area. A bone chilling shiver raked its way down my spine at the scene before me. My gasp caught Rooke's attention, his eyes discovering what was looming at the end of my spotlight.

The remains of a mauled body laid on the floor. Their grey-blue clothing indicated the deceased had been a Solarfleet employee. We slowly approached, anxiously flicking our eyes in the direction of every shadow and dark corner.

I glanced down at the decaying body. It must have been there for at least a couple of weeks. Blue and black patches plagued the sunken skin. Long, scraggly hair fell across the harrowing face where two eyes bulged unnaturally. The neck was punctured by multiple marks, exposing rotten muscle and bone beneath. The look of immense pain was frozen across the decomposing face. But the worst of it was the realisation that both legs had been ripped off at the thigh. Torn muscle, ligament, and clothing surrounded jagged, fractured bone. The red smear on the ramp had originated from this spot. This person's legs had been shredded from their body and dragged from the ship. The thought was horrifying.

Cora's distressed voice split through the haunting silence. "I

21

think I'm gonna be sick." She ran for the exit.

Zamya called after her, "Do not remove your helmet!" The only response was a whining hum.

Examining the corpse closer, Zamya bent down. "This is utterly barbaric."

Rooke scanned the area. "Where are the other crew members?" A hint of desperation coated his tone. "There should be four."

"Boss, there's one over here," Oz's voice rumbled through my earpiece. He was standing in the corner of the room, behind what remained of a computer station. "This one looks like their spinal cord has been ripped out."

Somehow my legs managed to follow Rooke over to the second body. The sight was just as horrifying as the first. Decomposing guts lay in a puddle surrounding a body that had fallen face down, split in half. Now I wanted to vomit.

I looked at Rooke. His mind was in overdrive. He hadn't expected this. To be honest, neither had I. I had expected something eerie or inconclusive, but nothing this distressing. What had killed these people?

"Rooke, we need to get out of here as soon as possible," I said.

Breathing deeply, he nodded his concurrence. "We can't take these mutilated bodies home. They need to be buried here."

"Agreed," Oz murmured. He appeared to be the only one unaffected by the scene. "I'll get Sym to help me dig a couple of graves outside."

Rooke nodded and turned to me. "Let's see if we can find any captain records or ship data. We can't return home without some form of explanation."

Chapter Three

We didn't find any more bodies, but we found the remainder of the bridge. Although half of it, including the driving panel, had disintegrated against the rockface, we managed to find some control computers in amongst the rubble.

We were quiet as we searched the area, hunting for any clues of what may have happened. There was no way of switching any of the data screens on, no way of accessing any information. Even with the absorption of the hot sunshine outside, none of the bridge computers worked. Looking in the cupboards and under the floor panels, the wires were singed, broken, or missing. Again, the missing part baffled me.

None the wiser, we left the bridge and headed towards the captain's quarters. All long-range ships were the same. The personnel quarters were a level higher than the bridge and main monitoring stations. The captain's quarters always sat at the rear of the ship, usually with an outward facing window.

We struggled up the battered staircase but found the room easily enough. The door was closed without any sign of missing panels or gnawed metal edges.

Rooke opened the door vigilantly. Slowly, he scanned the room, then seemed to relax. Strolling in, he made for the average sized bed in the corner. The bed was made, the room was pristine, nothing like the devastation downstairs.

Above the bed, stuck to the wall, was a brown envelope with the words, *For anyone who comes to rescue us*, written in large black writing. Rooke stood on the bed and peeled away the envelope. "I get the impression the captain knew they were going to die."

Still eyeing the room cautiously, I said, "What the hell killed them?"

"I don't know." Rooke peered into the envelope. "Maybe this will shed some light on the situation." He pulled out two hard drives and a digital signature chip. "This must be the captain's records."

Oz's voice rang through our earpieces. "Boss, we found a grave up on the clifftop."

I glanced out the window and realised the shipwreck was located in a crescent shaped bay. Sym and Cora were digging graves out on the sand below; Oz and Kobe were strolling back from the cliffs.

Rooke headed for the door, clutching the envelope. "I'm on my way down."

We exited the ship the same way we came in, passing Zamya, who was still examining the mutilated bodies. The red smear appeared far more disturbing now that we knew what it was.

"The grave was over there." Oz approached us, pointing to a lower section of rockface nearing the edge of the cove. "It was definitely one of ours. We found a Nux necklace dangling around a star made of sticks."

"How many graves?" Rooke asked, as we stepped off the ramp onto the beach.

"Just the one."

"So, we're still missing one crew member."

"There could've easily been two bodies in that grave."

"Or one could still be alive," I suggested.

Rooke looked at me pensively. "How could anyone survive out here on their own?"

"We could see a large forest to the east," Oz mentioned. "If these forests are anything like ours on Allura, it'll be full of food and shelter."

Rooke scoured the uneven clifftops surrounding us. He didn't look convinced. "I don't think we should stick around much longer. It's not safe. We don't know how swift the sun sets, and I don't want to be stuck out here after dark."

"Good point."

"We head back to Parvos, get airborne, and redock with The Orka. Kobe can leave sensors on the ground to give us more insight into activity in the area. It will pick up on any human lifeforms in close proximity. We can return tomorrow to scout the area from the air." He glanced over to Sym and Cora, who were still digging the graves. "But first, we put those lost souls to rest."

Within the next hour, the mutilated bodies were moved, the graves filled and covered by small rocks to keep the light, fairy dust ground in position. Standing in a circle around the graves, holding hands, we paid our respects the Alluran way. Kobe's voice filled the radio wave, "We honour your sacrifice of living the life you've endured. May your flesh and bone help replenish this land. May your soul scour the endless night and find its way back to the home where you belong."

This was an ancient verse Allurans recited at funeral services. The sacred words came from the time of the Nux Warriors. The phrases were to thank the deceased for their courage and hardship during life. In death, they would continue to support our people by nourishing the Alluran soil with their body. The last part was to encourage the immortal soul to find its way back to where our ancestors originated from…Earth. I couldn't help thinking how fitting the last part was for the two people laid to rest at our feet. But I hoped their souls found their way back to Allura, because even though this world was beautiful, it wasn't home. Allura was.

After a short, reflective silence, we packed up our belongings and headed to the edge of the cove, back towards the stretch of coastline where our ship awaited.

"Do you think the fourth crew member could still be alive?" I asked Rooke as we walked side by side.

"I doubt it. If they are, they would've seen our ship earlier. They would've found us by now. And if they are injured, they'd hold no chance against whatever mutilated their crewmates. I just hope the hard drive we found gives us some insight to what's happened here."

Cora caught my attention from up ahead. She stopped and slowly turned. "Has…has anyone else noticed that the sea has shifted considerably?" Her voice sounded nervous, hesitant.

"What do…you…?" I glanced along the shore, starting to understand her comment. The sea water was now lapping at the ground far closer than before. The waves were choppier, stretching further inland.

"How did that happen?" Rooke said, looking at Cora for an explanation. "It was at least ten metres out not so long ago."

Inwardly I cursed. "No, no, no!" I began to race along the soft, resilient ground towards the peninsula. Rooke called after me, but I didn't stop. If the sea had moved, that meant…

I turned the sharp corner at the tip of the cove, the sea almost blocking my path. There, two miles up the coastline, sat the Parvos, now partially submerged in sea water. I began to swear profusely.

Rooke's voice was in my ear, "Eden, slow down. What's wrong?" Then he cursed when the scene came into view. "Eden, wait up!"

He caught up with me when the ship was only a few strides away.

When we landed, I hadn't noticed how much of an angle the floor inclined towards the ocean. Sea water now slapped against the silver and blue hull on the port side of the ship. At the rear, the lower portside thruster and main engine output were sodden. They were supposed to produce water, not sit in it. This type of natural occurrence didn't happen quite so violently on Allura. The seas and their waters were far more stable. The tides only rose and receded by a couple of metres, not half a mile.

Standing on the dry side of the ship, I placed my gloved hands on my helmet and shook my head. "This is a disaster."

Rooke swung round looking for Cora. The rest of the crew were scurrying along behind us.

"Cora, why has this happened?"

"I…I don't know." She winced.

"How does the level of sea even move this much?" Rooke sounded vexed.

"I don't…"

"It must be the moon," Kobe said calmly, looking up into the sky.

"Oh my Nux, yes. That's it," Cora exclaimed. "Of course. Earth has a moon. On Allura there is a fairly insignificant tidal effect caused by our sun. Earth's moon dominates theirs causing a harsher effect."

Rooke cursed again and turned to look at me. I felt as though I was in shock.

"Eden, can we take off?"

I shook my head. "I…I don't think so, no. The thrusters are filled with water. There'll be too much excess weight to get airborne. The ship could break apart. It's too much of a risk."

Rooke groaned, turning back to the scientists. "How high will this *tide* go?"

Cora shrugged but Kobe took the initiative to scan the rockface and the ground around our feet. "Judging by the texture of rocks and the marks on the ground, I don't think it will rise much further."

Rooke gave a sharp nod. "Good. Everyone, get inside the ship. Let's hope this water recedes and the engines dry out before nightfall."

Both Oz and Zamya's groans of uncertainty rung through the radio. They obviously shared my doubts.

Chapter Four

Surveying the digital instruments on the driving dashboard, I brushed several strands of dark hair from my sweaty forehead. I was stressed. The engines were laden with sea water and one of the fuel tanks had a small, albeit dangerous amount of sodium chloride present.

"Damn, the water must be full of salt," I whispered to myself, rubbing my face with frustration. It would be too much of a risk to take off even if the engines dried out.

"I'm so sorry, Eden," Cora's soft voice carried over to me from behind. She was hovering in the open doorway of the flight deck, looking almost sheepish. A line of worry indented her freckled forehead.

"Hey," I reached back for her hand, "this isn't your fault, Cora. No one knew this would happen."

"But…I should've known. It's my job to know." She walked forward and plopped herself in the chair next to me. "Rooke is so angry."

"What's new?" I said, trying the lighten the mood, but it didn't seem to help. Cora sunk into the chair, wrapping her arms around herself. She looked so young and inexperienced. Being only twenty, she, somehow, had ended up being the last-minute, stand in astrogeologist for our previous mission. The mission we never returned from. Rooke had accepted our current, unplanned mission mid-flight.

To Cora, the whole situation must have felt overwhelming, like she'd been caught up in an unstoppable whirlwind. Yes, she was overly excitable, but when the pressure got to her, it was obvious she was struggling. And she was struggling now. Rooke and his lack of tact could be irremissible at the best of times.

I squeezed her hand, changing the subject. "Did you get a chance to speak to Troy?"

"Yes." She smiled sweetly. "Just before he went into blackout. I wish he was here." She averted her gaze to the sea glistening around us, her light green eyes illuminated in the golden light. "This place *is* beautiful. Look at that sunset."

I followed her gaze to my left. A scatter of puffy clouds sat near the horizon, edged with glowing pinks and oranges. The blinding sun was starting to deepen in colour, attempting to touch the endless horizon of water.

"It's going to get dark soon," Cora said, her voice suddenly laced with alarm. I aimed to calm her anxiety, but the words didn't come. This was going to be a long night and we all felt the consternation creeping in.

Zamya sighed heavily behind us. Looking over our shoulders, we found her leaning against the doorway. She held up a thermometer. "I need to check your temperatures hourly. Rooke is on a rampage. He wants everything done *properly*."

"I told you he's angry," Cora said to me.

I huffed loudly. They always came to me when Rooke was on his high horse, when they wanted him knocked down a peg or two. Standing up, I manoeuvred between the chairs, around Zamya, towards the doorway.

"Not so fast." Zamya caught my arm and pressed the thermometer forcefully into my ear. It beeped and I left immediately. She called after me, "You're fine, by the way."

"Pleased to hear it."

I found Rooke in the captain's study. The long, slim ship only had one dwelling level, made up of the flight deck at the front, a basic kitchen area just behind, then a narrow corridor separating two sets of sleeping quarters. When the corridor opened out further along, the analysing room was found, made up of a circle of research desks around the edges, segregated at four points, allowing access to the two docking doors and the corridor at either end. Between the analysing room and the loading bay at the rear, was a corridor that supplied access to the medical room, and opposite, the captain's study.

I knocked on the door and strolled in. Rooke was leaning against the wall on the far side, where his collection of old-fashioned bullet guns adorned the metal panels. One arm lay across his body, propping the other one up with his fist pressed to his lips. His expression was one of unmistakable concern, his eyes focused on the screen on his desk.

"Rooke?" I took a step closer. His gaze eventually shifted to mine and the frown across his brow deepened. "What is it?" I asked.

"I…they…" He pointed to the screen. "Maybe you should just watch."

I rounded the desk and sat down on the metallic stool. Rooke tapped the screen, and a recorded message flashed up on the monitor. I recognised the woman who appeared. She was Captain Emilia Lewison, the commander of the scouting ship. Her Solarfleet profile photo had shown a healthy-looking woman in her forties, but here she appeared pale and gaunt. Dark shadows circled a pair of anxious blue eyes. Her long blonde hair was a similar length to the corpse we found that afternoon…with no legs.

A deep chill infiltrated my bones as I watched the footage play.

"I am recording this because I believe by the time anyone gets here, it'll be too late, and you are probably wondering how we got here in the first place. Well, let me shed some light. We picked up an unusual signal when we were scouting the outskirts of Tridon. It was unusual in the sense it was transmitting ancient space coding. The same coding we stopped using over a millennia ago. I radioed the discovery into high command, but we were denied permission to pursue. Command assumed it was a lost satellite that had floated too far out.

"We continued on our course directive but after a few hours, Lieutenant Filo reported the ship had verged off course and was

bearing a different course entirely. We were unable to realign the course settings and discovered the ship flight systems were locked. It was then that we lost radio signal.

"After a distressing couple of days of flying further and further away from the Alluran solar system at a frightening speed, we discovered we were following a probe like entity. It appeared to be transmitting a metallic field, dragging us along in its wake. Fortunately, Lieutenant Zukola successfully rewired the distress signal, and we began transmitting. We had no idea where we were, or where we were heading. And even though we knew Solarfleet would pick up the signal, how long it would take to reach them was another answer we did not have.

"Months later, we found ourselves approaching this planet. A glowing blue and white world that somehow seemed familiar. Before we knew what was happening, our ship automatically began atmosphere entry. The descent was violent and rapid. Filo tried to take control of the driving panels, but something else seemed to be guiding us down. As you can probably tell, we landed...but the devastation was immense. Filo died immediately on impact. The last amounts of fuel we had leaked into the sea water and exploded, causing a severe fire. Thankfully, it didn't last long but we lost most of the supplies on the ship. We buried Filo on the clifftop."

Captain Lewison paused. A wave of pain and suffering filled her haggard features. She was trying to suppress the tears from forming, but as she began to speak again, a cluster of rogue droplets fell. *"There doesn't seem to be any intelligent life around. We've looked for food, but the only thing we've found are a few berries and seaweed. There are fish in the sea but they're too difficult to catch, and any animals we find in the forest are either diseased or mutilated. We are starving. The only thing keeping us alive is the water reclaimer, but the power supply is becoming unreliable."* She breathed in a deep, stabilizing breath. *"You see, our ship is being eaten...by...by these creatures. Creatures I can only describe as something from a horror story. At first, they only seemed to eat the metal coated in composite, and the wire cabling.*

In doing so they were ruining the wire connections to our power supply. But the worst of it was…was…" She placed her hand over her mouth, gasping for air, trying to control the emotion boiling up inside. *"They…they took Louisa…Lieutenant Chorlar. She…she was fixing the power coupling on the starboard ramp. They usually only come at night, but that day they arrived mid-morning. I heard her screams as they dragged her away. There was blood everywhere. With…without power, the laser guns weren't charged efficiently. We had no means to stop those bastards, and they took her. They took her.*

"The next thing we knew, they were inside the ship. They got in through the lowered ramp Louisa was fixing. Zukola and I keep to my quarters. They don't seem to disturb us up here. But as soon as they see or smell us, they start roaring ravenously, trying to reach us. I have no doubt what their intentions are. We have no food, no water. We are either going to die of dehydration or die trying to get out of here. Whichever is the lesser evil, I am still unsure. We've lasted two weeks. I doubt we'll last much longer. If anyone does find this, please don't make the same mistake we did. Leave this planet and its race of demons behind. I doubt I'll be here to warn you myself. Captain Emilia Lewison. Over and out."

The footage ended and I peered up at Rooke standing beside me. He was still frozen, a frown dominating his features.

"It explains the missing panels," I said.

"It explains the mutilated bodies," Rooke's tone was clipped. He exhaled and walked back to the wall he was initially leaning against. "We need to get this ship off the ground before nightfall."

"Unless you want to end up as a fireball in the sky, this ship is not going anywhere, Rooke. One of the fuel tanks has been contaminated."

Incredulously, he gawked at me, then cursed at the floor.

"The sun is already setting. I have enough fuel to drain the tank and refill it, but it'll have to wait until tomorrow. The sea is receding, and the humidity has dropped. The engines should dry out by the morning."

Rooke glared at me. "Did you not hear what Captain

Lewison said? These things come at night."

"Yes, okay, I heard. But the scouting ship is huge and was tucked away into a neat little bay. We are further out on the sea edge. These creatures may not have seen us."

Rooke chuckled sarcastically. "Look at you, being the optimistic one." There was a hint of disdain in his voice, one I did not favour.

"Well, I have to be," I snapped, "when you're acting like this."

"Like what?" he growled back.

"This! I can't keep up with you at the moment. You're either being a reckless risktaker or you're waltzing around in a brooding stupor. Which, I'd like to mention, is badly covered up with your aggressive orders. It doesn't help the crew when you start blaming them for everything."

I was expecting a brash comment in his defence, but instead Rooke pushed his head back and sighed deeply. "I'm sorry. I want to get this mission over and done with so we can go home."

"Pardon, what was that?" Tilting my head playfully, I slowly walked toward him.

"I want to go home."

"No, not that bit. The other bit." I smirked, teasing him. "The bit about you're...you're sorry?"

Rooke pointed at me. "Look, Eden, shush."

I knocked his finger away and smiled. "You never apologise."

Now he was trying to refrain from grinning. "Yes, I do. Just, not often."

"You mean never."

He finally chuckled. "Okay, Eden, I get it. I'm a terrible person."

"No, you're not." I stopped in front of him, smiling up at his handsome face. "Only a stubborn one." He scowled. "But I'm pleased Rooke the commander is back in the room. I don't like the brooding version of you."

"Hmm." He pushed away from the wall and walked to the desk, where the frozen image of Captain Lewison was still displayed on the monitor. He switched the screen off and said, "Until we are off this planet, be prepared for the brooding version to reappear." Rooke sat on the edge of his desk. His pensive expression had returned. "What do you suggest we do about the situation?"

"What choice do we have? We spend the night here, take it in turns to monitor activity outside, and hope for the best."

"I guess that's all we can do," he grumbled.

Chapter Five

Rooke stood in the analysing room informing the rest of the crew of the situation. I watched their faces transform to looks of trepidation as they processed the information Rooke spoke of.

"Captain Lewison didn't provide any information on what these creatures look like, so stay vigilant. Oz and Sym have left enough weapons in here to defend a small town."

"Let's hope it doesn't come to that," mumbled Oz, who stood with his arms crossed, towering over Kobe's desk of screens and keyboards. Even Kobe, who was renowned for his nonchalance, held an aspect of fear in his eyes.

"This is going to be a long night," groaned Zamya from across the room. Her frown, fuelled by anxiety, had deepened since this morning. She didn't look impressed.

"The myth must be true, then," cocooned in Sym's arms, Cora spoke timidly. She was shivering. Her frightened body looked tiny against Sym's muscular form, a complete contrast to his concerned facial expression set like stone.

"We don't know if any of this is connected," Rooke said. "Once we leave tomorrow, we'll stay in orbit for a few days, see if we can pick up any activity to confirm the theory."

"Cora and I will take the first shift," I said, meeting her eyes. She nodded in agreement.

"Okay, good." Rooke hovered next to me. "Me and Zam will take the second. Oz, Sym, Kobe, you take the third. Hopefully nightfall isn't much longer than ten hours."

Voices echoed their agreement and the room cleared. Rooke gently caught my elbow. His dark green eyes sank into mine, emphasising his instruction. "Make sure you wake me if there's any sign of trouble."

"I will. Try and sleep, Rooke. You look knackered."

The gentle smile he gave me didn't reach his eyes. I recognised it as his usual look of appreciation when he wasn't in the mood to voice it. I watched him head towards the captain's study, clearly intending to sleep there tonight.

Cora appeared holding a mountain of books. If research was her way of coping with the pressure, I was happy to sit and listen to her ramble. I doubted anyone else would tolerate it, especially Zamya.

We took a seat next to each other at the comms desk, in front of the monitoring screens. There were six screens in total, all surveying the circumference of the ship. Two cameras were positioned on each side, with another one at each end. Our surroundings were dark. Only the glow of the crescent moon illuminated the area outside. The waves seemed choppier than before, but they were undeniably withdrawing.

An hour passed and I returned from the kitchen with two cups of Eonian tea. I only drank this when Oz wasn't around, otherwise he would chastise me for drinking his enemy's beverage. But I loved this tea. It had a citrusy flavour that didn't leave my mouth dry. Its smell reminded me of my late grandma and her cottage in the Torlan valley, which bordered onto the Eonian tea fields.

This was the longest I'd ever been away from home. I could understand why Rooke was so adamant to get back. It had taken us five months to get here. It was going to take at least that to return, if not longer, which currently felt like a lifetime.

Cora started rambling again, "It's really quite fascinating how similar Earth and Allura are. Their air is made up of near enough the same number of gases. Even the time scale is similar. The Earth day is just under twenty-four hours, Allura twenty-six. The Earth year is three hundred and sixty-five days, Allura has three hundred and thirty-seven. That, theoretically, is the exact same length of time, just made up differently."

I smiled to myself and handed Cora her tea. She seemed far more relaxed now. The colour had returned to her cheeks, the smile of intrigue back in place.

"I'm going to ask Kobe to reconfigure our watches," she continued, "so they sync with Earth hours. That way we'll have more of an idea of how much time we have tomorrow before the sun sets again."

"Any more information on the tides?" I asked. It had dawned on me that the tide would come back in at some point, which could hold us up again.

Cora shook her head. "It's inconclusive. The tides vary day to day, area to area. And these books were written thousands of years ago. It may have changed."

A thud resounded behind us making us both jump. From the corridor leading to the sleeping quarters, Sym appeared. He was bare foot, wearing a pair of black shorts and a loose-fitting blue T-shirt. Surprisingly, his black mohawk was perfectly in place, but his brown eyes were hooded and tired.

"Are you alright?" I asked him.

He grumbled and slumped down into one of the chairs on the opposite side of the room. "I can't sleep. Oz is snoring."

"Ah, just put a pillow over his big head," was Cora's suggestion. I glanced at her, shocked by her words.

"At least on The Orka we had separate sleeping quarters." Sym yawned, his muscular arms stretching above his head.

"Hopefully, we'll be back there tomorrow night," I said.

"Uh-huh." He yawned again, setting me and Cora off. "I'm going to get some coffee. Think I'm gonna need it."

Thankfully, our three-hour stint passed uneventfully. Sym remained with us throughout. Sitting at a separate desk space, he sketched in his drawing pad, commenting occasionally on our conversation. When Rooke and Zamya took over the monitoring, Cora and I staggered to our sleeping quarters, leaving Sym engrossed in his artwork.

After redressing in a black vest top and a pair of black leggings, I sunk into one of the lower bunks. Cora took the one directly above. It didn't take me long to doze off into a deep, exhausted slumber.

The sound of screaming jolted me awake. I felt disorientated at first. It hadn't been my recurring dream that had woken me, which confused me further. Then an urgent male voice was heard. It sounded muffled, as if it was coming from outside the ship.

As my fogged consciousness cleared, movement from the bunk opposite caught my eye. Zamya forced herself up, listening attentively. She must've finished her watch a while ago. What time was it?

Cora stirred above as the echoless screaming and shouting came again, followed by what could only resemble laser gun fire. For a brief second, Zamya and I exchanged questioning looks before I launched myself towards the closed bedroom door, Zamya hot on my heels. I heard more shouting, more laser fire. My heart pounded in my chest. What the hell was going on?

The ship was dark, only the green emergency lights were lighting the floor. We found no one in the analysing room, the monitoring screens were flickering on and off, the blue overhead lights buzzed as if the redundant power system was trying to kick in.

A chilled draught of air hit my bare skin. It felt different to the gentle flow of air conditioning. It smelt unusual. It smelt fresh and…salty. My eyes widened and I found myself sprinting towards the airlock at the rear of the ship.

Stumbling to a halt as I entered the vast chamber, the airlock was open. Rooke, dressed in a grey T-shirt and a pair of black lounge pants, was hauling Oz's large body in through the open doorway. Kobe was standing at the top of the extended ramp, continuously shooting lasers into the darkness. There were unusual sounds coming from outside; growls, roars, clicks, and gnawing.

Gnawing?

I cursed and lunged forward to help Rooke. Oz's T-shirt was ripped on his left shoulder and arm, drenched in blood. His face was scrunched up, clenching his teeth in agony. Zamya crouched next to me as we placed him on the loading bay floor.

Rooke ran back to the airlock, gun in hand. "Kobe, get inside, now!"

The sound of laser shots reverberated through the air. The growls and shrieks grew louder, closer.

"Kobe!" Rooke leapt forward, firing his gun down the ramp, pulling Kobe backwards before hitting the airlock button. They fell into a heap on the chamber floor. As the doors slid together, I caught a glimpse of a monster; a wide, elongated head with a large, snarling mouth. Two rows of sharp teeth flanked by long, deadly fangs glistening with saliva. Four dark eyes were possessed with determination, hooded by a crown of scales. It roared as it slammed into the now thankfully closed doors. Another thud confirmed the large beast had fallen off the ramp, which had folded back into its redundant position under the airlock chamber.

I stared at the door for a moment wondering if I was dreaming. Captain Lewison had mentioned the terrorising creatures were like something from a nightmare. If what I had just seen was anything to go by, she wasn't wrong. The image stained my conscience with fear.

I averted my eyes to Rooke and Kobe laying on the floor. Their heavy breathing and groans indicated the extent of their exertion and relief. I glanced down at Oz on the floor next to me, he was pale, sweat beading his forehead. Zamya was pressing down on a large wound stretching across his left shoulder. Her hands were too small to cover the full area.

I flinched, regaining my focus. Pushing down on an exposed area of tissue and blood, Oz grunted under my weight.

"Sorry Oz," I whispered to him. A hint of a smile flashed across his lips in response as he panted.

Rooke and Kobe got to their feet and staggered into the loading bay, closing the inner airlock door as they did so.

"What the hell happened?" Zamya barked at them. "Why did you go outside? Without atmospheric suits on, nevertheless?"

Kobe appeared uncomfortable with his head hung to the floor, unusually lost for words.

Oz spluttered from below, "The power went out. We went to check the cables."

"What?" I gasped, looking at Rooke.

"They went outside without my knowledge," he confirmed, squatting down next to us.

"Rooke was asleep," Kobe mumbled. "We didn't deem it necessary to wake him."

"Are you insane?!" Zamya bawled, her expression full of shock and frustration. "You heard what Rooke said earlier. Those things eat metal. Why didn't you wait for the backup systems to kick in?"

"They weren't working." Oz groaned.

"You absolute idiots! We could've survived without power for another few hours."

"I know, Zamya," Kobe's voice was raised and angry. "You don't need to point out the obvious. It was clearly a mistake!" I'd never heard him sound so distressed.

"We hadn't seen…any movement on…the monitoring screens," Oz said, starting to shiver.

"They were stealth-like," Kobe stressed. "They pounced when Sym and Oz went outside."

"Where is Sym?" asked a small voice from the corridor behind. Cora stood on the threshold wrapping her arms around herself. She looked half asleep, her complexion a shade paler than white.

I scanned the room. Sym wasn't present. I looked back at Kobe and Rooke, waiting for them to answer Cora's question. Kobe remained silent, staring at the floor. Rooke had a solemn, distant look on his face. I touched his arm and asked the question again. "Rooke, where's Sym?"

He looked up at me, his eyes moist. "He's…he's still outside…Eden, Eden, NO!"

I launched myself towards the inner airlock door. I couldn't leave Sym out there. He was one of us, one of the crew. Why would they leave him outside?

I reached for the door's access button, but Rooke's arm locked around my midriff, pulling me backwards into him. His breath was in my ear. "Eden, please don't. He's gone. Sym's gone." His voice cracked on the final word. I could feel his heart pounding behind me.

As his words sunk in, a tiny whimper escaped me. Rooke wrapped his other arm around my shoulders, pulling me tenderly closer.

"We can't leave him out there," my voice quivered.

"We have to. We…have to."

I stared at the door, trying to make sense of it all. Sym was dead? His body was outside being mauled by giant, beetle like monsters, in a foreign world, trillions upon billions of miles from home. How could this have happened?

It was only when Rooke released me from his tender hold, I remembered Sym hadn't slept all night. He'd been exhausted. Anyone that tired could've made mistakes or misjudged the situation. Why hadn't I offered him to sleep in the spare bunk in our room? Why had I left him to endure the long night, relying on coffee to keep him awake? I felt angry with myself, angry with Oz and Kobe for their bad judgement. I was too angry to move, beyond anguished to cry, but too sombre to scream.

I glanced back at the rest of the crew. Zamya and Rooke were guiding Oz to the medical room. Kobe was still frozen on the spot, lost in his distressing thoughts. My gaze shifted to Cora at the back of the room. Her face was drenched in tears, her posture collapsing. I rushed over to her and pulled her into my chest. Letting her sob into my shoulder, I allowed my own tears to surface as the truth sunk in…

Sym was dead.

Sym was gone.

Chapter Six

Relief washed over me when Cora finally passed out from her hysteria. Leaving her sleeping in her bunk, I sought out Zamya. She was in the medical room, attempting to sew Oz's wound under a flickering overhead light. Finding a large flashlight in Rooke's empty study, I held it steady above Zamya and her patient, allowing her to work more efficiently.

Oz had been sedated. His complexion was unsoundly pale, his shoulder a mess of ripped tissue and punctured, oozing skin. When I realised the punctures were horrifyingly deep teeth marks, a shiver of fear scaled down my back.

"Will he be alright?" I asked, grimacing as I watched Zamya wipe and sew.

"Hopefully," Zamya rasped. "As long as the wound doesn't get infected." She sat back and sighed heavily. "Why were they so idiotic? Our orders were to stay on the ship and observe, regardless of what was occurring outside. It's bad enough losing Sym, but if we…if we lose Oz as well…we…"

I placed a gentle hand on her shoulder. She was hiding it well, but deep-down Zamya was petrified. She had been since before we left The Orka.

Zamya finished sewing the wound up. I helped her clean the small, clinical room, then left her to observe Oz's progress. I needed to find Rooke.

Walking through the ship, I could still hear the disconcerting sound of gnawing. I prayed to all the Nux Lords that those creatures found eating through thick metal harder than shredding flesh. The thought turned my stomach.

Kobe was sitting at his desk in the analysing room, his head lay in his hands. He was a practical man, intelligent. Even though he portrayed the phlegmatic, rational scientist, I sensed he was concealing a pool of emotion. I could barely imagine the extent of guilt he was feeling, nor what he'd witnessed while standing on the landing ramp earlier. The horror of it would affect any human soul. I squeezed his shoulder as I walked past, attempting to give him a reassuring sense of companionship, but he didn't look up; didn't acknowledge I was there.

After scouring the remaining areas of the ship, I eventually found Rooke on the flight deck, standing frozen behind the pilot chairs. He was watching the sunlight rise over the clifftops to the east. His fist was against his mouth, arm propped up by the other one resting across his chest. A tell-tale sign he felt troubled.

I lightly touched his flexed bicep, letting him know I was there. Without looking back, he dropped his fist and squeezed my lingering hand.

"This is all my fault." His voice was an unstable whisper.

"Hey." I reached around him, encouraging him to turn to face me. "No, it's not. You didn't order them to go outside."

His eyes locked with mine. The sadness swirling within them was heart wrenching. "I should've listened to you," he said. "We shouldn't have landed so quickly We should've…"

"Rooke, you can't blame yourself for this. No one knew what to expect."

"Which is why we should've surveyed the area from the air for far longer than I instructed…Nux, I'm such a selfish bastard." He dropped his gaze.

"Why would you say that? You risked your life saving Oz. I'm pretty sure you saved Kobe as well."

He shook his head. "I'm not the hero here, Eden. I wanted to get this mission over and done with in a day. I rushed everything. I want to get home to…to…" He pinched the bridge of his nose. "It's all my fault."

I pulled his hand away and peered up at his frowning features. I knew every line, every contour of his face, but I'd never seen him look so troubled, so ashamed. "Rooke, if you want to place the blame somewhere, then we are all guilty. I should've pressed you more to follow standard procedures. When we landed, *I* should've noticed the way the land declined towards the sea. Cora should've known about the moon and the tides, Kobe also. You could blame Sym and Oz for stepping outside this ship in the middle of the night, when you specifically gave us orders to remain inside. Stop blaming yourself. We all agreed to this mission fully aware of the unprecedented risks. And we all want to go home. You're not being selfish."

His forlorn eyes met mine. There was a vulnerability within, one I rarely saw. He stepped closer and pulled me into his chest. Pressing his face into my untidy dark hair, I wrapped my arms around his broad shoulders, in the way we always did when one of us needed comforting. And perhaps I needed this as much as he did right now.

"I'm so glad you're here with me," he said, his voice muffled against the crook of my neck.

"I'm not going anywhere." I stroked the back of his hair, resting my hand on the warmth of his neck. Closing my eyes, the smell of him overwhelmed my senses. He smelt citrusy and fresh. He smelt of comfort and security. He smelt like home.

We remained frozen for several moments, lost in the comfort of each other's arms. It was only when Zamya's voice echoed through the kitchen area behind us that we unravelled.

"Looks like the horror beetles are leaving," she called.

Rooke and I turned to the driving screen. I grimaced, viewing five yellow-white scaled backed creatures scuttling across the sand towards the lower part of the rockface, to where the cascade of rocks formed an access point to the clifftop. We watched them struggle to ascend the giant makeshift steps. Their six legs appeared too thin and spindly to support the bulk of their bodies.

"That's interesting," I said.

Rooke glanced at me. "They didn't attack the upper levels of the scouting ship, did they?"

"No. I'm guessing they can't climb easily."

"Well, well, well. That gives us a slight advantage."

We remained onboard for another hour. After confidently confirming the hostile creatures had left the area, four of us headed for the airlock. The atmospheric suits were stored in vertical glass cases along the walls of the airlock chamber. They were fully charged and ready for use. After suiting up and checking the comms, I followed Rooke, Kobe, and Zamya down the ramp. We left Cora inside, observing the scanners and monitoring screens, and regularly checking on Oz, who was still sleeping.

Rounding the end of the ramp, we paused and observed the carnage that lay before us. Several gaping holes were present in the hull's usually flush exterior, metal casing hung from bolted clamps, broken fragments littered the floor, and thick clusters of exposed wiring dangled towards the ground, some buried amongst the sand.

How these creatures could create such chaos in a few hours was beyond remarkable.

My gaze shifted to the landing gear on the port side of the ship. It had clearly been nibbled on. A loose wire hung from the main arm, but that wasn't the only issue. I ducked underneath the ship, moving towards the area. The large, portside wheel was now submerged in the damp sand. Only the top part of the tyre was visible. The tide must have dragged in a copious amount of sand, raising the bed and giving the creatures better access to the hull.

Trying to dislodge the wheel, I used my gloved hands to uncover it, but it was pointless. Even though the lower layer of sand held a stodgy, weighted consistency, the top layer had already dried, resembling the unwavering, powdery fairy dust. The wheel was well and truly stuck.

Zamya appeared next to me, pointing to the ground around us. "Look at these footprints. They're everywhere."

I glanced down. Dozens upon dozens of strange footprints lay indented in the damp areas of sand. We bent down to study them. From observing the creatures earlier, they had thin, spindly legs, but their footprints now indicated they had what resembled hands. They were small, thin palms, with elongated fingers and pointed tips. There were only three digits on each, widely spaced out.

"These points could be claws." Zamya motioned to one.

"They look as sharp as knives." I peered up at the ship's underbelly above us. "It would explain how they ripped the metal from the structure so easily."

"Among other things."

"Yeah…" Images of the mauled bodies we'd found yesterday prodded at my conscience. And then, as if following my train of thought, Rooke's voice rumbled through our in-suit radio, "I've found him."

I exchanged a look with Zamya before we both navigated the sand under the hull of the ship, towards the front landing gear. Rooke stood where the starboard wing began to loom overhead, and there, laid before him, was Sym's body.

I fought the urge to wince away. There was blood and flesh everywhere. What was left of Sym's body was positioned downwards, his head twisted at an unnatural angle, his face unrecognisable through the shredded skin. Only the curls of his black mohawk proved this body belonged to the man we knew. His blue T-shirt was ripped across the top part of his spine, where teeth marks punctured the dark skin of his neck. And if that wasn't bad enough, his left arm was missing, ripped from the socket.

I could no longer bear it. I had to look away, but to no visual benefit. One of his boots lay a couple of metres to the right. The rubber and metal sole had been chewed, but his foot and ankle were still inside. I muted the sob threatening to rip from my throat. The extent of his injuries was beyond comprehension, and the silence that swamped the three of us at the realisation was utterly haunting.

Kobe appeared from behind me. I glanced up at his face as he took in the sight. Behind the visor, he appeared as hard as stone, showing no sign of emotion. He gave me a sideways glance before turning and walking away. His reaction concerned me. His reluctance to stand with us, along with his silence, confirmed the guilt he was enduring. He was suffering. I called after him, but Rooke told me to let him go.

After another moment of silent reflection, I left Zamya to study Sym's condition in more depth, documenting the details with photos and digital notes. Rooke started digging a grave close to a scattering of boulders halfway between the ship and the cliff face, while Kobe and I began fixing the power issues.

Once Rooke and Zamya had respectfully moved Sym into the fresh grave, his body was covered in sand and rocks in a similar fashion to the graves we set yesterday, and Cora emerged from the ship. Aware of the risk that could appear from the clifftops at any moment, we swiftly said our heartfelt goodbyes to our dear colleague.

Sym was young, he was the same age as me. He was a good, decent person, a gentle soul. He didn't deserve such a horrifying death. It would take a long time to fully accept he was gone.

Several hours later, the ship's exterior was still a mess. The primary power was back online, and I had fixed the landing gear. But there was an excessive amount of metal debris that needed to be cleared, and the remaining hull breaches required covering.

The sun beating down on us didn't help the mammoth task.

Even in the shadow of the ship, the warmth was sweltering. Sweat slicked across my forehead proving an aggravating annoyance, and with wearing an atmospheric helmet, I couldn't wipe it away. My eyes stung from the continual body salt dripping into them.

My hands shook as I screwed another large bolt into the outer shell of the ship. I was exhausted, my muscles ached, my head pounded.

"Eden, Kobe," Zamya called from the edge of the ship, "you both need to take a break."

"Sure," Kobe replied. I ignored the request. I wasn't

stopping anytime soon. Too much needed to be repaired before the tide came in. We needed to get the ship off the ground before those creatures returned.

I noticed Kobe walk past. He tapped my arm. "Come on, Eden. Doctor's orders."

"I'll be in soon."

From the corner of my eye, I saw him disappear up the landing ramp.

I started repairing another metallic panel on the underbelly of the ship, cursing and spluttering at the awkwardness of its position. I knew I needed a break, but my stubborn adamance to keep pressing on was far stronger.

Ten minutes later Rooke's voice was in my ear. "Eden, are you still outside?"

I huffed. "Yes," I grunted, reaching up to insert a nine-inch bolt into an allocated hole.

"Eden, you need to stop and eat. We have muffins…" I heard the smile in his voice, but it didn't calm nor entice me. "Eden, come on."

"Rooke, I need to get this *finished*." There was a clear warble in my voice, resonating through my bones, causing my hands to shake. I sucked in a breath before screwing the bolt into place with the mechanical drill. For some reason, I was close to tears. The situation had become overwhelming. I felt stressed and under pressure, battling against a nagging ache in the back of my mind…

Those creatures will return.

Those creatures killed Sym.

He was mauled to death.

Sym is dead!

A rogue tear slid down my cheek.

With my mind ticking louder and louder as the seconds dragged by, I hadn't realised Rooke had gone silent until I caught sight of him standing in my peripheral view, fully suited up. "Eden, talk to me," he said compassionately.

I lowered my aching arms and slowly looked over at him. He was reaching up, leaning against the hull of the ship, peering down

48

at me. Squeezing my eyes together, I shook my head. "There's too much to be done. Even with everyone's help, we won't complete the repairs in time."

"Yes, we will." He ducked down, pulling me out of the awkward position I'd been crouching in for the past two hours. "We're nearly finished."

"It's getting late. I still need to transfer the fuel. I still need to…"

"Okay, okay." He placed his gloved hands on the bulbous glass of my helmet. "We have time."

"Do we?" I pointed towards the sea. The lapping waves were growing in strength. I could hear their roar vibrating through my suit. I whimpered at the realisation. "The water's starting to come in. The port side wheel needs to be dug out of the sand before the sea reaches the thrusters, otherwise I can't take off. Holy souls, this isn't going to work!"

"Eden, calm down." Rooke took me by the shoulders, pressing the glass of his helmet gently against mine with a thud. "Breathe," he said.

I took in a few deep breaths. The panic prickling in my veins slowly subdued. I raised my eyes, meeting his green gaze through our visors. His expression was soothing, affectionate. Nux, I loved this man.

"I'll sort the wheel. Kobe and Zamya can sort the last few hull breaches. You need a break, Eden. The fuel transfer won't take long. We can do this."

I swallowed before a feeble nod replaced my concern. Rooke took the large drill from my hand and led me up the ramp, opening and closing the airlocks while I ambled absentmindedly behind.

After I ate, I took my seat on the flight deck. Thankfully, the full expanse of the dashboard illuminated to life at my command. Typing instructions into the computer to initiate the flush through of the contaminated tanks, then transferring the remaining fuel from the redundant supply, a whirling sound was evidence the routine was playing out successfully.

My eyes flicked to the sea outside, calculating how much

longer we had until the water became an issue. We still had time.

We can do this.

On the dashboard, the fuel dials changed from red to green, confirming adequate fuel transferral. I felt my lips twitch with relief. Leaping from my seat, I headed towards the analysing room, preparing to contact Rooke outside with the good news.

I found the large, circular space empty. Movement on the monitoring screens caught my eye. Rooke, Zamya, and Kobe were scurrying up the landing ramp towards the airlock.

From behind me, Cora's small, wavering voice announced, "They're here already."

My heart sank as I took in her worried expression. "You mean the creatures?"

She nodded. "The scanners picked up their imminent presence."

"But it's not even sunset. Please tell me we're ready to leave."

A look of utter turmoil flashed across her face. "The wheel is still stuck."

I cursed inwardly, and with a despondent frustration, I dropped into the desk chair beside me.

All that work for nothing.

Chapter Seven

Rooke's rumble of frustration was heard from where I sat in the analysing room. Cora and I winced at the sound of the loud crashes and bangs that followed, reverberating throughout the metallic shell.

Kobe appeared, mumbling his disapproval. "As you can hear, Rooke's throwing a tantrum."

Zamya's voice echoed down the corridor behind him. "Just calm down! You'll only make things worse if you…" The sound of a door call button being slammed several times followed by another loud thud made us flinch.

Zamya marched into the room. She looked vexed. "He's gone and broken a suit helmet." She threw her hands in the air. "I understand he's annoyed by the situation. Who isn't? But he's not permitted to go around destroying vital equipment. He needs to calm down. Seriously! Did he ever attend that anger management course?"

"Rooke?" I scoffed. "No."

"Well, if we do make it home, I highly recommend he does."

Another thud was heard from the direction of the captain's study.

"He can probably hear you," Cora whispered.

Zamya walked to the corridor entrance and shouted down it, "I hope he can hear me!"

"Give him some space, Zam," I said, half watching for movement on the monitoring screens. I hadn't seen any yet. "He's under a lot of pressure. We're all his responsibility and Sym's death has hit him hard. Please don't take his actions personally."

"You always say that. But if he wants to be a decent commander, he needs *better people skills!*"

"Zamya," Kobe groaned from his desk, "at least he threw his helmet. He could easily have thrown you across the room instead."

Zamya bared her teeth at him, hissing her displeasure. She turned back to me and said in a slightly lighter tone, "I'm going to check on Oz."

"Good idea."

Zamya left, and the room fell silent. Both Cora and I scanned the screens searching for evidence of the creatures' return. The portside cameras indicated the sea water was starting to draw closer to the ship, but I chose to turn my focus to the starboard side.

It wasn't long until I saw them. A cluster of pale-yellow creatures littering the clifftop, briefly halting and rearing at the edge. They began to descend the ragged steps in the rockface. Some rolled violently down, while others carefully took one step at a time. There was at least a dozen of them, varying in size. The smallest was the size of a large, thickset dog. The largest, as terrifying as the one I saw through the closing doors last night.

I took a deep breath, attempting to hold back the fear prickling through my veins, waiting for the carnage to begin. The gnawing began moments later. Kobe slumped into his highbacked chair, whilst Cora mewed into her hands. Outside, the creatures were everywhere, but thankfully, they remained at beach level. My only hope was the landing gear wouldn't disintegrate easily.

Taking my eyes away from the troubling sight, I found Rooke standing directly behind me. His tall stature looked menacing from my seated position. His hard stare was digesting the live footage playing before him, the planes of his face were stern, emotionless.

He glanced down at me, his dark eyebrows shadowing the whites of his eyes. "Cora, go round up Zamya. Bring Oz as well, if he's able."

Without hesitation, Cora scurried to the corridor entrance, disappearing from sight. Rooke ambled to the opposite side of the room and perched himself on the edge of the desk space. Keeping his eyes fixed to the floor, he waited for the rest of the crew to emerge.

A pasty looking Oz entered first. He was shirtless, exposing an avalanche of toned muscles and tattoos. His left shoulder was heavily bandaged, his arm resting in a sling across his chest. Cora held onto his other arm, guiding him to the seat beside Rooke.

Still scowling, Zamya followed behind. She paused in the doorway, standing with a defiant aura surrounding her.

Rooke finally looked up, glancing around the room, meeting each one of our gazes with solid regard. "So, here's the plan," he said in a far more passive tone than his expression suggested. "We bunk in here tonight, all of us. We'll create makeshift beds using our mattresses, blankets, chairs, anything we can find. We stay together. If you need the restroom, or need to get anything from the kitchen, we go in pairs. And we go armed." He met my gaze. "Eden and I discovered that the horror beetles, as Zam calls them, appear to have issues with climbing steep and possibly flush surfaces. I doubt they will penetrate anything above the lower hull. I've sealed the stairs off to the engine rooms. If they get in, they won't be able to access this level. Tomorrow, I'll contact Troy. Ask him to bring the dropship down to collect us…"

"Isn't that a bit risky?" I queried, concerned Rooke's temper was hanging on the edge of a knife.

"It's more than risky," Kobe stepped in. "It's suicide." From under his eyebrows Rooke peered at the head scientific engineer. His unimpressed glare spoke volumes, but Kobe didn't back down. "The dropship is solely for use on moons and asteroids, which have none or very little atmospheric pressure. In an atmosphere this dense, there's a high risk the dropship will burn up on entry. And it will have to endure entry at least twice. There are only six seats."

"I am well aware of that," Rooke said.

"If you want my advice, it won't work. You risk losing Troy."

"It's a bit late for precaution, don't you think?" Zamya's snarl was aimed directly at Kobe. "Maybe you should've thought about that last night before allowing Oz and Sym outside. You were in charge."

"Zamya, leave it," Rooke interjected.

"If they had stayed onboard," she continued, "Oz and Sym could've helped with the repairs today, saving us valuable time. We would all be back on The Orka now, safe!"

"Zamya, shut it!" Rooke glared at her. Her eyes were defiant, but eventually she lowered her guard, folding her arms across her chest. Kobe turned in his chair, obscuring his face from view.

Rooke looked over at me, silently asking for my opinion. I cleared my throat. "I agree with Kobe. The risk is too high. Troy is our only communication link to Allura. If we lose him, we lose every chance of getting home."

"So, you'd rather wait another five months for Solarfleet to come and rescue us?" Zamya groaned, clearly disturbed by the direction the conversation was heading. "Do they even know we're stranded?"

"They will," Rooke said.

"I don't want to stay in this shithole for five months."

"I will," Cora said, shielding herself behind Oz. "If it means not risking Troy."

"Ha, wouldn't want to kill off your shag buddy, would we?"

"Zam!" Rooke threw her another authoritative glare. Zamya raised her hands in surrender before leaning back against the wall.

"We have enough food to last two years," I said. "If we remain organised with the wiring repairs and keep on top of the destruction that occurs every night, we'll continue to have power. The sun is strong. Solar energy will suffice."

"Until it starts raining," Zamya mumbled.

"What happens if those things get inside?" Cora asked, warily.

"We won't let that happen," Kobe said. "The scouting ship was in a far worse condition to start with. They didn't stand a chance. We do."

Rooke pushed away from the desk he was perched on. "Okay, we'll take a vote," he said, rubbing his hands together. "Who agrees to remain here and wait for Solarfleet to arrive?"

Kobe and Cora raised their hands. I joined them. Rooke nodded his acknowledgment, then asked, "Who agrees to risk using the dropship and return to The Orka as soon as possible?"

Zamya raised her hand, slowly followed by Oz. I looked across at Rooke. As the commanding officer, if there was a voting draw, he'd have the casting vote. He nodded his head in understanding. Biting his lower lip, he flared his nostrils. I watched his mind tick over in contemplation. Everyone remained silent, waiting for his decision.

"My vote…my vote is to use the dropship." A stir of mixed emotions murmured around the circular room. "But…only if Troy agrees to it. It's his life that's at stake."

I nodded my approval. Rooke passed me a look of gratitude before leaving the room. The others spoke amongst themselves and began to build the makeshift bunker. Without a word to anyone, I scurried to the flight deck.

I had made the transferral of clean fuel barely half an hour ago, but that didn't mean I was going to allow it to become contaminated with salt water again. No one had suggested that we may be able to complete the repairs tomorrow and leave on Parvos. I wasn't going to sit back and let that remote option become extinct.

I watched the sea drift closer, waiting for another fuel transferral to complete. The sun began to set over the horizon, and the sound of unusual growls filled the air outside.

The clattering of metal and running water coming from the kitchen area behind me shifted my attention. I glanced over my shoulder and found Rooke standing in the cockpit doorway, holding a kettle of water. The hilts of two small guns were visible in his hip holster.

"I thought I said not to go anywhere alone." He raised his eyebrows.

"I did hear you." The fuel dial on the dashboard changed to red, indicating the fuel had been redeposited into the redundant tank. "It was only for half an hour. I wanted to spare the remaining fuel. You know…just in case we can use it."

I stood up aiming to leave the restricted area, but Rooke was still lingering in the doorway, a soft smile dancing across his lips. Lifting his free hand, his fingers traced my jawline. "I like this confident, optimistic side to you."

Slightly taken aback, I scowled at him. "Stop mocking me, Rooke."

He laughed. "I'm not."

I pushed past him, snatching the kettle from his hand. Clicking it onto the power terminal on the kitchen side, I pulled six metal cups out of the cupboard below.

"Do you really think we could survive five months here?" Rooke asked. I looked at him. He was leaning in the doorway, hands in his jumpsuit pockets.

"Yes. As long as Zamya doesn't kill us all first."

He chuckled. "She does seem angrier than usual."

"Ha, coming from Mr. Angry, himself." I smirked, distributing the soup granules equally into each cup.

"I'm the commander. I'm allowed to be angry."

"And no one else is?"

"No." He chuckled again. "Everyone else needs to be on their best behaviour."

"Go around voicing that statement and you'll end up with a mutiny on your hands."

Rooke screwed his face up fractiously. "Ha, and I'm guessing you'll lead the charge…Commander Riley."

I stuck my tongue out at him and he started poking at my ribs with his finger. I elbowed him away, but he continued relentlessly.

"No, stop it. Stop it…Rooke!" I glared up at him. He stopped playing, dropping his hand on the curve of my hip. His face mere inches away, eyes locked with mine. Too close, he was too close for comfort. The look he held was solemn, unreadable, and for a moment, I couldn't breathe. My heart was pounding in my ears as

I gazed into his mesmerising eyes, shamefully glancing at his sultry lips, wondering what they'd feel like against my own.

Why did he always do this to me? Innocent moments like this became torturous.

His lips eventually curved upward, and he pulled away. "It has a ring to it, don't you think? Commander Riley."

Still batting away the image of those lips against mine, I forced a smile and began pouring the hot water from the kettle into the cups. Rooke stepped around me, opening the food compressor, pulling out several warm bread rolls.

"I've been thinking," I said. "There must be some form of intelligent life here."

"Why do you say that?"

"Captain Lewison mentioned that their ship was domineered by a probe-like entity, which guided them here. Well…where did it come from? Someone must've despatched it?"

"I have thought about it. I've asked Troy to check the satellites in orbit, to see if any are active. He hasn't found any live ones so far. It may have been a stray from several millennia ago."

"I doubt that's possible. Someone must have sent that probe out. With those beasts roaming around, I'm starting to wonder if it could've been a cry for help."

"Really? I was actually thinking the opposite. I'm wondering if it was a trap…to lure us in."

I chuckled. "Now who's being the sceptic?"

"There are giant flesh-eating beetles outside, munching on our ship. I have a right to be sceptical."

"Fair point."

He gently bumped my shoulder with his. "We balance each other out, you and me. You're the yin to my yang. We work well together. We always have."

I hummed my approval. Yes, we worked well together, but that didn't help with my everlasting internal battle of wills and wants.

We returned to the analysing room with the food. A cluster of makeshift beds were made up in the middle of the room, and a low seated area of cushions had been placed up against one of the curving desks in one corner.

Oz lay on one of the beds, his good arm across his eyes. Rooke squatted next to him. "Here, buddy, have something to eat."

Oz eyed Rooke, then the food, and grimaced as he hauled himself upright. He took a bread roll and started nibbling on it. I frowned at his unusual behaviour. He was renowned for being a gannet. That roll would normally have been devoured in two bites. I couldn't help noticing his deathly pale complexion. A fine sweat misted his neck and forehead and his limbs seemed laboured with every movement.

Placing a cup of soup on Kobe's desk, I lingered, observing his work. Using the cameras, he was taking screen shots of the creatures roaming outside, creating a calculated 3D digital illustration of a specimen. Scales covered the upper part of the body structure, the colour ranging from white to brown. The underside was lined with abdominal segments where the six rigid legs jutted out, and those skeletal fingers flexed in several places. The four eyes and mouth were flat against the front of the wide head, the fangs protruding at a vicious angle.

Zamya appeared next to me, sipping on her soup. "What I'd give to dissect one of those beasts."

"I'm not sure how easy they are to kill," Kobe mumbled, without removing his gaze from his work. "Oz and Rooke shot a couple last night, but they seemed unaffected, or just scarpered away."

Zamya chuckled. "I wouldn't be surprised if their injured become their prey. They reek of primal cannibalism." She began to walk away. "But I guess we'll never find out as we'll be back on The Orka this time tomorrow."

I exchanged a look with Kobe. A part of me hoped Troy would see sense and oppose the suggestion of using the dropship.

Long, tedious hours ticked by. It was zero two hundred Earth hours. Oz and Zamya were asleep on separate beds in the centre of the room, Kobe snoozed in his desk chair, while Rooke sat at the comms desk with Cora next to him, both reading from one of her dozens of books. The power had gone out over an hour ago, but, thankfully, the backup systems kicked in without issue.

I sat on the makeshift couch in the corner, my back propped up against the cushions with several guns cluttering the desktop above me. I had gotten used to the gnawing sounds still reverberating through the ship. Occasionally, the sound merged in with the background noise of the computers, almost disappearing from all acknowledgment. But sleep continued to evade me.

From under my weary eyelids, I watched Rooke walk over. Sitting down beside me, he placed an A4 pad on my lap. I rubbed my eyes and peered down at it. Recognising the thick, yellowing paper, I realised it was Sym's sketch book. I straightened up in my seat, eyeing Rooke questionably.

"Take a look," he said.

On opening the front cover, I discovered an amazing pencil sketch of Zamya's face. Everything about it was exquisite. Her frown, her large dark eyes, the shape of her petite face and hooked nose. It was a perfect depiction of her. I glanced up at Rooke. He nodded, encouraging me to continue.

As I flicked through the pages, I found more and more sketches of different people filling the cartridge paper, all drawn by Sym. An old, rotund lady sat by a window, dressed in heavily patterned clothing. Three young, similar looking women laughed with each other. A teenage girl with dark braided hair played a violin. Her smile was a brilliant wide flash of teeth, similar to Sym's. I could only imagine these women were Sym's family. I remembered him telling me he had four sisters and a mother at home.

A sad thought jabbed its way through my mind. How many people had Sym left behind on Allura? How many people wouldn't find out about his death for weeks, maybe months?

I continued, discovering more sketches of The Orka crew. Most were black or grey, but the odd one was drawn in colour. Cora being one of them. A vision of her sitting at her desk, smiling down into a thick book, with a loose strand of her golden curly hair falling over her eyes. I smiled at the sentimental detail.

Rooke turned the page. "This is my favourite," he said, pointing to a pencil sketching of my face. It really was me. An oval face, with high cheek bones, a pointed chin, and subtle dimples above the jaw line. My nose was straight with a curving bobble on the end, my biggest physical insecurity. My eyes were wide, sat under an arch of dark eyebrows and dark lashes, and my shoulder length hair was pulled back in a neat ponytail.

"I think he's captured you perfectly."

Scanning the image, I smiled. It was like looking in a mirror.

I turned the page, now meeting a large colour sketch of an eye. I gasped at the realisation it was one of mine.

My eyes were my most distinguishable feature. They were unusual, some called them strange, but most referred to them as stunning. The iris was made up of an amber, multiple-sided star circling each pupil. Each point of amber burst into irregular speckles of brown before meeting a sphere of vivid green. The green was surrounded by a gradient layer of blue, the darkest shade lining the circular edge. It was the reason why my parents had called me Eden. My father had claimed I didn't cry when I was born. I just stared up at him with my large, unusual eyes and he instantly knew how unique I was. I was their paradise in a world full of troubles.

I shook my head, trying to subdue the thought. I missed my father. I missed my mother and brother, too. All of whom had been taken from me by the time I had reached the tender age of twenty.

Rooke's arm slid around my shoulders, and he squeezed my arm affectionately. There was no doubt he'd followed my train of thought. I was grateful I had his support. His friendship was worth more to me than I could ever express. His warmth, his security, his guidance. Without him, I'd be lost.

Sinking into his side, I placed my head on his shoulder.

I must've fallen asleep, because the next thing I knew, Zamya was nudging me awake.

Sitting up, I blinked several times trying to work out where I was. Meeting Zamya's gaze, she pushed a cup of coffee at me and said, "Are you alright? You cried out."

"Did I?" I accepted the cup; aware my cheeks were flushing. I wasn't sure what I'd been dreaming about. It hadn't been Jacob's funeral…or Rooke's, or had it?

There was movement in the room. Rooke and Kobe were conversing at the comms desk. Oz was sitting in Kobe's seat, eating breakfast, while Cora tidied the blankets away.

"What's going on?" I asked, testing the coffee's temperature, suddenly aware the sound of light tapping had become the new continual background noise.

"It's raining," Zamya replied. "The horror beetles have left."

"Is it still dark outside?"

"The sun just came up. Rooke is preparing to go outside soon."

After drinking my coffee and changing into a spare jumpsuit, I followed Rooke to the airlock chamber.

Checking the two lines of atmospheric suits hanging up against the wall behind the glass cabinets, we discovered they hadn't charged sufficiently overnight.

From next to me, Rooke's voice boomed through the ship, "Zam, how necessary are the atmospheric suits?"

I heard her huff before her footsteps stomped towards us. She appeared in the shadows of the loading bay entrance. "What's the proper question here, commander?"

Rooke tilted his head back, smiling at her insolent tone. "Do we need to wear the suits?"

"They didn't charge," I mentioned.

Her mood obviously hadn't improved since last night. Her response was a loud, prolonged groan.

"Don't growl at me, Zamya," Rooke chided. "I understand your reluctance to allow us to step outside without a suit on, but I'm asking if stepping out there will cause any detrimental effect, other than enhancing your paranoia. And your foul mood."

Folding her arms across her chest, Zamya scowled at Rooke. "I resent your allegation."

"And I'm getting tired of your constant moaning."

I winced, turning away. Nux, he was playing with fire.

Zamya huffed and marched to one of the suits next to me. After examining it, she turned to Rooke and announced, "They will be useless. You'll suffocate."

"I know that much!"

"I don't advise leaving the ship without one. But as Kobe keeps specifying, the air is non-toxic and breathable, so you won't die instantly."

"Good." Rooke tried to fight the smirk forming on his lips. "Thank you for your advice, doctor."

Zamya mumbled something incoherent and left the chamber, closing the inner airlock door behind her.

"Do you think she may explode by the time we come back in?" Rooke chuckled, zipping up his navy-blue fleeced jacket.

"You love winding her up," I said, checking the charge on the laser rifle I was now holding. "You'll regret it when she starts stabbing us all in our sleep. You were worried I'd lead a mutiny. Maybe you should keep an eye on Zam."

"She wouldn't dare."

"Oh? And I would?"

He winked at me and walked to the closed outer door.

Standing side by side, armed and ready for what could potentially meet us on the other side of the door, Kobe's voice came through Rooke's handheld radio, "Area is clear, sir."

Rooke hit the airlock button. The doors hissed open, and the ramp began unfolding in front of us. A pink glow flittered over the rockface to the left. The sea, a mixture of greys and blues in the distance to the right. Walking down the ramp, delicate droplets of water hit my face. I glanced up at the sky. The edge of a grey raincloud loomed above, showering cool raindrops over my skin. I took a deep breath. The air was fresh and clean, almost tranquil. But that was quickly wiped away…

Stepping off the ramp and turning towards the main section of the ship, we viewed the immense carnage littering the ground under and around the ship's hull. The amount of stripped metal, hull breaches, and wire destruction were abundant. I admitted to myself, the possibility of fixing this every day was slim to none.

I glanced up at Rooke. "Have you contacted Troy yet?"

"No." His voice had turned gruff and flat. "I was hoping we may find an alternative solution."

"I don't think there is one, Rooke."

He looked at me, surprised by my words. "Yesterday you opposed the dropship option." We both glanced at the metallic and mechanical mayhem surrounding us. "There is no other option, is there?"

"Doesn't look like it."

Rooke sighed. "When I accepted this mission, why didn't I ask for a larger subspace carrier with an extra atmospheric ship attached? That could've solved all our problems."

"We've never needed an extra one before."

"We've never been on a mission like this before."

I walked over to the sunken wheel, sighing with disappointment. The repaired cabling had caught my eye, it was once again hanging from the mechanical arm.

"When does Troy come back into radio contact?" I asked, ducking under the underside of the hull back towards Rooke. He was dusting off a piece of metal on the floor. But his reply didn't register with me. My attention was drawn to movement on the distant clifftop behind him. I flinched; my adrenaline surged. A humanoid figure atop a horse was silhouetted against the brightening sky.

Noticing my reaction, Rooke stood, looking in the same direction.

The figure instantly retreated, disappearing behind the cliffs, leaving us gazing in wonderment. Rooke stared back at me, mouth gaping. "Did you…did you see that?"

I nodded. "I think we may have found a form of intelligent life."

Without taking a moment to contemplate the discovery, Rooke rushed back onto the ship, striding towards the analysing room with me in tow.

"Kobe, Kobe. Is the drone still functional?" The urgency in his tone was a mix of what sounded like excitement and panic.

Kobe swung round in his desk chair. "Uh, yes. I believe so."

"Can you get it airborne. Immediately?"

"Sure." Kobe scurried to the comms desk and started typing commands into the computer. Rooke hovered behind him.

"What's going on?" Cora appeared next to me.

"We saw a human, or what looked like a human."

Cora gaped at me. "The Nux texts mention every human left Earth during the mass exodus."

"Like I said, it looked human."

"Go southeast," I heard Rooke instructing Kobe. I moved closer to the single monitoring screen on the edge of the comms desk. It displayed a vast grassed area, falling away into a mass of endless trees. But there was no sign of a horse and a rider.

Kobe flew the drone over the forest. It was too dense to see anything beneath the top canopy. He veered back towards the water's edge, scanning the coastline. Rooke peered closer. "Go back," he commanded.

Kobe turned the drone southwards. I held my breath as it skimmed the coastline, relaying the real time imagery. Then it came into view. A mountainous construction of rock jutting out of the cliff face into the sea. There was a scatter of movement from the beached area either side. Kobe flew lower, and figures became visible enough to identify they were humanoid. Some were hauling boats in from the sea, others scurrying towards the pronounced giant rock.

"Bingo." Rooke grinned at the discovery. "We have found intelligent life on Earth."

The screen unexpectedly flashed, and the drone began to plummet to the ground. Kobe grimaced as he tried to regain control of the remote machine, ignoring Rooke's pointless instructions.

The screen flickered, then went blank, and we all stared in shock.

"I think they may've seen us spying," Kobe said, his fingers still hovering over the keyboard.

Filling the silence, hurried footsteps grew louder behind us. We all turned as Zamya emerged from the corridor. She was frowning, but not with the same agitated intensity as earlier. "Rooke." Her tone was soft but uncomfortably perturbed. "It's Oz. He's had a relapse."

Chapter Eight

"I thought he was improving," Rooke said, entering the medical room.

"He was," Zamya replied. "I came to check on him after I left you in the airlock and found him like this."

Oz lay on the solitary bed in the middle of the small room. Covered in a grey blanket, he was shaking fiercely. His face was pale, glistening with sweat, whilst his lips appeared dry and colourless.

I moved to his bedside, grasping his hand. His closed eyelids flickered, and I caught a flash of blue, as if he was trying to open them to acknowledge my presence.

Zamya appeared next to me, peeling back the blanket covering Oz's injured shoulder. The bandage across his wound had been removed and the row of red and bruised incisions oozed with yellowing pus.

"It's infected." Zamya looked at Rooke standing behind me. "This bacteria isn't anything I've seen before. I doubt any Alluran medication will work."

"Can you at least try?" Rooke insisted.

"I have been, but…I'm worried it won't be enough."

Staring at our colleague, our friend, we all watched as his chest rose and fell rapidly. His breaths were short and ragged. There was nothing healthy about his condition.

There was a desperation in Zamya's tone when she said, "We need to get him back to The Orka."

"Do you have alternative treatment for him on The Orka?" Rooke asked.

Zamya fell silent. I glanced up at her. Her eyes were wide, fearful. Looking between us, she shook her head. "No."

Rooke cursed. We couldn't lose Oz, not like this. "How long does he have?"

"If he's lucky, a couple of days. But...seeing how quickly he's deteriorated, possibly only a few hours." I heard the waver in her voice.

Rooke cursed again. He pensively stared at Oz, then departed the room in haste.

I continued to stroke Oz's hand, attempting to ignore the grotesque injury on his shoulder. Normally, he was a visually intimidating man, but here...here he looked vulnerable. I felt the frown form between my eyebrows. *We can't lose Oz, he's the strong one.*

I watched Zamya clean up the excess pus. There was so much of it. The unsightly mess turned my stomach, and I was fighting the urge to retch. I felt Oz's hand squeeze mine with a little more force than expected. Whether the procedure was causing him pain, or he was merely checking I was still there, I didn't know. But I squeezed his hand in reply, hoping my company was somehow comforting.

Zamya remained silent as she worked, her expression distant and grave. After a few minutes, she placed the apparatus on the medical table beside her. Removing her surgical goggles and mask, she took a deep breath and stared at the wall. "There's just too much of it," she said. I noticed her hands trembling as she pulled off her medical gloves.

Before I had the chance to cross the small area to comfort her, Rooke returned.

"Pack up as many supplies as you can carry," he said, placing two large, Solarfleet branded rucksacks on the floor. "We're leaving."

"Is Troy coming to get us?" Zamya asked, turning to face him.

"No, we're going to get help."

I watched Rooke move towards the bed. "What type of help?" I asked.

"We're going to find that human colony."

"What human colony?" Zamya asked, glancing at me.

"We think we've discovered a form of intelligent life. Human life," I replied.

"What? No!" Zamya's eyes flew wide, looking back at Rooke. "Are you crazy? They may be as hostile as those horror beetles."

"They may know how to treat Oz's infection. It's a risk I'm willing to take." He looked down at Oz. "Can you bandage him up again? We'll have to move him."

Zamya gaped at Rooke. Her expression matching my own.

"Rooke," I stood up, grabbing his arm, "are you sure about this?"

"Absolutely. If we get Troy to bring the dropship down, Oz will still die."

"He may *not* die," Zamya whimpered.

"He's dying, Zam. You know that better than I do. If I send for the dropship, Troy may die attempting the manoeuvre and then the five of us remaining will be stranded here. If we find the humans, there's a chance we can save Oz *and* keep Troy safe. And I have no intention of splitting us up. We stay together."

"But…but," I stammered, completely taken aback by his decision. "How far is the colony?"

"Eleven miles."

"Eleven miles? And you want us to carry Oz eleven miles? Have you seen the size of him?"

"Yes. That's why we're taking the life raft."

"Holy souls," Zamya mumbled behind us.

Rooke shot her a pointed look and began to walk through the door into the corridor. I followed him closely. "Rooke, we haven't studied the intensity of the sea. The currents could throw us off course. It could be treacherous. We don't know what type of life forms reside in the water. We may get attacked. And Zamya's right. The humans shot the drone down. How can you be certain they won't do the same to us as soon as they see us?"

Rooke halted before we entered the analysing room. Turning, he placed his hands on my shoulders and peered into my eyes. "We're doing this, Eden. We can't stay here, we'll all die, starting with Oz."

Silently staring at him, I mentally dissected his words.

"Please, Eden. Please give me your backing; your support. I need you."

I swallowed down the rational objections jumping around my head, and somehow nodded my acceptance. A brief, appreciative smile twitched across his lips before he stepped into the analysing room, leaving me standing in the shadows of the corridor, fighting the doubts and anxiety.

An hour later, I stood with Cora at the water's edge, holding the oval shaped life raft afloat. With both Oz's tattooed arms draped about their necks, we watched Rooke and Kobe stagger towards us with him wedged between them—his feet dragging along the sand, his head slumped forward.

Stepping backwards onto the small, makeshift boat, they hauled Oz over the side and laid him down along one of the edges, avoiding the two large canisters of water dominating the centre. Zamya climbed in after them, covering Oz with a hoard of blankets. He was still shivering feverishly.

Rooke returned to the ship to seal the airlock. I watched the ramp retract as he marched back towards us. He was wearing a comms earpiece with a connecting wire running down his jumpsuit into his chest pocket. Kobe and I wore the same, connecting us to Troy on The Orka. The ship was in a prime position to navigate us towards the human colony, using a signal Kobe had wired up barely an hour ago.

"Troy, we're all set," Rooke's voice echoed in my earpiece, and from directly in front of me.

"Roger that," Troy's voice crackled through. "The sea's

current is still moving in your favour. You just need to get across the wave break."

"I can see it, it's not far." Rooke glanced at me, noticing my tight expression. It must have given away my doubts. He tapped my shoulder trying to reassure me before he gripped the same piece of rope Cora was holding. Letting go, Cora scrambled onto the boat and together, Rooke and I pushed the raft into the sea.

The waves slapped against the thick fabric of my jumpsuit, labouring my movements. The cold sensation bit at my skin sending shudders down my already stiff body. Ten metres out, with the water now up to my waist, we passed the area where the waves began to break, and instantly the boat resisted the urge to retreat towards the beach.

With Rooke's help, I jumped into the floating piece of inflated rubber. I clambered to one side and sat down next to Cora. She wrapped a blanket around my water sodden legs keeping me warm. Rooke landed at the back of the boat near Oz's feet. Repositioning himself, he grabbed one of the oars from the rim, ready for use if needed. His expression was remarkably calm. He appeared focused, competently in control. In comparison, I felt as if I was going to vomit.

The raft began to drift southwards, and Troy's voice confirmed we were moving towards our destination. The thought of where we were going still harrowed at my nerves. I scanned the clifftop in the distance, eager to catch a glimpse of the figure I spotted that morning. Who were they and were they still watching us?

We were unprotected, floating out on the vast ocean. Even with the hordes of weapons each of us carried, we were sitting ducks. Although our blue-grey uniform blended in with the surrounding water and skyline, the raft was a conflicting comparison, displaying illuminous yellow and orange. Any life, intelligent or not, would see us coming for miles, but I got the impression from Rooke that was all part of the plan.

Drifting past the cove where the scouting ship sat crumbling against the rockface, my eyes swept over to Rooke again. He was conversing with Troy and Kobe, his eyes continually scanning the whole area with commanding obligation. Kobe sat at the very front of the vessel, Zamya to his right. She was intermittently closing her eyes and clenching her stomach. It baffled me how she could endure space travel with no ill effect yet suffered profusely on the open sea.

Cora tapped my arm. I found her glancing behind us towards the never-ending horizon of ocean.

"Look," she said pointing outwards, "can you see?"

I turned towards the waves, following her line of sight. At first, I only saw the outline of white tipped waves, but after several seconds of scouring the distance, I saw what she was excited about. Well over a mile away, a large form skimmed the surface of the water. It sprayed water upwards, creating a prominent mist. Then another even larger form jumped out of the water, exposing its dark grey skin and white underbelly. It twisted mid-air before crashing into the waves. The penetrating clap alerted the rest of the crew.

A wide grin of excitement spread across Cora's mouth. "Whales," she said in awe. "They still exist."

My concerned frown turned into a smile. There were few ocean-faring mammals on Allura, and none that originated on Earth. Only golden hoffs, which were long beaked sea otters, lived in the Alluran oceans, along with multitudes of small fish. But they were miniscule compared to these large, hopefully gentle beasts, and nowhere near as majestic.

"What the Nux is that?" Zamya groaned, a hint of trepidation in her tone.

Cora turned, rolling her eyes. "It's a whale, dummy."

"No, not that...*that*."

We all caught a glimpse of what Zamya was fretting about. A glint of turquoise light flashed sporadically from the top of a lone standing, eroded stack, which stood separately from a rock-faced peninsula. The flashing sequence was not constant, nor was it repetitive. I heard Rooke's heavy breathing through my earpiece. His posture had stiffened, his eyes seemed even more alert than before.

"It could be some form of communication," Kobe said, watching the light intently. "Similar to a lighthouse or Morse Code."

The current took the raft out wide, around the tall slab of rock protruding out of the sea. As we drifted past, I peered up at the top, assuming we'd be given some identification of the intelligent life form we were seeking. But the area was barren. The light continued to flash unaided.

It was only when the life raft juddered, surfing the change in the current, we saw what we'd been anticipating. The mountainous mound of rock stood between us and the next headland several miles along. Two small, narrow, low laying boats, each with one turquoise scalene shaped sail, were moving swiftly towards us.

I took a deep breath. It was a poor attempt to stabilise my racing heart.

"Remember what I said," Rooke's voice called to us all. "Stay calm. No challenging movements, no weapons. We don't want to rile them."

"I'm guessing they've spotted you?" Troy asked through the comms.

"Yeah. We're likely to go dark for a while."

"Copy that."

We sat in silence, watching the boats grow nearer. Figures stood along the open front and sides, looking in our direction. As the distance closed, the haze fell from around them. The boats wooden hulls were decorated with swirls of blue and coral. Their sails were embroidered with blue and golden thread, again in large, intricate swirls.

The sound of low voices drew my attention back to those occupying the boats. They were still too far out to identify, although their general stature signified they were human. Taller perhaps, and broader. But I became alarmed when a glint of light reflected off them. Several long spears were aimed directly at us, ready to engage. I heard Zamya muttering curses under her breath, while Cora inched closer to me. Remarkably, Rooke and Kobe remained calm and sangfroid.

A voice hollered over to us, using a strange unknown language. We all stared as one boat headed towards the port side of our small raft, the other to the bow. A hooked line flew towards us from the ship to the left. It landed barely inches from Oz's semiconscious body, puncturing the rubber of our life raft. Rooke stood up raising his hands in surrender. Remaining seated, the rest of us followed suit.

The line lurched back, dragging us closer to the boat. Unusual faces came into view, peering down on us as our vessel began to deflate. I couldn't help but gawk as one stepped to the edge of the boat deck, squatting down to grab the line when it stopped retracting. His pale limbs were long and lean, with an exposed, muscular, upper torso. A blue spiral, like those displayed on the hull and sails, covered most of his right pectoral. He wore a baggy pair of grey trousers, rolled halfway up his calves. His feet were bare.

I watched his long white-blonde hair swirl about in the breeze as he barked a series of harsh words at us, none that any of us could decipher. We remained silent, passing glances between each other. He barked again, this time pointing his spear at Rooke, who had remarkably continued to stand on the destabilising rubber floor.

"We wish you no harm," Rooke replied. "We need your help." He gestured towards Oz. With one hand still raised in the air, Zamya removed Oz's blankets, exposing the yellow stained bandages wrapped across his shoulder. The boatman sneered his disgust and began conversing with one of the other boatmen. After a couple of minutes of anticipating their resolution, the boatman looked back, eyeing each one of us warily. He pointed at me, Cora, and Kobe, then pointed to the boat at our bow, which steadily drew closer. Then pointing at Rooke, Zamya, and Oz, he grunted towards the deck he was standing on.

Rooke glanced over his shoulder at me, and I nodded in

understanding. We were to be separated. I was in command of Cora and Kobe.

Within seconds, the three of us were abruptly loaded onto the second boat. Our backpacks, radios, and weapons were removed immediately, and our hands were bound in front of us. After being forced into a sitting position in the middle of the wooden deck, I grimaced at the sight. The floor was cluttered with rope, nets, and what looked like fish guts. Shuffling to avoid a patch of blood and entrails, I peered down at the itchy restraint around my wrists. It had the same appearance as seaweed but was clearly reinforced. My hands could barely move under the restriction.

As the first boat began to sail off in front with Rooke, Oz, and Zamya aboard, I glanced back at our sad excuse of a life raft. It was partially submerged, sinking further as we sailed away.

I glanced at Cora beside me. She sat cross legged with her head hung to the floor. Whether she was crying or sweating, I was unsure, but I noted a water droplet fall from her cheek and into her lap. Kobe sat next to her. With intrigue, he silently observed the new humans flanking us.

There were two of them watching us attentively. My eyes roamed over one of them. It was uncanny how human he looked, although it was clear we were not of the same species. A pale skin, with the faintest blue tinge covered his face, exposed chest, shoulders, and feet. A small blue spiral was displayed on his right pectoral, far smaller than that of the boatman barking orders on the other vessel. I could only assume this signified rank amongst them.

I continued to visually examine the guard. He had a mop of white-blonde hair which fell to his shoulders. His head was long with sculptured cheekbones and a sharp chin. The nose was flatter than a standard human's, with thin, elongated nostrils, and his mouth was wide, displaying teeth similar to my own. The only difference was his canines were longer and far sharper.

The most human attribute about him was his eyes. They were a beautiful turquoise in colour. When he met my gaze, I gulped, flicking my eyes to the deck. But I was overly fascinated. Glancing back, I flinched at the realisation he was studying me. These people were probably just as curious about us as we were them.

I levelled my gaze, tracing his rounded shoulders with my eyes, running them down his lean, muscular arms. My eyes lingered there, squinting at the several slits of skin above and below his elbow. They were inch long openings on the insides of his arms. A flap of skin wavered over the top, in the same way a fish gill did. Glancing down at his bare feet, I noticed a piece of translucent skin webbed between each toe. I inwardly gasped at the revelation. Was it possible these humans could swim and breathe under water? I wondered if he had more gill-like openings under his trouser legs.

I caught Kobe's eye, his eyebrows raised showing the same intrigue I felt. Mumbling under his breath, he said to me, "Fish-men?"

To our surprise, a low, intimidating chuckle rumbled from both guards. We peered up at them. The one I had been observing was shaking his head. "Neb," he said, in a raspy, unusual accent. Pointing to himself, he said, "Akquarian."

PART TWO

Akquarian

Chapter Nine

The mountainous rock towered above us, blotting out the warm sunshine as we sailed towards it. A chill prickled my skin as darkness suddenly engulfed us. Squeezing my eyes together, I blinked repeatedly, trying to adjust my vision. After what felt like several delirious minutes; light streamed across the ceiling and walls ahead of us, exposing the jagged interior of a dark tunnel.

The restricted height eventually opened out to reveal an enormous cavern full of pale limestone stalactites and jagged chalky walls. The roar of water filled my ears before I noticed a glorious waterfall falling from a dark facet at the very top of the far cavern wall. I glanced at Cora—her eyes were wide with wonder.

The boat came to a halt and the Akquarians began to shout to each other, exchanging what I could only perceive as orders. A brutish hand landed at the nape of my neck, tugging at the collar of my jumpsuit. I haphazardly stood up, only to be abruptly escorted along a slatted, wooden gangway, before ducking into a narrow tunnel at the opposite end. The potent smell of seaweed and dampness filled my nose, causing my eyes to water. Strange blue lights hung at intersections along the dark, moisture-soaked walls. My eyes remained focused on the Akquarian in front of me, aware that the one still holding the back of my jumpsuit was carrying a long-handled spear. The point glistened in my peripheral vision. But I refused to panic. I had to stay strong for Cora and Kobe. There was no sign of Rooke and the others.

A cascade of steps appeared in my pathway, gleaming with moisture in the dim light. The Akquarian at my back noted my hesitancy and pushed me on. The steps were slimy and unstable under my booted feet. I clenched my teeth, attempting to keep my balance even though I was being brashly coerced forward by the brute at my back.

The steps spiralled upwards for several agonising, dizzy minutes. But when we emerged at the top, so did an array of sunlight. A large hole in the rock stood to my left, looking out onto the horizon of ocean, and the smell of fresh salty air hit me. The tense muscles in my back relaxed slightly, allowing my body to twist with ease as I glanced behind. Cora and Kobe were still with me, both being escorted by their own personal guard.

We continued, passing under the threshold of an archway carved into the dark rock, entering into a wide, open corridor. The walls continued to display the natural roughness from the indigenous rock, but the floors were smooth and flat. The black-brown marble effect looked as though the ragged rock had been scrubbed down with precision. It was gleaming, reflecting the surroundings.

I glanced upwards. Looming metres above, sunlight hit the ceiling in several places. A line of turquoise-coloured stones were suspended halfway down, twinkling in the daylight, reflecting intricate patterns on the floor and walls. The aura of this place felt like a palace, relishing in raw, earthly elegance. It was extraordinary.

I was abruptly pulled to a halt. Too fascinated by my surroundings, I hadn't noticed the Akquarian in front of me had stopped before a towering, arched door. Again, it was made of dark rock, with a sizeable spiral engraved into the exterior—the same design I had seen several times now. The door jarred open, screeching as the uneven bottom sliced across the floor beyond.

My personal guard grabbed my upper arm and hauled me inside. The room was lined with more armed guards, all with a golden spiral tattooed across the right side of their bare chest, dressed in bronze-coloured trousers clasped at the ankle. An empty throne, constructed of shards of rock and azure glass sat at the far end of the vast room. Two heavily armoured Akquarians stood at the base of its dais, staring at us while they conversed discretely.

Much to my relief, Rooke and the others were present. Rooke and Zamya were on their knees, each with a guard looming over them. Zamya was closer to the door, Rooke further along, closer to the dais, and Oz was sprawled out between them, unconscious but still guarded.

I was led up the walkway towards Rooke. The grip on my arm tightened, bringing me to a stop two metres to the left of him. A foot jolted into the back of my knee, forcing me down. I grunted at the shock of my knees hitting the unforgiving floor. Catching Rooke's eye, I realised his eyebrows were knitted together, worry etched across his face. If I wasn't mistaken, he was momentarily regretting his decision to come here.

A spear prodded into Rooke's shoulder, and he obediently hung his head. I glanced up at the guard behind Rooke, recognising him as the boatman who spoke to us on first contact; the one with the large blue spiral plastered on his chest. He sneered at me, and I instantly turned, dropping my head.

We waited several silent minutes, my heart pounding in my ears. The sound of low, guttural murmurs echoed around us in a language I could only describe as a mixture of throat scraping and grunts. But the voices fell silent as a loud, screeching door opened, piercing the tension. Slapping footsteps followed, and every Akquarian in the room bowed towards the dais.

Without moving my head, I peered forward under my eyebrows, noticing a pair of pale, subtly webbed feet standing at the edge of the raised platform. A cluster of small, sparkling gems dangled on a golden chain around one ankle. The other was painted with colourful swirls.

Movement around me suggested those bowing had returned to their upward position. I glanced over to Rooke, catching his fleeting gaze, before a hand grabbed his collar, pulling him upright, still on his knees. A hand landed on my shoulder, commanding I did the same.

In front of us, on the dais, stood a male Akquarian draped in an elaborate gold and bronze tunic and matching trousers. Two golden clasps sat on his shoulders, pinning a coral cape into place, allowing it to flow behind him. I lifted my gaze to his face. Sharp eyes studied me as another Akquarian—one with a curving sword at his hip, wearing a cape in a dark shade of blue—whispered in his ear. He nodded his head, shifting his gaze to Rooke, then to me. Both had long, clean blonde hair, pulled clear from their faces with a handful of tight braids.

The blue caped Akquarian stepped back, placing his hand on the hilt of his sword as he stood to attention. His abdomen, shins, and forearms were dressed in gold plated armour. The way he remained close to the other one indicated he was a personal guard, or a highly ranked soldier.

"I hear you speak the ancient tongue."

My eyes darted to the Akquarian at the front of the dais, the one who I now realised was wearing a crown of interwoven gold and green. *Did he just speak Alluran?*

I glanced at Rooke who was staring at him, just as surprised as I was. Our silence seemed to confuse him, and he reverted to his own, strange language to speak with the blue caped guard.

He stepped forward, down one step, and said coherently, "I did not think my dialect was so poor. Do you not understand me?"

My breath hitched, completely baffled at how this new species of human knew our language. Was he an evolved version of what we had been three thousand years ago, here on Earth?

Aware the awkward spate of silence was concerning the regal being before us, Rooke's voice suddenly echoed around the room. "Yes, your words are perfectly coherent. I apologise. I…we did not expect to hear our own language spoken here."

Again, the Akquarian looked confused. His eyebrows drawn together, studying Rooke for a matter of seconds. "Where are you from, stranger?"

"We…we come from a place called Allura," Rooke said.

"I have not heard of such a place."

"It's unlikely you have. It is not of this world, but of

82

another, in a neighbouring solar system."

The Akquarian raised his eyebrows and snorted. "Not of this world? Is that why you arrived in that loud, flying monstrosity?"

Rooke's face froze. They knew we had arrived days ago but chose to spy on us rather than help us? Had they done the same with the scouting ship? And left them to die at the clutches of those ravenous beasts?

Eventually Rooke replied, despondently, "Yes."

"Hmm." The Akquarian turned, walked up the step, and seated himself regally on his throne. "So, who are you and why are you here?" His tone was cold and challenging.

Rooke raised his head a touch higher. "I am Commander Maddox." He pointed to me with his bound hands. "This is Lieutenant Commander Riley…and my crew. We are here simply because one of our scouting ships went missing from the edges of our solar system, and it was our mission to find it. Its tracking beacon brought us here, but the crew were dead by the time we arrived."

The Akquarian nodded his head in understanding. "And what are you intending on doing now that you have found Earth?"

Rooke fell silent. He was looking at the king-like humanoid lounging on his throne, wondering where the motives for his questions were coming from. Was it possible they were worried we had come back to conquer their home after all these years?

"We wish you no harm," Rooke said.

"You wish us no harm, however, you come laden with weapons!"

"They were purely for our defence. We…were unsure of how welcoming you would be. We risked coming here in hope you'd help heal our fallen crewmen."

The Akquarian eyed Oz's unconscious body laying behind Rooke. "I see you have encountered the Igknamai?"

"Pardon?"

"The Igknamai. The beasts."

"Is that what you call them?"

"It translates in the ancient tongue to *demon of paradise*.

Rather fitting if you ask me." He sighed before landing his gaze solidly on me. "If I am not mistaken, you appear to have females among your crew. Are they not of use to heal him?" Even though his eyes raked over my slouched body, his question was aimed at Rooke.

Rooke glanced at me. "Our medicines do not seem to be working. And the women of my crew are skilled in many things. They are highly regarded."

"Skilled? In what way? What is their purpose? Are they soldiers? Do you give them the same rights as the males?"

Rooke paused while I met the Akquarians gaze. I didn't warm to the prejudice in his tone, and the look of disgust he was giving me stripped away any sense or reason I had.

"Yes," I said gallantly, "I am a soldier." The irritation laced in my voice caused him to wince. He seemed shocked I'd spoken. "And, yes, I am treated with the same dignity and respect as any male, if not more so. I am the second in command aboard my commander's ship."

His gaze hardened. "You don't look as strong as your male counterparts, young female."

"I'm strong enough to pull my weight among men, and I'm intelligent enough to fly a ship across the expanse of space, defying the laws of physics." I doubted he could even comprehend that.

He scowled at me, his gaze suddenly far colder than before. It would appear he'd never been spoken to in such a way by a female. Somehow, it didn't surprise me.

I held his turquoise gaze with a defiance Zamya would be proud of. Ruffled by my audacity, the Akquarian abruptly stood. He strutted down the steps in a fluent, flowing movement, his coral cape swishing in waves behind him. I caught sight of Rooke's warning look in my peripheral vision, but I ignored it, still holding my nerve, watching the tall, lean Akquarian stalk dominantly towards me.

With his feet mere inches from my knees, he snatched my chin in his cold fingers, pulling my head back and to the side. I held my breath as he examined my profile, tracing his other hand down my neck and behind my ear. He seemed to hiss his disapproval and let go. "We honour our weaker sex by protecting them, keeping them safe. Maybe you don't deserve that honour."

Walking back to his throne, I looked at Rooke. His face was like that of an open book. He was beside himself, concerned, unnerved; heavily sighing with relief.

The Akquarian lounged in his throne again, deep in contemplation, stroking one of the glass arms. "I will help your fallen crewman," he finally announced, "but there will be terms."

Rooke swallowed hard and nodded, as if he had expected this. "And what are your terms?"

"You and your crew," the Akquarian shot his eyes briefly to me, "are to remain here under my supervision. Which means you abide by my rules. And you will allow me to…what is the word? Yes, study you. We do not have visitors often, especially those from distant worlds."

Rooke briefly glanced at me, before asking, "What do you mean by study?"

"I like knowledge, to be educated. I'm intrigued by you. I want to learn about you, your culture, your habits. I want to learn about your species."

"So, nothing…intrusive? Nothing physical?"

The Akquarian mused for a moment, surveying the crowd. "Nothing physical, unless consented to by yourself."

Rooke and I exchanged a look. My initial instinct was not to trust this male, but if it meant saving Oz's life, then it was a risk I was willing to take.

"Do we have a deal?"

I nodded and Rooke answered, "As long as your studies of my crew are chaperoned by myself, then, yes, we have a deal."

The Akquarian chuckled. "Oh, believe me, commander, you will always be chaperoned here." He clicked his fingers and the guard at my back stepped around me, cutting the bonds around my wrists. He pulled me to my feet, and I realised the others had also been unshackled.

Looking over my shoulder, Oz was being transferred from the floor onto a wooden stretcher by several guards. I watched them carry him away as I scanned the remainder of the room. Other than myself, Cora, and Zamya, there were no females present. All the guards appeared to be male.

I glanced back at the dais, to where their leader was no longer visible. Now descending the steps was the blue caped, golden armoured soldier—his eyes on me.

"Come," he said, his words spoken in a stronger accent than his leader. "I will show you to your rooms."

My guard grabbed my arm tightly and coerced me to follow the blue caped male exiting the main doorway. Heavy steps resounded from behind, and Zamya's hissing indicated I wasn't alone. But it was several minutes later, after climbing three sets of claustrophobic stairwells, I realised Rooke and Kobe weren't with us.

Walking along a wide hallway, I glanced at Cora and Zamya behind me, both being hauled along by tall, bare-chested Akquarians. "Where is Rooke?" I asked, my voice shaking. "Where is our commander?"

The blue caped soldier made no movement to acknowledge me, continuing to lead us down the hallway. I cursed under my breath. I couldn't ignore the overzealous churning in the pit of my stomach. Everything about this situation felt wrong, horribly wrong.

The soldier eventually stopped and opened a door to our left. Watching us with scrutiny, he said, "Your commander and the other males are being escorted to their rooms. The first rule you must become accustomed to is males and females do not mix here. Unless they are escorted by an approved chaperon, or during the seasonal festivities."

"Approved chaperon?" Zamya chided.

"Yes." He glared at her. "Anyone with a blue cape or sash is an approved chaperon. You'll do well to remember that." He rested his gaze back on me. "Rule number two. You remain in your rooms unless summoned. If you are found outside your rooms unauthorised, you will be reprimanded."

Reprimanded? How severely reprimanded? I stared up at his tall stature. Judging by the emphasis in his crystal blue eyes and the hard expression chiselled onto his face, it was something I did not want to challenge. There was a brutal scar, bluish in colour, slashed across his chin. I considered asking him where he'd gotten it from? Was it a battle scar or merely an example of punishment?

He gestured with his hand to the open doorway leading into a bright room. I swallowed down the knot forming in my throat and reluctantly walked over the threshold.

The sight that met me stopped me in my tracks. The room was breath-taking, almost overwhelming. It was spacious and light with a marbled floor and rustic looking walls, that twinkled as if they were made of crystal. A large balcony lay on the far side, allowing sunlight to stream into the room, and a soft breeze played with the loose strands of my ponytail. Pale, smooth surfaced rocks jutted out of the floor. Each had an array of cushions and throws sprawled across them in shades of green and blue. A similar structure, in the shape of a table and dining chairs, stood in the corner. A large glass vase sat in the middle, displaying a cluster of unusual purple flowers.

"Wow," gasped Cora, appearing next to me.

"I know," I whispered back, my eyes still finding beauty in everything they looked upon.

We both jumped at the sound of the Akquarian soldier's harsh voice behind us. "Your attendants will be along soon." I turned to face him. "Enjoy your stay," he said before pulling the door shut, sealing us inside.

"Attendants?" Zamya stared at the closed door. "Is this really a palace?"

"It would appear so," Cora said, walking towards the balcony.

"A palace full of pompous, sexist aquamen. I haven't seen one female here. What do you think they do with them? Lock them up and throw away the key until they're needed for breeding?"

Zamya folded her arms across her chest and huffed. "Palace or not, I still feel like we're prisoners."

"Maybe we are," I said, "but we have to endure this for Oz's sake."

Zamya cursed under her breath, her expression tightening. "What was Rooke thinking? We should've got Troy to bring the dropship down…"

"Zam! It wasn't an option."

"We have no idea where the others are."

"Zam!" I grabbed her arm, trying to prevent her panic from rising. "For now, it's the three of us. We need to stay strong. We need to have each other's backs. We'll get through this."

She met my gaze and huffed. "Let's hope this doesn't turn out to be the worst idea Rooke's ever had."

Chapter Ten

It felt as though several hours passed and still we had no word from Rooke. From where I stood on the balcony, the sea seemed to stretch out forever before me, twinkling against the orange and purple setting sky. The view had become breathtaking, if not surreal.

My mind was a jumble of thoughts, fluttering around on waves of anxiety. Were Rooke and Kobe safe? Was Oz's wound being treated, and could he really be saved? Were the Akquarians trustworthy? Was it the Akquarians who had sent the space probe which lured the Challenger here in the first place?

For every question I asked, I had no answers.

Zamya's steps sounded behind me. "I think I found the lavatory. It's a strange contraption behind the door on the far side of the bedroom."

I turned to look at her. "Strange in what way?"

"It's, it's…" She screwed her face up. "It's a small hole in the rock. There's flowing water beneath."

"Sounds wonderful." Cora came to stand with us.

We all turned towards the sun setting horizon, drawn towards its beauty.

"I'm starting to get hungry," Cora said meekly.

"Do you think they'll feed us?" Zamya asked.

"Depends on what class of prisoner we are, I guess," I said, trying to ignore my own grumbling stomach.

Zamya groaned. "I checked the door. It's not locked. We could leave and find some food."

"You heard what *Captain Blue Cape* said. If we're discovered outside this room unauthorised…"

"I know, I know. I just don't fancy dying of hunger, that's all."

The screeching sound of a door opening resounded through the open archway behind us, followed by a scurry of bare feet. We all turned and stalked into the room. Two Akquarian guards appeared in the main doorway holding our backpacks. They threw them down on the floor as three more Akquarians entered. These three were far smaller, clothed from the neck down in flowing fabrics of shimmering pastels. Their unusual garments covered the length of their arms and legs. One had a blue sash wrapped around her waist, accentuating how tiny it was. Their faces were small and feminine. Their blonde hair was pulled back and clasped on top of their heads in a thick spiralling braid. If these were female Akquarians, they were tiny in comparison to the males.

We watched them walk over to the table, placing trays of food upon it. The one with the blue sash smiled at us, and said gently, "I am Yuska, and this is Woohla and Bibska. We will be your attendants for the duration of your stay. We have brought you dinner. My apologies for the lateness in its arrival."

I prevented myself from gawking at her. Her Alluran was impeccable. "Umm…thank…thank you."

Yuska pointed to the backpacks on the floor. "We have returned your possessions, although not all, I'm afraid. The weapons are not deemed necessary. Your commander has requested that you, um…raid-ee-o him? Does that make any sense to you?"

I smiled and nodded.

"Good. Please eat, sleep. Tomorrow will be a new day." The three of them bowed subtly then swiftly departed the room, followed by the two guards.

Zamya approached the table. "Well, she seemed unbearably nice."

I was still staring at the closed door, utterly bemused by how pleasant that female was. "How do they know our language?"

"I don't know," mumbled Cora around a mouthful of food. "Mmm, I have no idea what this is either, but it's delicious." She pointed to a large plate full of pink and yellow fruits. My stomach growled and I joined her.

Once my appetite was sated, I opened the backpacks, searching for my radio. I found the small contraption buried in amongst my spare clothes. Detaching the earpiece from the main body, I held it up in front of my mouth and pressed down the call button. "Rooke, are you there?"

Instantly Rooke's voice was hissing through the small speaker. "Eden, are you okay?"

"Yes, we're fine."

"Thank Nux."

"Where are you?"

"We've been taken to an apartment. Kobe's with me."

"What about Oz?"

"He's being treated elsewhere."

"Do you think we can trust these people?"

"I think so. As long as we abide by their rules. At least we're safe from the horror beetles here."

"True. Are we to remain segregated?"

"I don't know. They seem to be strict on this gender segregation crap. Just keep your heads down and stay in contact with me. The radio batteries will last a few days. Hopefully that's all we need."

"Okay." I sighed. "Rooke, I'm sorry if I spoke out of turn earlier."

"It's fine." I heard the smile in his voice. "I was rather shocked at your outburst, but he was being a chauvinistic pig. Their culture is obviously far removed from ours."

"You can say that again."

"Just…hold your tongue in future." He sighed. "By Nux, Eden. When he approached you, I thought he was going to strike you."

"To be fair, so did I."

Rooke laughed. "You're braver than I am."

"Commander Riley really is starting to sound realistic."

He laughed again. There was a short pause before he said, "I'm going to try and get some sleep. I suggest you do the same. Radio me in the morning."

"Sure. Sleep well."

"You too."

The radio crackled before it fell silent. Speaking with Rooke had reassured me he and Kobe were safe, but it didn't ease the anxiety boiling away inside.

Surprisingly, I did sleep well. No dreams, just a deep, restful slumber.

The bedroom was just as large as the living area. Three beds made in the same way as the chairs next door filled the space. The rock bases were topped with a mattress of what I could only describe as sponge foam. My body had melted into it as I laid down, and once I was covered in the luxuriously soft blankets, I must've fallen asleep within minutes.

Opening my eyes, a soft golden light filled the room, reminding me of home back in Runeia, Torla. High in the rustic hills, the mornings there were always filled with an aura of golden calm. The thought began a heart tugging battle, and I realised how much I missed my small, one storey cottage, the sound of the yellow kites calling to each other in the distance, the smell of freshly baked bread wafting from the bakery down the road, and Rooke knocking on the front door every Saturday morning when he was in town, with a box full of pastries from said bakery and two coffees. I smiled to myself. How I longed to be back there now.

For several moments I stared at the high ceiling, reminiscing about the life I rarely felt contented with. The life, I now realised, I took for granted.

Eventually, I pulled the covers off and swung my legs over the side of the rock bed. I could hear the waves through the glassless windows, crashing against the shore far below. Cora was still sound asleep in her bed in the far corner. Zamya, however, was nowhere to be seen. Her sheets were crumbled as if she had laid there, but knowing Zamya, she hadn't slept a wink.

After attempting to radio Rooke to no avail, I found Zamya in the main room. She was in the middle of a workout.

"Don't stop on my account," I said, smiling.

Her face was flushed and sweaty. She wiped her forehead with the back of her hand and said, "I'm glad you're up. I've been awake for hours."

"Didn't sleep well?"

"On the contrary. I slept like a baby. That bed was ridiculously comfortable. Best night's sleep I've had in months."

"Not a bad prison then, huh?"

"Give it time." She walked to the chair and picked up a Solarfleet towel. Wiping her face, she said, "At least we didn't have to endure listening to the endless gnawing of those horror beetles last night."

"Very true."

"This place is absurd." Zamya shook her head. "I can't work out if these Akquarians are a new human species or an evolved one."

"I had the same thought. The latter may explain how they know our language so well."

Zamya narrowed her eyes towards the door. "I'm not so sure. If they are an evolved species of our ancestors, then why aren't they living in towns. Earth was full of them, far larger than what we have on Allura."

"Maybe the horror beetles, what did the Akquarian call them…Igknamai? Maybe they made it too difficult to remain in such places. A lot of time has passed."

Zamya groaned in frustration. "There's so much I want to know."

Yuska and the other attendants arrived an hour later with trays of food. Cora and Zamya impatiently dug in as soon as it was laid out on the table, but I stood in the balcony archway, staring at the radio in my hand.

"Eden," Cora called, "come eat."

I approached the table, still frowning at the handheld contraption.

"Is Rooke still not answering?" Zamya asked.

"No. I know he likes his sleep, but wouldn't Kobe answer instead? I'm sure he said they hadn't been separated." I placed the radio on the table and Cora began to fill my plate with an array of colourful foods. I stared down at the strange concoction. I didn't feel like eating. "What if something's happened to them? What if they've…" I glanced at Yuska near the door. She was watching me. Even though her genteel persona was welcoming, could I trust her? Could we trust any of them?

What if Rooke and Kobe were being interrogated or worse, tortured? Was Oz being treated with the correct care we'd been promised, or was he being *studied* inappropriately?

I picked the radio up again. "Rooke, it's Eden. Are you there? Rooke, *please* pick up…*Rooke?*"

Nothing.

I cursed, slamming the radio against the tabletop. Burying my head in my hands, I flinched as cold fingers touched my shoulder. Yuska was now standing beside me. She gave me a small smile. "Your male crewmates are well. They have been taken to the springs to bathe."

"Bathe?" Zamya chirped. "When do we get to go?"

Yuska chuckled, flashing her small, yet sharp canines. "The springs are allocated to the males in the morning and evening. I shall take you this afternoon."

She walked away and I chuckled at myself. Rooke always referred to me as *Miss Pessimistic*, and in that moment, I could understand why.

I checked my watch. Thanks to the time reconfiguration Kobe had conducted before we left the Parvos, our watches displayed the Earth time zone, as well as the Alluran space time. On Earth, it was currently 13:52, and I'd still had no communication from Rooke. If Yuska had been truthful about where they had been this morning, then where were they now?

"How long does it take two men to have a bath?" I said impatiently.

"They did smell," chuckled Cora, lounging in the chair opposite me.

I groaned and stood up, glancing at the sparkling horizon of sea through the balcony archway. "I can't cope with this." And I couldn't. Not knowing if Rooke was safe was starting to eat away at my sanity. Rooke was my family, my world, and even though I felt an overwhelming concern for Kobe and Oz's wellbeing, my heart pained thinking something awful could be happening to the man I adored; just like my recurring dream had suggested. If anything happened to him, I wouldn't be able to…

A short, yet distinctive electromagnetic hiss caught my attention and I glanced at the table. Another hiss, then a crackle, and a hint of muffled words trickled through the radio speaker. I leapt towards the table, and it came again, "Groundcrew, this is The Orka. Please respond."

Troy.

I picked up the black receiver. "Orka, it's Eden…Troy, do you copy?"

"Loud and clear, Lieutenant. I was starting to get worried."

I sighed and looked at Cora, who was now standing beside me, beaming.

"You seem to be in a shielded location. I've been in your radio silence far longer than normally expected."

I frowned. "That's strange."

"Is everything okay? I lost your signal within minutes of you being found."

"Yes and no. But we're safe. Although Rooke and Kobe are off the scope at the moment, and I don't know why. We're being kept apart."

"I'll see if I can get a trace on their position."

Cora leaned closer, her bright eyes gently pleading with me. I laughed and spoke into the radio. "I have someone here who wants to speak with you."

"Ahh, put her on. I've kinda missed her."

95

Cora grabbed the radio. "Kinda missed me! Only kinda?"

I smirked and left them to their lover's banter.

Another couple of hours passed and still no word from Rooke. I'd given up trying, hoping he would radio me instead. I felt agitated. I couldn't sit down, I couldn't eat. The worry was churning away at me.

From behind the pages of a book, Zamya peered up at me as I paced past her for the umpteenth time. "Eden, you are doing my head in. Just sit!"

"How can I sit? We haven't heard from them for nearly a day. This just…this just doesn't feel…right. I need to know they're safe. I need to see with my own eyes…"

"Look, why don't you ask Yuska if you can request to see upper management when she returns."

I glared at her. "Don't make fun of this situation, Zam! Yesterday it was you who was losing your shit."

"Hey, okay, I'm sorry." She stood up, catching my arm. "Eden, please…please, sit down. We'll ask Yuska when she…"

"And what will we be asking Yuska?" said a soft, female voice from the doorway. Yuska was holding the door open, allowing Woohla & Bibska to enter. They were both holding garments high above their heads, in an attempt to keep the flowing material from dragging along the marble floor. With intrigue, Zamya and I watched them march into the bedroom.

"What's going on?" Zamya asked, looking back at Yuska.

"You shall be dining with our divine lord this evening. Which means you shall be appropriately dressed." She eyed our attire disapprovingly.

I looked down at my black leggings and vest top. I hadn't bathed or brushed my hair for days. I must've looked like a giant wildling compared to her petite, elegant self.

"We will be taking you to bathe now."

"Ah, yes." Zamya smiled. "I was worried you'd forgotten."

"Not at all. We needed to clear the route, so there won't

be any unauthorised presences when we take you through the fortress."

I looked at Zamya, my eyebrows drawn. *What did that mean?* She shrugged and followed Yuska into the bedroom.

Within minutes we were being escorted through a labyrinth of corridors and stairwells towards what Yuska referred to as the springs. Closely surrounded by Yuska and the two other attendants, three male guards led the way, with three more at our rear. All six were bare chested with golden swirls tattooed on their right pectoral. No deadly looking spears were in sight, but they were all burdened with a large curving sword, sheathed and hanging from the belt on their bronze trousers. I wasn't sure if their presence was to dissuade us from escaping, or to protect us against something or someone else.

As Yuska had suggested, the corridors were empty. Other than our party, I didn't see a single being. The silence falling around our footsteps felt eerie.

After climbing another spiral of steps, an open iron gate appeared, exposing a long expanse of stone before us. The walls of the corridor fashioned multiple open archways in the stone on either side.

The wind hit me as we scurried along it, ripping strands from my bound hair. Glancing through the archways, I felt a sudden pang of vertigo. The rockface below narrowed, almost disappearing from beneath the corridor floor, with the beach and the waves hundreds of metres below.

At the opposite end, another dark stairwell descended into the rockface. This one was far more enclosed than any of the previous ones. Each step was steep, and the ceiling felt low and claustrophobic. I had to duck to prevent myself from hitting my head. My back and legs ached by the time we got to the bottom, where a low, yet wide chamber met us. Strange blue lanterns illuminated the area, revealing several openings in the rock wall, big enough to step through. A gentle trickle of water echoed around us, signifying running water was somewhere close by.

Yuska dismissed the guards, and as they returned up the stairs she turned to us, the blue light dancing across her long, pale face.

"Each of these openings takes you to a different bathing pool. You may either bathe separately, or together. The choice is yours, but you must remove your...*foot protectors* before entering."

Zamya snorted. "If you don't mind, I'd rather go separately." She began to unlace her boots. "Not sure about you, but I'm not comfortable enough with our friendship yet to start stripping naked in front of each other."

A laugh escaped me, and I nodded my approval. Looking across at Cora, she seemed nervous, almost scared. I reached for her hand. "I'll join you if you want."

She shook her head. "No, it's fine. I'd rather go alone. Like Zamya said, it would feel...awkward."

"And the guys would have a field day if they ever found out we got naked together," Zamya japed. "It would probably explode their tiny brains." She looked at Yuska and pointed to an opening to the left. Yuska nodded and Zamya ducked over the threshold, closely followed by Bibska.

"Not completely alone then," mumbled Cora, just as Woohla coerced her forward towards a different opening.

I watched her go, content she was safe, before unlacing my boots and stepping through another opening after Yuska.

Wet, uneven rocks met the soles of my feet as I steadily made my way down a shallow stream of steps. They ended at the edge of a small bathing pool moulded into the rock floor. Sunlight filtered in from two small holes in the rock several metres up, but it was the four hovering blue lights that gave the space a tranquil atmosphere. It felt almost peaceful.

"You may undress."

I realised Yuska was holding her hand out to me, awaiting the disposal of my clothes. Peeling off my garments, I tried to ignore the pang of self-consciousness, before dipping my toe into the clear water. It was pleasantly warm.

Without hesitation, I slipped into the pool, submerging my

shoulders. The warmth and softness of the water made me sigh. I hadn't realised how tense I'd become.

Leaning back against the edge, I watched Yuska as she placed my clothes and boots into a netted bag. She was unusually pretty but I couldn't work out how old she was. She seemed knowledgeable and had a position among the Akquarians. The blue caped soldier had specified all chaperons wore blue capes or sashes. Well, every time I'd seen Yuska, she was wearing a blue sash. That in itself must've meant she had some kind of authority amongst the males.

She noted my attention and asked, "Do you need assistance in cleaning oneself?"

I chuckled. "Oh, no. No...but thank you." I reached for the bar of soap on the uneven floor behind my head. Well, I think it was soap. It felt more like foam or sponge. Bringing it up to my nose, I sniffed it, discovering a pleasant fragrance which emanated the freshness of the sea. I began to scrub myself, aware Yuska remained by the steps, watching.

After several minutes, and washing the remaining suds from my now clean hair, Yuska moved to the edge of the pool, holding a teal robe out to me. Clearly signalling the end of my bathing session, I reluctantly stood, climbing the shallow ragged steps, and allowing her to wrap my body in the warm robe. Tying the soft material securely, I watched Yuska climb the steps to the exit, leaving my Alluran clothes in the netted bag by the pool. I followed her, keeping my questions to myself.

We didn't wait for the others. Yuska guided me back to our quarters with two guards in tow. Guilt overcame me as I entered the apartment. I should've demanded that I wait for Zamya and Cora. But here I was, back in our rooms with neither of them in sight.

It was as if Yuska sensed my unsettling thoughts. She asked me to sit at what appeared to be dressing table. It was situated in a small room at the far end of the bedroom, one I had not known existed.

"You worry too much," she said gently, beginning to brush my hair. "Like a mother hen."

I frowned. "Are they safe?"

"Yes. As is your commander."

"You've seen him?" I met her gaze in the murky glass before me.

"Yes." But that was all she would give me.

I tried to calm my thoughts while she brushed, untangled, and arranged my hair. But it was only after a strained few moments, then hearing the sound of Cora's laughter and Zamya's hissing from next door, that I allowed myself to relax.

Yuska tapped my shoulder as if to say, *I told you so*.

I wasn't sure how long I sat at the dressing table, but Yuska's delicate fingers in my hair seemed to sooth me into a trance. I wondered how Oz was, if his wounds were healing. I thought of Troy alone on The Orka. How must he be coping with us down here and the lack of radio communication? I thought of Sym and what he'd make of the Akquarian people, how he would try to mimic their hair styles. Knowing Sym, he'd probably pull off the long locks and braids the males seemed to fashion. I smiled. Nux, I missed him already.

I hadn't noticed Yuska had finished until she appeared next to me with a long, midnight blue dress draped across her arm. I looked at her then at the dress, my eyes dancing with questions.

"Havav has asked you to wear this for dinner."

"Havav?"

"Our lord."

Oh. Him! I snapped my eyes away, catching a glimpse of myself in the mirror. Wow, my hair looked good. I looked good. I went to stand, gently touching my now thick, wavy locks and the intricate braiding on each side. Tiny shells and gems sat in amongst the plaits adding detail. The style made my eyes stand out, my eyelashes and brows a dark contrast against my pale skin.

Taking in the dress laying in Yuska's arms, I untied my robe, reluctantly losing the comfort of its warmth. Uncomfortably naked, I bobbed down to allow Yuska to heave the heavy dress up over my head. The fabric fell to the ground in a ripple of waves. I looked down at the dark, shimmering material, stroking its smoothness over my hips and legs. It hugged my body, accentuating my lean curves.

The sleeves were long and loose, clasped at the wrist with a thick golden band. The neckline swept low at the front, forming an acute V near the bottom part of my breastbone. An intricate chain of gold links, clasped at the base of the V, dropped down to my waist. It was all a little too much for my modesty. I tugged the material closer, trying to conceal the roundness of my breasts.

Yuska smiled at me as she pulled my hands gently away. "This is a popular Akquarian style. Although, Akquarian females are only blessed with a subtle bump of breast. You appear to have ample."

I peered down at my chest. "You make it sound like mine are huge."

Yuska's eyebrows elevated in amusement. "I did not say huge."

"Are they…are they too exposed?"

"No." She tapped my hand away again. "It suits you."

I looked at her petite face. Eyeing me from head to toe, she seemed genuinely impressed. Did I look that good?

The nerves hit me. Why had Havav asked me to dress this way? Would it only be him and me at dinner? I hoped not. I wanted Rooke there, but now I was starting to think it was best if he wasn't. What the Nux was *Rooke* going to think if he saw me dressed like this?

Yuska opened the door to the bedroom, and I stepped through glancing behind me to appreciate the swishing of my skirt. I found Zamya and Cora standing in the middle of the bedroom. They both looked beautiful, their hair in neat arrangements of loose curls and braids, their long dresses less revealing than mine but still made to flatter in shades of green.

Cora gaped at me. Zamya smirked. "I do not recall ever seeing you in a dress. Especially one quite so elegant," she eyed the plunging neckline, "and revealing."

I tried to pull the fabric together again and Yuska slapped my hand away. "Stop that," she said.

Zamya laughed. "You might as well flaunt it."

I sighed deeply, closing my eyes. I felt so out of my comfort zone.

Within fifteen minutes, we were being marched down the halls and stairwells by an entourage of guards, with Yuska and the other females beside us. The soles of my bare feet screamed at the sharp chill as they continually slapped against the hard floor, and my stomach was churning with anxiety more than hunger.

Zamya nudged my shoulder and whispered, "Did Yuska give you any underwear?"

"No."

"Is it me, or does it feel a little breezy without any on?"

I chuckled. "I strongly advise not to start any table dancing later."

A wicked laugh escaped Zamya, causing Yuska to shoot us a stern look.

Our entourage halted before a wide double door. The dark stone screeched open and Yuska guided us over the threshold, into an artificially lit room. The glow held an orange hue, with the smell of incense hanging in the air. It felt strangely welcoming. And then I realised I could hear Rooke's voice, speaking with another. Where he was, I couldn't tell. A line of guards shielded my eyes from the extent of the vast room.

I pulled my gaze to a guard who was approaching us. It was the same one who had escorted us to our rooms yesterday. His gold armour gleamed in the light, his blue cape shifting behind him. His crystal blue eyes met mine and I swore I caught a glimpse of shock flashing across them. I held my breath in question. Was he shocked at how different I looked? Had I appeared so utterly untamed yesterday? The thought horrified me.

"Welcome," his tone short but amiable. "Please follow me, I will show you to your seats." In a swish of blue, he turned and walked further into the room. I followed, glancing at the line of guards as we passed. All of them held weapons—deadly spears or curving swords.

Rooke's voice grew louder, Kobe's too, and a wave of relief washed over me. No sign of discomfort or terror from either one, only civilised conversation.

The blue caped guard led us through a line of marble pillars, and I spotted Rooke sitting at a long rock-table at the far end of the room. He was laughing with the Akquarian leader, Havav. *Laughing.*

Still walking, I glanced at Rooke again. He looked…different. A smile tugged at my lips at the realisation he'd been groomed. Wearing a dark, high-necked jacket, his hair had been trimmed and combed. But the biggest shock of all, was his stubbled beard was gone. Only smooth golden skin remained.

"Ah, finally. The ladies are here." Havav stood up at the far end of the long table. The fabric of his turquoise jacket glistened with his sleek movement. Locking his eyes with mine as I drew closer, he smiled, gesturing to the chair to his right, opposite Rooke. "Will you do me the honour?"

The blue caped guard pulled the chair out for me. Even though I was a purified mess inside, I took the seat with confidence, still holding Havav's friendly, yet assessing gaze.

While Havav welcomed Cora and Zamya, signalling where they should sit, I caught Rooke's stare from across the table. He was looking at me as if it was the first time he'd laid eyes on me. I raised my eyebrows in question, but his lips twitched into a smile; a teasing smile. I felt the colour rise in my cheeks and I tugged gently at the material exposing my open cleavage. Further amusement danced across his face. I knew he'd find my attire laughable, but then, he looked ridiculous without his facial hair.

Zamya, seating herself in between Rooke and Kobe, shifted my attention. Cora was now sitting to my right. Several guards lined the walls on either side of the room, standing stiff and responsive, and the blue caped one stood to my left, behind Havav. I felt his eyes constantly surveying the room, landing on me several times.

103

"Thank you for joining us," Havav drawled, inclining his head towards me. "Your commander informed me you were finding the segregation from your male comrades rather…distressing."

I flicked my gaze to Rooke, who was trying to conceal his smirk. "Did he now?"

"I suppose after living in such close proximity to each other for months, it must feel strange not to have them close by."

"Yes…quite."

Havav nodded, assessing the look I threw Rooke. "Miss Eden, I feel you and I did not get off to a good start yesterday."

Slightly shocked, I forced a smile, looking down at the place setting in front of me. The table had the same marble effect as the floor, dark and swirling. The cutlery looked like pieces of reinforced coral tied together by a piece of decorative string. The drinking glass had a short neck with a wide, crystalised bowl. Eyeing it, I wished it was full of wine so I could drink as a distraction.

"I apologise if I came across abrupt or rude," I said, albeit half-heartedly. "Yesterday, I was exhausted and more than a little harassed about the situation. However, your hospitality has been overly generous, and our attendants are nothing but kind and attentive."

Havav hummed his approval as a flurry of bodies entered the room, carrying plates of food and glass bottles of what I hoped was wine. I caught Rooke's eye. He subtly nodded his head, pleased with my show of apology and appreciation. This was all an act in the name of diplomacy. We had to keep on the right side of Havav, for Oz's sake more than anything else.

Once the wine was poured and the bright, colourful food distributed, we began to eat. I went straight for the peach-coloured wine. To my surprise it tasted spicy yet smooth, and exceptionally morish.

"I have spent the day with your commander and Mr. Kobe," Havav went on. "They explained who Allurans are and where you originally came from."

"So, you know it is said we originated from Earth?"

He nodded. "The Akquarian people were emerging from the waters when the human race was fretting about the Igknamai. They were too focused on the beasts to notice our species' presence."

I noticed Zamya's attention pique. She sat up straighter in her chair, her dark eyes glistening as she listened. But it was Cora who spoke, "So the Igknamai were the reason the human race left?"

"I believe so. My species was intellectually young at the time. But we were evolved enough that we no longer relied solely on the ocean."

"So, you are an evolved species of fish?" Zamya asked.

Havav shot her a glare. He appeared offended. "No. We are the same as you, with…some physical differences."

"Which explains the intellect, I guess."

"Indeed." Havav smiled at Zamya. A smile that relaxed the harsh lines of his pale face. He looked oddly handsome. And in a way similar to Yuska, his features were young yet carried an older, wiser expression, especially around the eyes.

Cora spoke again, "So why did the Igknamai drive the humans from this world, yet your people remained?"

"Firstly, we did not have mechanical transportation as the humans did, and secondly, we are water people. The Igknamai do not like water. They avoid it as much as possible. Even when it rains, they tend to disappear."

Well, that explained why they only munched on the dry underside of our ship, and why they scarpered early yesterday morning when it had started raining.

"This fortress is surrounded by sea. It is a safe haven from the savage beasts who roam the land."

"Have they ever attacked your people?" I asked, still sipping on the heavenly wine.

"Yes. They attack anything that lingers on dry land. We have lost many of those who farm the fields in the past. We have better defences now, ones the Igknamai tend to avoid. But yes…we have lost many." There was a sudden sadness in his eyes. He'd lost someone close; he must have.

"So, if the humans left without making any semblance of contact with you," Zamya said, cutting into her food, "how do you know our language so well?"

"Ahh." Havav smiled and lent back. "Your ancestors lived in cities, bigger than imaginable. And when they left, they didn't take any superficial commodities with them, including their libraries. My ancestors found these exquisite buildings full of knowledge and retrieved many books before the Igknamai found and destroyed them. Through those books we learnt their languages, including the one you speak. The one we call the ancient tongue. We have a large library here full of said books."

Cora practically squealed. "A library? Full of ancient texts?"

"Indeed. I can take you there. Tomorrow, maybe, if your commander allows it."

Cora beamed at Rooke. He rolled his eyes at her silent persuasion, followed by an accepting nod.

"Wonderful," Havav boomed, smiling at Cora, causing her to blush. "I shall look forward to it."

Both Zamya and Cora continued to ask questions about the Akquarians. Once dinner was finished, Havav gestured for us to follow him through another doorway into a luxurious sitting room. The balcony doorway was open, allowing a cool breeze to filter into the room. I stood by the opening, gazing out into the darkness, glimpsing the stars through the scattering of dark clouds, wondering what direction Allura lay in.

Slow, padded feet sounded from behind and Rooke appeared next to me, handing me another glass of the peach-coloured wine. "I get the impression you like this drink."

"I do. I could easily become addicted to it." I took the glass from him.

He chuckled. "I always knew someday you'd stoop to my level."

"Hey, I can handle my drink just fine."

"So can I." He chuckled again and looked at me, *really* looked at me. "You look so different."

"So do you. Baby face." I smiled, gesturing to the non-existent beard. "Why'd you shave it off?"

"I had to. Akquarian rules. I get the impression they don't allow them because they can't grow them themselves."

I snorted, glancing at the guards scattered motionlessly around the room. All six of them were fair and pale without a trace of facial hair. Maybe Rooke had a point.

Rooke's tone shifted to a softer one, "Are you alright, though? No issues with anything?"

"Everything seems fine. Other than your radio silence today." I sighed, pushing away the traumatising thoughts that had whirled irrationally around my head earlier.

"I've been accompanying Havav since mid-morning. He seems very inquisitive about us."

I glanced at the Akquarian leader, lounging in a large armchair, casually talking with Kobe and Cora who sat on the rock-based sofa next to him. "To the point we should be worried?"

Rooke shook his head. "I don't think so." He flicked his eyes about the room and said in an undertone, "He took me on a tour of the fortress. I didn't see any tech. None what-so-ever. I don't believe they could've been the ones who drew the scouting ship here."

"They may keep said equipment hidden elsewhere."

Rooke scrunched his nose up and shook his head in doubt.

"If they weren't the ones who lured the scouting ship in, then who did?"

Rooke shrugged his shoulders. "Havav wants to meet with each one of you individually. Maybe we could probe him with our own questions."

I nodded but froze when I caught the scrutinising glare of the blue caped guard, standing a couple of metres behind Havav. *Definitely a personal bodyguard.* I swallowed and looked back at Rooke's distant, contemplative daze. "Even though we feel comfortable here, we still need to remain vigilant."

"I completely agree."

"Any news on Oz?

"I saw him this afternoon." There was a hint of relief in Rooke's expression. "He's only semi-conscious, but…stable. A lot better than yesterday, so improving."

"That's a relief."

"And Havav has agreed to help us with fixing our ship."

"Really? That's good. Very good."

"It is." Rooke smirked. "So, you agree it was a risk well executed, then?" He lifted his eyebrows in anticipation of me chiding him. But I smiled and nudged him with my elbow. "You're an arrogant, risk-taking bastard."

"One you can't live without, though, yeah?"

I smirked at the undeniable truth to his words, one he clearly had no idea about. When I remained silent, watching the smile fade from his handsome face, he touched my arm gently and said, "I'm not going anywhere, Eden."

I took a deep breath and met his concerned eyes. "I thought the worst today when I couldn't get in touch with you."

"I can imagine, I'm sorry. Everything is fine. We are safe here."

I forced a smile and nodded, only to be swamped by gold armour. *Captain Blue Cape* forced himself between Rooke and I, towering over us. Those crystal eyes full of authority and demand. "No touching," he said with an icy tone.

"We weren't." *Were we?*

"You are too close. Take a step back," he insisted, "both of you." We complied.

I scowled at the Akquarian as he strode away. Rooke hung his head, a smile dancing across his face. He peered at me, and we burst into laughter.

"What the Nux is all that about?" I said, before downing my wine.

Chapter Eleven

The following day Cora was whisked away to the fortress library by Havav. She returned late afternoon, beaming from ear to ear. Two guards followed her into the apartment with arms laden with books—books that looked older than life itself. They smelt it too.

"Put them over there, please," she said sweetly, indicating to the table. She watched them stack the multitude of books in three piles, before they were swiftly ushered out by Yuska.

"How did it go?" I asked, rising from the sofa I had been resting on all afternoon.

"It was *amazing*. The library is huge, and considering how old they are, the books are in such good condition." Cora gestured to the piles on the table. "Havav only allowed me to take these. The others are too delicate."

"Did you find anything interesting?"

"I didn't really have the chance." Cora walked over to me and seated herself in a lone chair. "Havav, he…he doesn't stop asking questions."

"About what?" Zamya asked, from where she lay on the sofa opposite.

"Everything." Cora shrugged her shoulders. "Literally everything about Allura. What part I come from, what the people are like, the temperature, the humidity, the size of the mountains, literally everything."

Zamya glanced at me, inquisitive worry dancing in her eyes. "Do you think he's going to use this information somehow?"

"I suppose he may want an alliance with Allura…if we eventually get off this rock."

"What if he…" Zamya stared into her thoughts. I could see her mind ticking over at a hundred miles an hour, distorting her delicate skin.

"What?"

"What if he sent that probe? What if he wants to get off this rock himself, away from the horror beetles?" She sat up abruptly. "What if he wants Allura?"

"What if he does?" I sat down again. "What's he going to do when he gets there, if he gets there? Attack? There's probably only a few thousand Akquarians here. They can try and conquer Allura, but they won't succeed. To start with, their weapons are obsolete."

"Maybe they aren't quite so ill educated and defenceless as we think." Zamya lowered herself into an alpine position again.

"Zam, I don't think it would be possible."

"All right, I know. But…I'm trying to get my head around this."

"Aren't we all."

"Maybe you could ask him why he is so interested in us yourself," Cora piped up. "He wants to see you tomorrow."

Zamya groaned. "How wonderful for me."

Yuska escorted Zamya to Havav's social quarters early the next morning. She was gone most of the day, leaving me to scroll through some of the books Cora borrowed from the library. A large majority of them were geology books, which didn't surprise me, but one that caught my eye was a book on modern space engineering. Modern, as in twenty-second century Earth modern. The language in which it was written was slightly different to what Allurans used, but it was understandable enough.

There was a section on interstellar travel and the ingenuity of the vessels they used to transport miners to and from the edges of the solar system. Saturn and its moons being the furthest out they'd venture. The book suggested mining on Titan had become an international venture. But what astounded me was the complexity of their spacecrafts. It was as though they over complicated every system, every aspect of space travel. The modern Alluran ingenuity of spacecraft was complex, yet far less convoluted than what I was reading. I began to wonder how they succeeded in leaving Earth and finding a new home.

The door screeched open, pulling my attention away from the faded pages. Dressed in a flowing blue dress, Zamya breezed in with a forced look of nonchalance on her face.

"How'd it go?" I asked, watching her take the seat next to me. I realised her eyes were twinkling, she was ready to burst.

"Havav is a nosy bastard. But…" She glanced at Yuska, who was closing the door, lowering her voice. "It seems I can out question him." She smirked, a flash of triumph flickering across her face. "After hours of subtle interrogation, I concluded we are dealing with a really young species. I'm talking *really* young. Havav says they are the same as us, but they aren't. If anything, they are at least one hundred thousand years behind in evolution, and certain physical traits are very different. The Akquarians still possess their raw, natural, primitive instincts which, I presume, humans lost many millennia ago."

I glanced across the room to the where Cora sat at the table. She was frowning at Zamya with as much confusion as I was.

Zamya chuckled and said, "Havav could tell that I was about to enter my phase of *bleeding*, so he called it. And he isn't wrong."

"What? How?"

"He could smell me, which is seriously off putting, but I discovered this is why the males and females are segregated."

My frown deepened, as did Cora's, who now joined us around the coffee table. Zamya huffed a laugh. "Havav told me that Akquarian females only ovulate three specific times of the year. It's only during these three periods that the males and females mix. During the rest of the year, a strict segregation is put in place because, occasionally, some males become aggressive in a primal…sexual way. It's a phase called Tektrasc. Their testosterone levels dangerously peak and if they come into contact with, or even smell, a female who attracts them, they can become dangerous…uncontrollable. The females are at risk, as well as any male who gets in their way. This is why they have chaperons. They're able to detect any males showing signs of Tektrasc and are capable to subduing them."

I looked to where Yuska was in the adjacent room, arranging the beds. She was so petite, almost fragile looking. She always wore a blue sash, identifying herself as a chaperon. Could she possibly protect the females from the burly males?

"Other than Yuska," I said, "the only chaperons I've seen are males themselves. Do they not suffer from Tek…whatever it's called?"

"They're deemed less likely to."

"So, what happens to the males who are detected?"

"Anyone showing signs of Tektrasc are isolated until the phase has subsided."

"How long?"

"As long as it takes."

I swallowed down a daunting thought. "Would the Akquarian males be affected by us?"

"Oh, yes." I shot a glance back at Zamya. Her eyes were wide with concern. "Havav could smell me, which means the rest of them can. Which also means they'll be able to smell us when we ovulate."

"Which is a lot more often than three times a year," Cora mused.

"Exactly." Zamya sighed. "And because of that, Havav is concerned that we could be the cause of sporadic Tektrasc behaviour. Rooke is now concerned too."

"But we're a different species," Cora said. "Why would they find our smell attractive?"

"We smell similar, apparently."

"Nux. So, what do we do?" I asked, understanding why Yuska cleared the route to the springs the other day.

"If you can both try and work out when you're next due on. We need to take our temperatures every morning and evening. It will display a pattern of our cycles. As soon as we show signs of either, we need to stay in this apartment for a few days. No social dinners, no tours, no spring baths…"

"I thought we weren't planning on staying that long."

Zamya shrugged. "Rooke seems to think we may be here a while, especially if the Akquarians are to help with the ship repairs."

Circling my temples with my fingers, I sighed with irritation. I wanted to get off this planet. I wanted to get back to The Orka and Troy. Even though we felt safe here from the Igknamai, how safe were we?

"So, we'll be prisoners for two weeks of each month," Cora groaned. "*Great.*"

The following day I woke early, jolted awake by that damn recurring dream. But Rooke hadn't been in Jacob's coffin this time. He was lying dead on a beach, covered in blood.

Leaving Zamya and Cora sleeping soundly, I ambled into the living room, searching for a glass of water. My head throbbed. The unsettling feeling in my gut had become unbearable.

I'd tried radioing Rooke yesterday evening but Kobe had picked up. Rooke had gone to dinner with Havav, alone. The thought had spiked my anxiety, probably instigating the dream. Rooke alone with Havav surrounded by armed guards? How safe were we here even without the daunting announcement that there were primally crazed psychopaths walking around?

I shook my head and walked out onto the balcony. The ground was still wet from the rain fallen during the night. I glanced at the beach and land surrounding the fortress, scanning for signs of Igknamai. I saw none…but…in the corner of my eye…

Up on the clifftop to the left, silhouetted against the pink glow of the brightening sky, a lone figure atop a horse sat motionless, almost picturesque. It looked identical to the one Rooke and I spotted a few days ago. Was it an Akquarian? A part of a scouting or guarding party perhaps?

I peered closer, trying to block out the morning haze from

distorting my vision. If I wasn't mistaken, the figure was looking towards the fortress, towards me.

"Who are you?" I whispered to myself. And as if they detected my attention, the horse and rider turned, disappearing beyond the clifftop.

I stood there for a while, gazing in the wake of the rider, trying to piece my thoughts together. Whoever it was, I felt drawn to them. Intrigued.

Yuska appeared a few minutes later. "Havav has requested your presence today," she called to me through the archway. "I have an appropriate dress ready for you to wear."

Luckily, the dress was far more conservative than the one I wore to dinner. I felt comfortable with the slashed neckline and long, tight sleeves. The hem of the dress brushed the floor, the shimmering green material felt soft and warm.

Yuska escorted me down the spiral stairwells to a part of the fortress I had not seen before. Zamya had checked my temperature beforehand, noting it was no different from my previous stats a few days ago. To be honest, I had no idea where my cycle was. Space travel always interfered with it, slowing the process. Now that we were on Earth, I assumed my body may start reacting in the same way it did on Allura, but when, I had no idea.

Following Yuska down a corridor of ornate walls and glassless windows, we approached a double door, guarded by two of Havav's men. They opened a door each, neither taking notice of me, calming my paranoia of what Zamya explained yesterday. But a part of me chuckled at the thought. As if any of these males would find me attractive, Tektrasc or not? To them, I was just a strange human with dark hair and weird eyes.

Yuska opened another door, revealing a wide, empty corridor with a number of closed doors to the right. At the far end, a large, oval window looked out onto the beach and headland beyond.

"If you wait here," Yuska said, gesturing to a low chair to one side, "your commander will call you in shortly."

Passing her a grateful smile, I watched her leave the way we came in. Ignoring the plush chair, I walked towards the window opening at the far end. The sun was rising higher in the sky, the breeze was warm but refreshing. Sea birds circled the sky above the ocean, their calls challenging the sound of the waves. But my attention was drawn to the illuminous yellow and orange object laying at the edge of the sea, being tackled by three large Igknamai.

The object was our life raft. It must have been dragged in by the strong tide. From the way the beasts were shredding at the material, it brought back memories of the mutilated bodies we'd found on the scouting ship…and Sym. Dear Sym. Mauled to death by those terrorising demons. *Demons of Paradise*, they were called. Very fitting indeed.

"Savage beasts, aren't they?"

I jumped at the low, foreign accent close behind me. Whirling ninety degrees, I found *Captain Blue Cape* standing in the corridor, barely a metre away. He was gazing over my head, towards the Igknamai outside. Where he'd appeared from, I had no idea.

"I'd say savage is a far too polite a term to describe them."

His crystal blue eyes met mine and I saw a hint of a smile. I glanced back to the view, observing the creatures who appeared to be fighting with one another over the piece of deflated rubber. "What are they doing?"

"Calling dominance before they feast." He appeared beside me, still surveying the scene. He was tall, far taller than Oz even, and just as powerful. His gold cuirass armour glistened in the morning light. I contemplated how much of his armour exaggerated his physique, but judging by the thick set muscle and bulging tendons along the exposed part of his arm, I doubted the outline was anything but a good representation.

His facial features were more pronounced than most other Akquarians. The bridge of his nose was higher, the angle of his chin stronger. Apart from the scar across his chin, even his pale skin held less of a bluish tinge. If I wasn't mistaken, he looked almost human. It was only the long white-blonde hair and elongated canines that claimed him to his Akquarian lineage.

I pulled my attention back to the Igknamai. "Do they eat everything?" I asked.

"Not everything, no. They leave grass, rock, sand, wood untouched. But crops, low lying plants and shrubs are devoured, along with any animal…any living being." He looked down at me. "Since your kind arrived here, the Igknamai have found a new taste for the materials you brought with you. Tell me, what is it they're eating?"

"That's rubber, coated in a composite plastic. Our ships are made of a metal compound, also coated in composite."

"Artificial materials?"

"Yes."

"Their appetite has certainly become insatiable since tasting it."

We stood there for several moments, watching the Igknamai rip the life raft apart. It astounded me how they could consume such materials without any ill affect.

"You will be safe here," he said softly. "They can't touch you here."

I squeezed my lips together. "We appreciate that, thank you."

"Forgive me," he shuffled on his feet awkwardly, turning towards me, "I've been in your presence a number of times now, yet I have failed to introduce myself. I'm Dybgofor—" He pronounced a word—a name I had no ability of reciting. The look on my face must have confirmed my bemusement and he laughed…actually laughed. A deep throaty rumble. His most human attribute yet. "But you can call me Dybgo."

"Dybgo." I let out a breath. "Oh, good. I can pronounce that. Otherwise, I would've had to make something up." I chuckled, sending a ripple of amusement across his face. "But saying that, up until now, you have been referred to as Captain Blue Cape."

Frowning, he stiffened for a moment, before a smile illuminated his face. "That isn't very imaginative."

"Well…it's far less insulting than some of Zamya's suggestions."

He laughed again, a sound I realised I could relish in. "Ah, yes, Miss Zamya. The brutishly inquisitive one."

"That's one way of describing her…in the nicest possible way."

Dybgo smiled widely, exposing those pointy canines, and the sound of Rooke's harsh, authoritative voice suddenly shot over us. I glanced over to where the voice came from, unsure of what he had said. Rooke was standing in an open doorway on the corner of the corridor. Dressed in an Akquarian tunic and pair of dark trousers, an unusual frown rippled across his forehead. "I'm not interrupting, am I?" Rooke glanced between me and Dybgo, his words laced with a hint of sarcasm.

"No," we said in unison, only to look back at each other and smile.

Dybgo straightened, pushing his shoulders back, and walked towards Rooke. "I need a couple of minutes with Havav."

Rooke stepped aside, allowing Dybgo to pass, only to shoot me a hard look as I approached.

"Ah, Miss Eden," Havav drawled, spotting me in the doorway. "Come in, come in."

Before I stepped across the threshold, Rooke caught my elbow and said into my ear, "Be careful, Eden."

I looked back at him with a questioning expression.

"Zam told you about the males here?"

"Yes. We were only talking."

"Just be careful."

I nodded my head gingerly and walked into the long, elegant room. At the far end Dybgo was speaking to Havav in their own strange language. The deep rumbles and clicks almost mimicked a type of underwater song. But I picked up on a couple of coherent words that were repeated several times—red and wood, always said together, as if red-wood was a name or a place.

The conversation was brief, and once Havav barked a final order, Dybgo inclined his head, turned on his heel, and left the room without a single glance in our direction. Before the door clicked shut, Havav tapped the seat beside him. He watched me as I sat on the long chaise, keeping a decent distance between myself and the Akquarian leader.

"Well, don't you look exquisite, Miss Eden." His charming smile seemed devilish.

A little shocked, I flicked my eyes to Rooke, who was now sitting in a large chair to Havav's right. The hint of a smirk flashed across his lips. He was probably used to listening to Havav's charm by now, but it didn't stop the blush rising to my cheeks.

I flicked my gaze back to Havav. "It should be Yuska you thank for my appearance, not me."

Havav eyed me with an incredulous look. "Indeed." He leant forward, grabbing a drink from the table beside him. Offering me the glass, he said, "Welcome to my study. I do apologise for leaving you until last to interview."

"No need."

"I am intrigued, though." He leant back against the chair's rolling arm. "I've discovered Mr Kobe's expertise is in physics and engineering, Miss Cora in astrogeology, and Miss Zamya in biology. So, what do you bring to your crew, other than your beauty of course?"

Rooke rolled his eyes.

Suppressing my laugh, I shrugged. "I'm just the pilot."

"Just the pilot?"

"A damn good one, too," Rooke said, peering at me.

"I was under the impression you flew the ship, commander?" Havav adjusted his position, only to look back at me when I said, "There's a rota. Rooke helps me fly the ship, along with Tr…"

"Kobe." Rooke's voice cut across mine. Our eyes met and I sensed the exaggerated meaning within his. He hadn't told Havav about Troy and The Orka, and clearly wanted it to remain that way.

Quickly, covering my mistake, I said, "Yes, Kobe sometimes helps. He can't be left for too long on his own, he gets distracted." Kobe hadn't flown a spacecraft for years.

Havav seemed to buy into the ruse and chuckled to himself. As he continued his random questioning, I flicked my gaze to Rooke again. He was mentally noting every question, every comment and hidden incentive. Something was going on. I needed to talk to him in private, but with his presence constantly domineered by Havav, finding the time would be difficult.

Sensing my attention, Rooke's dark gaze shifted to my face. He moved his elbow, resting it on the arm of his chair, tapping his ear twice, before leaning into his fist in a casual motion.

A double ear tap—Solarfleet directive for radio. It seemed he needed to talk to me as well.

Chapter Twelve

I sat up late with the radio earpiece activated in my left ear, not wanting the radio speaker to crackle loudly this time of night. And I got the impression Rooke didn't want this conversation to be overheard by any Akquarian. I only hoped they were as technologically underdeveloped as we assumed and didn't possess the knowledge of how to intercept radio frequencies.

Eventually, Rooke's voice, soft and low, crackled through, "Eden, are you there?"

I tapped my ear. "I'm here. What's going on?"

"To be honest, I don't know. Over the past few days, I've been feeling more and more uncomfortable about the situation."

"Why? What's happened?"

"I can't explain it. Havav seems genuine enough, but I can't shift this feeling that he is up to something."

"Have you noted any modern tech anywhere?"

"No, which baffles me. But his questions aren't random, they're generic. Which is making me wonder what information he is attaining."

"Zam thinks he wants to conquer Allura."

Rooke chuckled. "I don't think that's it."

"So, why are you keeping The Orka a secret?"

"He doesn't need to know. And if things do go south, Troy and The Orka could be our only means of escape." He sighed heavily.

"Have you spoken to Troy recently?"

"Yesterday. He's finding it hard to make contact with us. There's a huge amount of lead in the fortress walls. But occasionally he does get through, although for how much longer, I don't know. Our battery charges are running low."

"Yeah, mine too."

"Kobe doesn't think he can muster anything up to recharge them here. We need to go back to the ship."

"So, what's stopping us?"

"Havav may not allow it."

"Then, let it be a test. Ask him. See what he says. He doesn't need to know the exact reason why we need the radios. At least that way we'll know for certain if we are prisoners or guests in his eyes."

Rooke agreed it was a good plan, however it didn't ease my scepticism when Yuska came to me two days later, bearing my Solarfleet uniform in her arms. "Your commander asks that you'll be ready by midday."

I took the clean clothes, noting she had only brought one set. "Are Cora and Zamya not joining us?"

"No." Yuska frowned at me, as if I was being downright idiotic. She pointed towards the balcony, to where both Cora and Zamya were lounging about in the sunshine. "They are both currently indisposed and sanctioned to remain in the apartment for a few days." She shook her head. "I cannot believe your species are unable to detect such things on each other."

I frowned at her as she busied herself. Turning abruptly, I walked onto the balcony. Zamya was sprawled out on a sun lounger, whilst Cora sat at the table, under a large, leafed parasol, reading.

"In future, can you both keep me informed of your changing…conditions."

Shielding her eyes from the intense sun, Zamya looked up at me. "I told you a couple of days ago it was due."

"I know, I know." Nux, this was frustrating. Clearly Havav did not see us as his prisoners, but being a female amongst these people was the same as condemning us to a prison. Although, it

121

appeared both my female colleagues were enjoying the isolation and relaxation. I, however, found it an inconvenience.

I rubbed my forehead with my thumb and forefinger. "I'm going back to the ship to charge the radio batteries with Rooke and Kobe. While I'm gone, maybe both of you could do with a workout. We need to keep our bodies strong and active."

Zamya groaned. "Yes, master."

Cora, on the other hand, ignored my suggestion entirely. "If you're going back to the ship, could you retrieve a couple of books for me please? I'm sure I left them on the flight deck. There should be two."

I sighed and went to get dressed.

Just before midday, Yuska escorted me down the dark, spiral staircases. Down and down we went, deeper into the fortress until I started feeling nauseous. When we finally emerged at the bottom, I recognised the area as the wide corridor we had been aggressively marched along when we first arrived a week ago. The turquoise crystals hung from the high, caustic ceilings. The floor smooth and polished under my black boots.

An Akquarian male stood at the far end with his back turned to us. His upper body bare, exposing the deep contours of his back muscles. A blue sash sat around his slim trouser waist, with a curved sword buckled to his left hip and a cluster of smaller knives on his right.

As we approached, he turned and I realised it was Dybgo, without the cape and golden armour, revealing a large golden swirl tattooed onto his right pectoral.

His crystal blues swept over my face before he thanked Yuska. And as if they tag-teamed, Dybgo suddenly became my escort.

The smell was the first thing that hit me as I followed Dybgo down the moist, uneven steps into the caves below. Seaweed and potent dampness stung my nose. It was so gloomy down here, even with the blue lanterns hanging along the damp walls.

Exiting the claustrophobic tunnel, a boat very similar to the one we arrived on, bobbed at the end of a gangway. The sails were lowered and closed, and a line of Akquarians sat on either side, ready to row the boat out of the large cave.

As we walked up the small incline to the boat, Rooke appeared at the edge in front of us. Eyeing Dybgo, he smiled. "Didn't recognise you, buddy," he said, slapping Dybgo on the shoulder, "without your usual golden glow."

Unimpressed, Dybgo frowned at him, while I tried to suppress my snigger. Thankfully, he didn't look back. He continued onto the boat, barking orders at the small crew.

"Nice to see you looking more like my second again." Rooke winked at me, taking in the blue-grey T-shirt, combat pants, black boots, and the usual high ponytail.

"Did you not approve of my elegant side?"

"Well…I suppose I did like that dress. You know the one with the really low-cut neckline, that showed off your…" I slapped his hand away from where he was pointing at his breastbone. He laughed. "What?"

"Stop it. Anyway, you can talk. Still no beard?"

"It's not permitted, unlike flaunting one's breasts."

I rolled my eyes. "I didn't flaunt them."

He winked, taunting me again. I hummed my disapproval as he walked towards the stern of the ship. I followed. "You seem in good spirits today."

"I am," he said quietly. "We finally get away from this prison for a few hours. And Nux knows, it's been a long week."

"You're not worried about the Igknamai?"

"Look around…we've got a small platoon of trained Akquarian warriors with us. I'm pretty sure we'll be okay." He handed me a small handgun; one from his own collection. Not laser, but bullet. His preferred type. "Our laser guns have lost their charge. So, keep this with you. Just in case."

I pushed the relic into my belt and the boat started to move.

It took just under an hour to reach the stretch of land where our ship sat. Out at sea, it was obvious the sand surrounding the

Parvos was littered with materials. Caught in the tide, some floated out towards us. But as we drew closer, the extent of the damage was horrifying. Rooke cursed profusely as we waded through the sea, pulling a small, wooden longboat to shore.

Fuel leakage stained the dry sand. Cables were scattered everywhere, their plastic casings no longer protecting the wiring inside. All three of Parvos' landing gears were submerged in the sand, lowering the height of the hull considerably. Metal from the underbelly and exterior walls had been shredded, displaying several large holes big enough for a horse to get through. Big enough for the Igknamai to gain entry onto the ship.

A haunting revelation shuddered through my bones; we would be dead if we had remained here. Rooke's risky plan to find the Akquarians had saved us all from the same fate as Sym and Captain Lewison. Even Zamya wouldn't be able to deny that.

I walked towards the rear of the ship, to where Rooke stood pointing the remote at the landing ramp to open. He cursed. "Kobe, it's not working."

"I thought as much. There's too much wiring damage." Kobe appeared from behind me. "We'll have to get in through one of those holes." He nodded to the jagged opening to the left of the landing ramp. Sharp pieces of metal sat at odd angles making the access point seem hazardous.

Rooke spun round looking for Dybgo. The Akquarian was striding from the grounded longboat at the edge of the surf, studying our alien vessel with those assessing eyes.

"What are the chances the ship's being inhabited?" Rooke called to him.

Dybgo stopped next to me, now surveying the large hole. "It's possible. But the sun's hot today. The Igknamai won't linger for long if it's warm inside."

"Without the air coolant running, it'll be stifling," Kobe said.

"Then, there's a good chance they would've left for the day. They don't function well in the heat."

"What do you mean by that?" I looked up at Dybgo, shielding the harsh sunlight from my eyes with my hand. He moved, shadowing my face with his tall body. I gulped at his closeness—at the pale, toned chest directly in front of me—realising he was merely being a gentleman, blocking the sun from blinding me. Would either Rooke or Kobe have even considered doing that? I doubted it.

"The heat slows the Igknamai down. They're rarely seen between the hours of ten and fourteen." *Ten and fourteen?* He meant 10 a.m. and 2 p.m. "They prefer the coolness of the night."

"So, you're saying," Rooke added, "the Igknamai don't like the heat nor the rain?"

"That's correct."

"It's always hot and raining here. How the hell do they thrive?"

"That's a question my ancestors have been asking for centuries." Dybgo looked round at his men, barking an order in his native tongue at them. He turned back to us and said, "My warriors will make sure the ship is secure before you enter."

I looked at Rooke, who was staring at Dybgo with stern ferocity. Whether or not it was because of a reluctance to bow down to Dybgo's authority, or if he was digesting the intel regarding the Igknamai, I couldn't tell.

Two Akquarians hauled themselves up into the irregular ship cavity, disappearing into the darkness. We stood in silence as we waited, listening attentively. After several minutes, a harsh voice shouted down to us.

"He says it's clear," Dybgo interpreted.

Rooke immediately headed for the opening. He entered, followed by Kobe and two more Akquarians. As the opening was only a metre off the ground, I easily pulled myself through, but a sharp pain pricked my skin as I skimmed the edge. I must've snagged my leg on a sharp piece of metal. I stifled the hiss trying to escape from my lips. With Dybgo behind me, I was more than aware the Akquarians regarded their females as weak. I had no intention of proving that about my species.

Climbing in the darkness, I followed the others upwards, gripping gnawed cables and jagged edges to gain height.

Eventually my head appeared through the floor of the dully lit loading bay. Pulling myself clear, I noticed the area seemed untouched. It would appear the Igknamai had concentrated on feasting on the lower levels. Maybe the climb was too strenuous for their feeble looking legs. It had left me breathless. And it was hot up here, really hot.

"Main power is out," Kobe said from the panel on the far wall, "but auxiliary power is working." He pulled a lever and the room fully lit up.

Leaving Rooke in the loading bay with the Akquarian warriors, I accompanied Dybgo and Kobe down the short corridor to the analysing room. The consoles illuminated as soon as we entered. Again, everything appeared untouched.

I made a beeline for the comms desk. Rooke had instructed me to charge the three radio sets, while Kobe downloaded any information The Orka had sent during its orbits around the Earth, albeit without drawing attention to the task.

In the corner of my eye, I could see Dybgo strolling around the circular space, surveying. One hand on the hilt of his sword, the other holding a long spear. He certainly held a domineering presence.

To my surprise his voice echoed through the room. "This…this isn't what I expected."

I glanced at him over my shoulder. "What did you expect?"

His eyes swept the computers. "I pictured your ship to be more…more futuristic."

"Sorry to disappoint," Kobe retorted as he stood up. He looked over at me. "Eden, can you keep an eye on this?" He indicated to his desk screen. "I need to check something with Rooke."

"Sure." Kobe left and I moved over to his desk.

"I'm not disappointed," Dybgo went on. "Just surprised."

I smiled. "I think you've been reading too many ancient human Sci-Fi books."

He chuckled and I leant back on the desk, obscuring the screen from his view.

In the dull light Dybgo looked human. A rather tall, muscular human with a sculptured face, but the similarities were there.

"Can I ask you a question?"

He inclined his head. "Of course."

"Why do you not wear your armour outside the fortress, where it would possibly be useful?"

He raised his eyebrows and glanced down at his chest, to where, I realised, I was staring. *Eyes up, Eden.* Nux, what was wrong with me?

"I never wear it out on the sea. If the boat capsized or I fell overboard, the weight of it would drag me down. And even with my Akquarian lungs, I would drown."

"Ahh, I see."

"I only tend to wear it around the fortress. Havav insists I wear it to show authority and rank."

"So, what, exactly, is your rank?"

He smiled, almost bashfully. "I do not know if there is a word for it in your language. Possibly protector or…general."

I nodded. Exactly what I assumed. "And the large golden swirl signifies that?" I gestured to his chest.

"That is correct."

"I do feel like a fraud for taking your attention away from your duties. You seem to be here guarding me. I am honoured, but I really don't need protecting."

There was a hint of primal possessiveness in the way he stared at me. "All females need protecting."

"But you are the Akquarian general…"

"What if I am?"

I huffed a smile. "Don't you have more important things to do?"

"Your crew's appearance has been the highlight of Havav's reign. Believe me, he defines you as important."

I narrowed my eyes at him, trying to work out if there was a deeper meaning behind that comment?

The computer pinged behind me. Turning, I found the download was complete. I removed the small, portable hard drive and placed it in my back pocket. I faced Dybgo again and found him watching me. *Damn, had he seen something?*

I smiled, motioning to the closed door to the sleeping quarters and flight deck. "I need to retrieve a couple of books for Cora. I won't be long."

His eyes softened and he regally inclined his head in understanding.

I tapped on the door panel. It scanned my thumb print and the door opened. *Now, where had Cora left those books? Flight deck, that's what she'd said.*

I strolled to the front of the ship. The door to the cockpit was open. Quickly scanning the dashboard, I couldn't see any books, but stepping forward between the pilot chairs, something light in colour caught my eye. A small book sat in the co-pilot chair, its pages creased and strewn open. I leaned down to pick it up when I noticed another, larger book on the floor. I tutted, astounded at how carefree Cora was. I knelt to retrieve it but froze when I realised the edges had strange marks embedded in the leather cover, as if it had been chewed on.

Snatching the book up, I turned it over, assessing the damage. The marks seemed too dainty to be anything to worry about.

A clonking noise from the kitchen caught my attention. Dybgo must've followed me in, probably amazed at how little space we had to eat on board. No palace luxury here. I stood and turned, ready to ask him his opinion, but I didn't find Dybgo standing there. Instead, I was staring at the white–yellow scales of an Igknamai. Its head was facing away from me, its front four legs up against the kitchen side emptying out the cupboard with its skeleton fingers. It was the size of a large dog but far wider, and the smell that was resonating from it was making me want to retch.

But I couldn't move. If I remained motionless, it may not notice me. But even if it remained oblivious to my presence, I had no clear means of escape. It was positioned between me and the short corridor which led to the door to the analysing room. That's when I realised the door was shut. It must've automatically closed behind me after I entered. I was locked in here with an Igknamai.

128

I watched it pull the metal containers out of the cupboard. They clattered against the metal floor causing my muscles to constrict. I closed my eyes, sensing the panic rising up my legs, into my body. How was I going to get out of this? It was pointless shouting for help. As well as alerting the creature to my presence, with the door closed, the area was practically soundproof. And even if Dybgo did hear my plea, he wouldn't be able to open the door. It needed fingerprint authorisation. I didn't even know if he had fingerprints. I was stuck in here with no radio, no way of letting anyone know I needed urgent assistance. What the hell was I going to do?

I felt my heart pounding in my ears. The heat was stifling, and the smell was growing worse as the Igknamai moved around the kitchen, scuttling closer. I was too scared to breathe in case it sensed me.

Glancing at the door panel to the flight deck, I wondered if I could get close enough to shut the door before the Igknamai had a chase of pouncing, but the button wasn't illuminated. None of the lights on the dashboard were either. There was no power in the cockpit.

I felt my breath shudder as the beast shifted its position, edging closer. Then, it looked at me.

Four large black eyes widened at the sight. My breath caught as it hunched and roared, so loud I thought my ear drums had perforated. Its sharp fangs glistened in the light pouring in through the driving screen behind me. Any moment now, I was going to be shredded and ripped apart just like Sym had been.

My mind accelerated through vague memories of my parents, my brother, my grandma. Regret filling me that I hadn't been to see their graves in years. Memories of nights out with Rooke and mutual friends, full of laughter and bickering—Rooke, my dearest friend. Why had I never told him what he meant to me? If I died now, he would never know. My heart ached at the thought.

The Igknamai danced on its legs, riled and excited at the prospect of my capture. Still frozen on the spot, the two books I was holding slipped from my hands and I reached for Rooke's gun lodged in my belt. Flicking the safety catch off, I prayed it was loaded. It had to be loaded. Rooke wouldn't have given me a dud gun, antique or not. I took a step back and aimed with both hands. And the Igknamai launched itself at me.

Chapter Thirteen

I'm not sure how many times I pulled the trigger, but I hit true.
The Igknamai screamed, stunting its movement for a brief second,
but it didn't retreat. It lurched at me again. I ducked down behind
the pilot seat, pushing my body into the cramped footwell under
the dashboard. I felt the breeze from the snap of its jaw. The smell
of its breath was so rancid it was tempting me to pass out. Its head
loomed closer, and I kicked at it, only for its fang to penetrate the
tip of my boot.

Shit!

With all my strength, I kicked against its powerful jaws with
my other foot. If I didn't get my foot free, this beast was going to
rip my leg off. I felt the grunts emanating from my lungs, my
throat, as I jarred against the beast's head. I wouldn't let it win, I
couldn't.

With one final, bone crunching thud, the Igknamai halted for
a millisecond. Long enough for me to snap my boot free.

It roared again, trying to inch forward into the confined space.
It was getting closer, and I was running out of room to retreat into.
How its large body could fit between the pilot chairs, let alone
down here under the dashboard, I didn't know. There was so much
noise, so much blood pumping through my head, I was struggling
to think.

A whimper escaped me as its jaws snapped, snagging my
trouser leg. So close, it was too close. Nux, I was going to die!

I had no choice, I needed to get out of the tiny space of the
footwell. I struggled to move, frightened by the frenzied beast far

too close for comfort. One inch at a time, I shuffled to the outer edge of the chair, but the Igknamai had already tracked my movement. It jumped up onto the seat and roared down at me. Gloopy, rank saliva dripped into my hair, down my face. I felt sick.

My body tensed at the sound of the Igknamai growling, snapping its deadly jaws overhead. I looked down at the gun in my hand. The bullets hadn't penetrated the beast's skin whatsoever, it was useless. But it wouldn't be useless against me, my body. I looked at the barrel, flinching at the Igknamai's attempts to gain those last few inches to sink its teeth into me. I could end it. Take my own life. Surely that would be the lesser evil, if not the coward's way out. Suicide had always felt like the coward's way out. That's what I'd always been told, even when I'd tried to justify what happened back…I didn't want to think about that.

A tear slid down my cheek thinking of Rooke and everything he had done for me. How had it come to this?

"I love you, Rooke," I whispered, placing the barrel against my temple.

As if the Igknamai knew what I was about to do, it suddenly screeched, followed by a heavy thrashing. And then there was silence. Silence that took me a while to register.

Lowering the gun, I slowly looked up from my hunched position and found the tip of a spear inches from my face. It was jutting out of the Igknamai's head, directly between its two sets of eyes. Red blood trickled down from the wound. For some reason I imagined its blood would be yellow or green. Not red. Not like my own.

Dead. It was dead.

Relief and shock struck, causing my limbs to feel tingly and numb. My breath wavered as a figure emerged from the doorway—*Dybgo*.

He reached forward to offer me his hand. I looked down at the smooth, pale skin and stared. Not at his hand, but at the realisation of what had just happened. What was about to happen if he hadn't….

"Are you hurt?" Dybgo's voice was commanding yet

compassionate. My watery eyes looked up at him. He saved me. "Are you able to stand?"

Eventually, despite the pounding in my head, I nodded and took the hand he offered. It was warm, strong, comforting. After helping me to my feet, he guided me into the kitchen where we found Rooke, Kobe, and two Akquarians rushing through the doorway from the analysing room. Rooke stopped and looked at the metal door sitting at an odd angle. It had been pulled off its mechanical hinges. Dybgo must've ripped it open to get to me.

"What's going on?" Rooke demanded, approaching us, eyeing Dybgo sceptically. "We heard gun shots." He then cursed when he saw the dead Igknamai behind us. "What happened?"

Dybgo explained his side of the story. I couldn't speak. I was too lost in my horrifying thoughts. I was so close to ending my life, so close.

Familiar, dark green eyes appeared directly in front of me, pulling me out of my trance. "Are you alright?" Rooke asked sternly.

I nodded, but I wasn't. All I wanted was for Rooke to hold me. But instead, he barked demands at Dybgo to have the Igknamai removed from *his* ship, then turned on his heel and headed back to the loading bay.

Another reluctant tear fell down my cheek. I wiped it away quickly. I felt weak. I felt…ashamed.

An hour later, we were back on the boat. I was in shock. I knew I was. I felt cold, detached from reality. Standing on the bow, I watched the sea lapping around us, welcoming the whooshing of the wind and the roaring of the waves.

A hand grabbed my elbow and I found Rooke standing beside me, a harsh look on his face.

"Why did you leave the analysing room?" He glanced over his shoulder, keeping his voice low.

"What?"

"Why did you leave Dybgo alone in the analysing room?"

"I…" I frowned. Why was he asking me this? He seemed

angry.

He raised his eyebrows abruptly, waiting for my response.

"Cora asked me to retrieve a couple of her books."

Rooke groaned and shook his head. The tendons in his jaw tightened. He was definitely angry. "You left Dybgo in the analysing room, unattended, to retrieve Cora's sodding books? He could've found anything."

"The download had finished…"

"But the screen was still on." He lowered his voice further. "He could've seen something."

"He doesn't know how to use a computer."

"And you know that for certain? They could be playing us."

Was he being serious? I had almost died, yet here he was, chastising me for something he could not prove. "I think you're being paranoid, Rooke."

"Don't turn this around on me!" he snarled. "You knew the situation. You messed up. Do you still have the hard drive, at least?"

I pulled the slim metal block out of my pocket and handed it to him. Without another word, he marched away, slipping the hard drive into his back pocket. I stifled the urge to break down into a blubbering mess. How could he be so heartless?

Kobe appeared, eying me tentatively. "Here's your radio. Keep this solar pack outside when it's sunny and it should keep it charged."

I took the radio pack, nodding absentmindedly.

He went to leave but chose to turn back. "Rooke *was* genuinely worried about you, you know."

I met Kobe's brown gaze. Somehow, I shrugged, pretending it wasn't a concern; pushing the thought away.

Back at the fortress, without saying a word to Rooke, I was ushered from the boat by Dybgo. Yuska met me at the top of the stairs, and whilst I followed her up the dizzy stairwells to my rooms, I drowned in my thoughts.

Outside the apartment door, I glanced down at Cora's books

in my hands, tracing the strange marks in the leather with my thumb. "Yuska?" She turned, attentively. "Can you take me straight to the springs? I feel…" I swallowed nervously, "I feel grubby."

She scrunched her blonde eyebrows together. "I agree with you." I met her gaze. "Grubby doesn't suit you," she began to open the door, "and you appear in a far worse state than a mere *grubby*." How much she knew about today, I was unsure.

Cora and Zamya had hardly moved since this morning. I was too angry to say anything. Cora looked up at me as I dumped the books on the table, leaving immediately afterwards, ignoring her questions about the state of them.

In the quiet gloom of a spring bath chamber, I undressed and slipped into the warm, inviting water. The horrors of the day still swam about in my mind. I couldn't blot them out. I nearly died…by my own hand, nevertheless.

Aware of Yuska's presence behind me, folding my clothes into a net basket, I said, "Yuska, could you…could you give me five minutes alone, please?"

There was a short pause before she agreed. I heard the gentle padding of her feet disappearing up the stone steps before I sunk lower into the water, wrapping my arms around myself. It was only then I allowed myself to release the emotion. Full heartedly, I sobbed.

To her credit, Yuska left me for at least twenty minutes, allowing me to compose myself before she returned.

By the time we arrived back at the apartment, my head felt clearer, but I chose to ignore my female colleagues eating at the table. Both watched as I marched across the room to the bedroom, both eyeing each other with question.

I stopped at the foot of my bed, ready to collapse into it. Sleep…that's what I needed. But Yuska had other ideas. She ushered me into the small room on the far side, gesturing me to sit at the dressing table. I shook my head. "I don't need assistance, Yuska. Please, I…I can brush my own hair."

Unexpectedly, she pushed me down into the seat. "I need to

135

get you ready for dinner."

"Dinner?"

"Havav has requested your presence."

"Oh, no, no, no." I met her eyes in the mirror. "There is no way in this world, or any other, that I'm leaving this room this evening."

"You have no choice in the matter. What Havav requests is always obligated."

"Yuska, please?" I swallowed down a sob. It wasn't just the thought of Havav questioning me all evening that I couldn't bear, I knew Rooke would be in attendance, and I couldn't stomach seeing him. Not after what he accused me of. Not after…oh, there was so much conflict whirling around my head.

I rubbed my face with the palms of my hands. I hated this place. I wanted to go home, back to my little cottage and its log fire, where I could be left in peace.

Yuska began to brush my hair. "I'm sorry. Havav has insisted." And as if that was the definitive line drawn under the discussion, Yuska began her work.

My mind was elsewhere whilst Yuska arranged my hair. It was only when she asked me to stand, I refocused on the present. After removing my robe, she pooled a black dress over my head.

"Very fitting. It reflects my mood," I groaned, remarking at the colour, only for her to scoff. The dress was slick, long, and heavy, with a flattering heart shaped neckline. Beautiful, fluted sleeves started halfway down my upper arm, exposing my sleek shoulders. To finish off the look, Yuska placed a dainty chain of blue pearls around my neck, matching the ones already in my hair. I knew I looked elegant, almost regal, but I felt ridiculous. I felt like a fraud.

Surrounded by guards, Yuska escorted me to Havav's dining room. Much to my despair, everyone paused as I entered. Rooke, Kobe, even the guards lining the walls, flicked their eyes in my direction.

Unsure where to look, my eyes locked with Dybgo's. He

stood in his usual spot, on the opposite side of the room behind Havav's chair. His expression was stoic yet strangely comforting.

You saved me.

Lost in his crystal blue gaze, my attention was pulled to movement between us. Draped in layers of red and orange, with a golden twigged crown upon his head, Havav glided towards me, his arms sprayed wide. "Dear Eden. What a horrible ordeal you endured this afternoon." His voice was patronising, and overly dramatic. I forced myself to look at his alabaster skin, those turquoise eyes full of…was that amusement dancing there? *Bastard.*

Havav motioned me to my chair. "How are you, my dear?"

"I'm fine, really," I replied meekly, taking my seat.

"You shouldn't have been left on your own." He seated himself at the head of the table to my left. "I assure you, punishment has been dealt to the one whose duty was to protect you."

Attempting to disguise my shock, I glanced at Dybgo before dropping my eyes to the table. Havav had reprimanded Dybgo for leaving me unattended? Even though he was the one who had saved me? A knot twisted violently in my stomach. I wanted to be sick.

"This is why I strongly advise you remain in the fortress."

Of course he'd say that. "We needed to return to the ship for supplies," I mumbled.

"Your commander could've gone alone with Mr Kobe and my warriors," Havav continued. "Your presence wasn't essential."

"Wasn't essential?" Still staring at the table, heat flooded my cheeks. I suddenly felt hot, angry. "Why? Because I'm a woman?"

"Females should remain in the safety of the fortress, my dear."

I finally met his gaze. "I am *not* one of your females."

"Indeed. Yet the events of today have proven you are just as vulnerable as the females who were born and bred here."

I finally shifted my eyes to Rooke sitting opposite. He was

giving me a hard stare; one I couldn't read. Was he really going to sit there and let Havav dictate this sexism? Or was he still mad at me for leaving Dybgo unattended in the analysing room? It appeared both Dybgo and I were paying for that circumstance in more ways than one.

"Today was a coincidence," I said through gritted teeth. "It could've been any one of us facing that Igknamai."

"But it was you, and it was lucky my *male* warrior rescued you from a terrible fate."

"Yet you reprimanded him regardless?" I flicked my gaze to Dybgo, who continued to stare ahead, seemingly unfazed by the conversation.

"That is how seriously we take female protection here."

I huffed irritably. "And I am grateful for his heroism, truly I am, but that is not sufficient evidence to prove I am vulnerable and worthless. I am *not* a weak link."

"No?" Havav raised his blonde eyebrows. Again, his eyes danced with patronising amusement. "I was informed you wept for a good half an hour at the springs when you returned." I wanted to curse. Yuska, the little bitch. Most definitely one of his spies, informing Havav of everything we said and did. "If that is not a sign of weakness, dear Eden, I don't…"

"Crying is not a sign of weakness." I noted Rooke's gaze on my face. Was he shocked or concerned?

Havav chuckled. "Oh, I believe it is a sign of a weak mind."

Clenching my teeth tightly together, my jaw ached. "It is a way of releasing one's pent-up frustration, so one can move on with a clear head. And I was not crying purely about the attack. I miss my home. I miss my miserable life back on Allura. The life that held a sense of freedom and normality. I can't cope with being imprisoned on a different world purely because of my sex."

"Eden," Rooke's voice rumbled in warning.

I looked at him. He was scowling at me. "What do you want me to say, Rooke?"

"You're being disrespectful."

"I'm being disrespectful? Me?" I looked at Havav who was

138

lounging back in his chair, eagerly watching mine and Rooke's interaction. He genuinely looked as though he was enjoying this. "Am I not allowed to voice my opinion?"

Rooke's dark eyes flashed with authority as he gave one subtle shake of the head. Nux, I'd never felt so exasperated with him, or at least since adolescence. I felt hot and irritable. I wanted to shout at him, tear him apart. Why was he standing up for this male chauvinistic pig?

"You two," Havav drawled from his seat, "have an extremely interesting relationship." Both Rooke and I looked at him. He was smirking, glancing between the two of us. His wide nostrils flared several times as if he was smelling—scenting us.

He sat forward, still with a pompous smirk on his face. "Miss Eden, I sense you are not in the mood to socialise this evening."

I swallowed down my aggression, only for it to be replaced by a wave of sorrow. "I…" I glanced at Rooke. His eyes had softened. "Yes, you are correct. I'd rather be alone."

"Very well." Havav sighed. "Although I do enjoy your company on most occasions, you may leave us." He clicked his fingers and Dybgo stepped forward. "I sense we won't be seeing you for a few days anyway." A frown pulled at my brow, and he smiled, exposing his elongated canines. "We shall catch up in a week or so."

Avoiding Rooke's eyes, I stood up as gracefully as I could. Without a single acknowledgment to anyone, I strode down the long room towards the door, my head held as high as possible. I hated this place. I hated Havav, especially.

Dybgo appeared at my side, opening the main door to the corridor. We walked in silence back to my rooms, plodding down corridor after corridor. My mind was a jumbled mess. The silence only made it worse.

Dybgo's golden armour shining in the light of the blue lanterns caught my eye as he made a motion to open the door to my apartment. I placed my hand on his arm, halting him. "Dybgo?"

He peered down at my hand, which felt frozen compared to

139

his warm skin. I pulled my fingers away immediately. No one touched here. Only when they mated. *Nux!*

"I'm sorry. I forget," I whispered.

"Don't be." His voice matched my own.

I peered up at the tall Akquarian, aware his eyes were glistening. There was so much meaning hidden in them, so much sorrow I hadn't noticed before. "What did he do to you…because of me?"

He shook his head. "It doesn't matter."

I wanted to cry. It did matter.

Glancing at the floor, I forced a stabilising breath into my lungs. The thought of him being punished because of my actions was gut wrenching. It was then I noticed his pale feet. They weren't webbed like Havav's or the other Akquarians, they looked the same as a human male, or was it just the angle the light caught?

"Eden, I shouldn't have left you on your own. It was my duty to protect you…"

"And you did." *You ripped the frigging door off to get to me.* I looked up at him again. "You did."

His eyes wandered the planes of my face as if he wanted to say something else. Fighting the urge to reach up and embrace him, I reached for the door handle instead, halting as the door cracked opened. "Thank you, Dybgo…for saving my life."

A forlorn smile briefly touched his lips, and he inclined his head. "It was my honour."

I slipped in through the crack in the doorway and closed it gently behind me. Resting my head on the cool stone of the door, I suddenly felt alone, scared. I loathed the feeling that gnawed at me when Rooke and I were in conflict. I despised Havav and this palace. I hated being the cause of someone else's grief. And with that thought, I heard Dybgo's delayed footsteps leave on the other side of the door.

Chapter Fourteen

I didn't wake until after midday. I felt exhausted, mentally more than physically, and after last night, my mind had taken forever to switch off.

Trying to ignore my grumbling stomach, I forced my eyes to remain shut, encouraging another bout of sleep to take over. However, hushed voices next door caught my attention. Several moments later, I heard a dual set of footsteps enter the bedroom.

Under my eyelashes, I watched Cora and Zamya approach. Cora was holding a steaming glass of what looked like…was that tea? I opened my eyes fully, sceptical by Zamya's frown and Cora's fake smile. "What are you two up to?"

I felt the foam mattress bounce beneath me as Cora perched on the edge of the bed. Zamya pulled a wicker stool closer, sitting directly in front of me.

"Why didn't you tell us?" Zamya asked gently, resting her elbows on her knees.

"Tell you what?"

"That you nearly died yesterday?"

I froze, the memories replaying again in my mind. I sat up attempting to shake them away. "I…" I scratched at my scalp. "I don't know. I didn't know how to. I…I needed time to reflect. To digest what happened."

"Are you okay?" Cora shifted closer, offering me the glass of tea.

I closed my eyes, sucking in the warm, citrusy fresh aura of home. "Is this?"

"Eonian tea." She smiled. "Just how you like it. Yuska fetched us the hot water. Rooke gave her the box of teabags this morning. He apparently retrieved it yesterday from the ship."

I stared down at the orangey brown beverage trying to understand Rooke's motives. Yesterday he had been disappointed...no, angry with me. And today he was offering sentimental gifts? Did he feel bad for what happened last night? Nux, I wanted to slap him across the face...hard!

I took a sip, sighing gratefully. "Thank you. It's a lovely surprise."

"We always run to you when we have troubles," Cora said. "Please understand that we're here for you, too, Eden. We have each other's backs, remember? And we're terribly sorry for being unhelpful over the past few days."

"She means, we're sorry for being lazy-ass cows," Zamya stated, sincerely. "We'll start exercising today. I was thinking we could ask Yuska if we could go for a run on the beach."

"I doubt going outside is an option," I groaned, thinking of Havav's opinions and comments from last night. "No thanks to yesterday."

"Well then." Zamya slapped her thighs with her palms and stood up. "We'll have to run in the corridors."

"Ha, I'm sure he'll love that."

"Frigging bastard." Zamya flashed me a smile. "Speaking of egotistical males, Rooke has asked you to turn your radio on."

I hummed a non-comprehensible answer as I sipped the tea. I didn't want to speak to him. Not today.

My mood didn't improve. If anything, it worsened. I felt frustrated and irritable, snapping at everything and everyone. Zamya and Cora were no longer required to isolate, and Cora had been summoned by Havav. She'd been gone most part of the day.

I watched Zamya jump about the room in an attempt to exercise. I knew I should join her, but I was restless with no motivation. A horrible, contradicting combination which worsened my frustration even more.

The door opened and Cora breezed in with more books in her hands, no doubt from the library.

Zamya stopped and panted. "Everything okay?"

"Yep." Cora smiled, placing the books on the coffee table. "Havav wasn't quite so interrogating today. He actually helped me find some information I was seeking."

I groaned at the sound of Havav's name. Zamya peered at me.

"Judging by the information we received from The Orka and what I found in the library today, it looks as though our current position is somewhere on the western side of North America."

"You didn't tell Havav about The Orka, did you?" my tone was brusque, ignoring her information I would've normally found interesting.

"No," Cora replied. "Rooke made it clear to keep schtum."

I grunted my approval, but it sounded more like annoyance.

"And because of that, he's told me I can no longer speak with Troy over the radio. Rooke also insisted that I tell you to turn *your* radio on. He actually asked me using a large variety of colourfully explicit words."

Zamya glared at me. "Have you still not done it?"

"Nope."

"Eden!"

"Look, Zam, if you want to talk to him, why don't you turn it on?"

"Why are you being so petulant? Have you and Rooke had an argument?"

I didn't respond. I merely looked down at the ancient engineering book laying in my lap.

Zamya huffed and marched into the bedroom, I assumed to find the radio. I knew I was being unreasonable, but I couldn't shake this irritable mood. The past couple of weeks were weighing on my shoulders and I wanted to cry most of the time. Nux, what was wrong with me?

I looked over at Cora. She was gazing out through the open archway, lost in her thoughts. Every aspect of her from her button nose to the way her toes wiggled playfully, showed how young and innocent she was. She must've been desperately missing Troy, yet she was embracing this situation with as much enthusiasm as possible. I envied her.

A cold poke in my ear made me flinch. I hissed when I found Zamya standing next to me holding the ear thermometer. "What the hell, Zam!?"

"Uh huh." She examined the digits on the thermometer display. "That explains a lot."

"What are you talking about?" I snatched the contraption from her hand.

"Your temperature's up. I believe your monthly is about to arrive, hence your foul mood."

I scanned the digital display. Well, that *did* explain a lot.

And she wasn't wrong. The following morning, I woke in extreme pain, more severe than I'd had in years. No doubt the prolonged space travel and return to natural gravity had aided the severity of my stomach cramps. I could barely move.

It didn't help that I felt exhausted. The past two nights had been filled with vivid dreams. As well as the recurring dream about Rooke, I also dreamt about the Igknamai attack. But more disturbingly, Dybgo and Rooke had both been there, watching me being torn apart. Both said and did nothing. It all seemed to mess with my head.

I admitted it; I felt pathetic and weak. Scared and insecure. I felt out of control.

Soft footsteps approached as I laid in my bed, curled up like a ball. Yuska appeared holding a glass. "Here, drink this."

I sat up and took the glass from her hands, grimacing at its odd smell.

"It doesn't smell or taste very pleasing, but I assure you, it will make you feel better."

I downed the whole glassful, wincing at the grim aftertaste. Yuska held out a hand, ready to take the glass back but I held onto it, watching the dregs swim around at the bottom. Looking up, I eyed her blue sash tied around her tiny waist. It still baffled me how she acquired it.

"Yuska, may I ask you a question?"

"Indeed, you may." She took the glass from me and clasped it in her hands.

"The sash you wear, does it…does it give you extra entitlements?" I watched her brows knit together. "What I mean is…it has become apparent that the females here aren't given a great deal of freedom. I wondered if you are?"

Yuska stared at me. Her strange young-old turquoise eyes calculating my question, the same way Dybgo always did. Eventually she said, "I can understand why you think our ways are unusual, maybe overbearing, but you must understand, this is the way we have lived for centuries."

"And you are okay with that?"

"I have to be. We have to be. Our movements are restricted because there are so few of us?"

"As in Akquarians?"

"As in females."

As her words sunk in, it was my turn to stare. Other than Yuska, Bibska, and Woohla, I hadn't seen any females here whatsoever. Zamya always japed they were locked away somewhere. Maybe we hadn't seen any purely because, the reality was, there wasn't many to see.

"How few?"

Yuska moved to the window and placed the glass on the ledge. "Havav rules over this fortress and several other settlements along the shore. There are approximately fifty thousand Akquarians. Over forty-five thousand are male. You see, if Havav allowed the females to fight with the warriors, or even venture outside, that number *will* decrease, and the knock-on effect will be less births, less growth as a species. The rules are there to protect us all."

I nodded my understanding. It did make sense if the numbers were so depleted, but it still felt like a prison sentence.

"If anything, Eden, we feel shocked that you are treated in the same manner as a man." She pointed to my stomach. "They don't endure this, yet they expect you to perform the same tasks as they do."

"It's a choice."

She cocked her head as said, "Are you certain about that? I get the impression you feel obligated to compete with your male counterparts. Females are protected here because we are classed as sacred. We aren't bound by marriage or commitment. We are givers of life and because of that we get to choose what occupation we take up. The males don't. It is also the females who choose who they mate with each season. It's our choice and our choice alone. Any male who tries to intervene with that choice will be executed."

I couldn't believe how much information Yuska was divulging. It was an insight for sure. "Well," I smirked, "where I come from, women are certainly not seen as sacred. But it is generally a fifty-fifty split on our planet…maybe slightly more men, but not by much."

Yuska nodded and glanced towards the open doorway where Zamya had appeared. She was holding my radio in one hand, pulling the headset from her ear with the other.

"It's Rooke," she said. "He really needs to speak with you."

I sighed heavily, flicking my eyes to Yuska. She tapped my arm with her cold hands, giving me a boost of confidence. I hadn't spoken to Rooke since that horrible evening, days ago.

Watching Yuska leave, I sat forward, then frowned at Zamya, who was holding the two pieces of the radio in front of my face. "I don't have a choice, do I?"

"Not today."

I grabbed it and hooked the earpiece onto my ear. Noticing Zamya's immediate disappearance, I inwardly grimaced. How bad was this going to be?

I took a deep breath. "Rooke, it's me. What do you want?"

"I want to know how you are…and *hello* to you too."

The corner of my lips twitched upwards. Nux, I wanted to stay mad at him, but how could I when he made me smile with a simple tone of voice. "I'm fine, and hello."

"Heard you've become recently incarcerated."

"So what if I have?"

"Wondered if that was the reason we had a moody matron at dinner a few evenings ago?"

"Do you want me to hang up, Rooke?"

"No, no, I want to work out what's going on with you."

For Nux Sake. "I nearly died. And I could've done without the *I told you so* speech from Havav. The way he spoke to me made me question if he'd instigated the whole situation just so he could demoralise me. Nux, he is so…insufferable…"

"And he knows exactly how to get under your skin."

"As do you."

There was a short pause. "I know. I should've stood up for you but…I'm trying to remain on Havav's good side. He's appointed his shipbuilders to make a floating raft big enough to transport Parvos back to the safety of the fortress caves. That way, we'll be able to fix the ship with no detrimental interruption from the Igknamai."

"That's good," I mumbled. "I suppose Havav has his uses."

"He isn't all that bad."

"Hmm."

"I promise you; we'll fix the ship. We *will* get home."

I squeezed my eyes together, praying that was a promise he could keep.

"Oz is awake."

"Is he? That's a relief. How is he?"

"Weak but improving day by day. I'll work on Havav, see if he'll allow you and the girls access to the ward."

"Please. It'll be good to see him."

"I've also had a lot of contact with Troy over the past couple of days."

"Is he okay?"

"Yes. He's being kept busy. He's found an active satellite."

"Active? As in…"

"As in active and in orbit around Earth. But it's not relaying signals to another satellite, it's transmitting into space."

"Do you think that's what guided the probe?"

"It's a possibility, and the ground signal is transmitting from a site only forty miles from here."

I felt my adrenaline pulse through my veins. "Do you think it could be the Akquarians?"

"It's too close to disregard them."

"Rooke, Yuska told me Havav has more colonies along the shore. Could it be the same location?"

"No. Troy has pinpointed it to a wooded location, further inland."

"Outpost?"

"That was my thought too, but…ah…the Akquarians don't seem technologically savvy…at all."

"What about your theory regarding Dybgo and the ship computer?"

"I…I don't know. I may have overreacted that day. Uh…believe it or not, I was a little shaken. Another one of my crew nearly died."

"Oh." I smiled to myself. I knew he wasn't a cold-hearted bastard. He did care.

"I'm just baffled, Eden. It doesn't make sense. None of it does."

"Let's concentrate on getting the ship back. You'll have to work out if we can trust Havav, but you need to play this cool and calm."

"My speciality, then."

I scoffed.

Rooke laughed. "I've missed you, Eden. Please don't turn the radio off again."

"In that case, you better not piss me off again."

"I'll try my hardest not to."

I spent most of the next four days sitting by the open archway, either watching the storm clouds charge across the sky, reading about ancient engineering, or discouraging Zamya and Cora from bickering. Spending so much time stuck in the apartment together was taking its toll. On The Orka we had our own quarters we could retreat to for some alone time. Here, even sociable Cora was starting to feel harassed.

All three of us attempted to exercise for at least an hour a day, but we couldn't do much in the restricted area. We wanted to go outside, to run, to breathe.

Thankfully I'd been left alone in the apartment for the afternoon. Cora and Zamya had been escorted to the springs by Yuska and Woohla. I envied them, though. What I'd give to have a bath. It had been five days of rock basin washing and I felt disgusting.

It had been raining for days now. Sitting by the open archway, watching the water droplets hit the balcony floor, I couldn't help pondering whether the Igknamai had taken shelter inside our ship. I still had nightmares about the attack, about the gun trigger I was moments away from pulling if Dybgo hadn't made an appearance.

The craving to go home had become a persistent nagging. Even though I had spoken to Rooke every evening for the past four days, I missed him. I missed our interaction. I missed home and going to the pub for a drink, and hiking through the mountains for a weekend just because we could. And it worried me that even if we did manage to get the ship back to the Akquarian fortress for repairs—how long would it take, and would there be enough resources to fix it? I was trying not to feel despondent about the situation, but the more I anticipated the outcome, the more I dreaded failure.

Breaking me out of my daze, I heard the heavy door scraping across the floor. I glanced over the back of my chair and found Bibska holding the door wide, her head bowed slightly.

Havav entered with his usual graceful and fluid movements. Ripples of gold flowed behind him as his cape flapped in the breeze. I immediately stood, anxiously fighting my thoughts. The last time I'd seen him, he had purposely degraded me.

As he strolled across the room with an amicable smile softening his face, I noticed the four armed guards entering after him. No Rooke. Rooke hadn't accompanied him. This was unusual, unnerving. I suddenly felt alarmed. What did he want?

Flicking my gaze back to the regal being, he eyed my attire and raised his eyebrows. I must have looked an untamed mess in my black vest top and leggings. "I apologise," I said, "I did not realise I would have company today."

"Think nothing of it." He looked to the chair across from mine. "May I sit?"

"Of course."

I glanced towards the door as I heard it groan shut, and my heart rate increased. Standing by the door, dressed in his golden armour and blue cape, was Dybgo. His hand rested on the hilt of his curving sword, poised with the stature of protection. Thankfully he didn't look my way. After the dreams I'd been having recently, although innocent enough, I wouldn't know how to interact without blushing profusely.

"I hope you don't mind the intrusion," Havav drawled, "but I wish to speak with you, alone."

I slowly lowered myself into my chair, giving him my full attention.

He smiled, crossing one leg over the other. "Your unexpected arrival to our world has been a delight to me and my people. It's simulated something along the idea of a prophecy. However, I get the impression, you especially, do not reflect that same elation."

I stared at him, fully aware of the emphasis he'd put on the word *unexpected*. I swallowed nervously. "I never intended on giving you that impression."

"And I believe you. Your commander has explained about your world and the way human females live the same life as a male, with the addition of procreation as and when they feel the time is right. So, I empathise with your need for freedom. And I can understand how claustrophobic you must be feeling…but," he put a finger up to stop me from interrupting his speech, "I am going to tell you something that may give you an insight into why I am so accustomed to enforcing my rules. I haven't told your commander this, and to be honest, I rarely speak of it." An expression of sorrow filled his eyes and I felt myself drawn to him with a compassionate intrigue. "I believe Yuska has informed you of the lack of females we have here."

"She has."

"Each female can take as many mates as she likes over her life span, it gives them a better chance of breeding success. Males do not take wives, but as a ruler, over the past couple of centuries, it has become customary to do so. It shows our perseverance and strength, our ability to love and cherish. I had a queen. She was perfect. But I lost her…to the Igknamai. Several years back, we were returning from a…colony visit when we stumbled upon a hoard of them. They chased us down. She fell from her horse and…" His eyes moistened and, for a moment, he dropped his gaze. "I couldn't save her."

Oh Nux. "I'm…I'm so sorry."

He shook his head and gave a sad smile. "I reinforced the protection rule to include all females that day," he met my gaze, "and we haven't lost a single female to the Igknamai since. Although," he raised his head slightly, "we nearly did seven days past."

"You mean me."

Havav gave one slow nod. "You may not be one of my own, but you are treated with the same regard."

I understood, I did. A species so limited with female life protects and honours them, even if it did mean harsh, patronising restrictions.

"However," Havav shuffled in his seat, "I cannot force my rules on you, especially when they're causing such adverse effects…"

"I'm fine, really, I…"

He held his hand up to stop my words again. "I will allow you to leave the fortress as and when your commander permits your presence. But on two conditions…" My eyes widened in utter surprise. "You will take at least two of my finest warriors with you, of which both will remain with you at all times."

Okay, that may be awkward if I needed to relieve myself. I

151

glanced across at Dybgo wondering how he felt about that.

"And secondly…" I looked back at Havav as he pulled a golden dagger out from beneath the folds of his cape. He handed it to me. "…you accept this gift as a token of my utmost dedication to your protection."

I stared at the beautiful dagger twinkling in the grey daylight. The short, golden hilt was engraved with an elaborate design of Akquarian swirls, where a turquoise jewel sat embedded into the base of the blade. I took it from Havav's cold fingers, examining it with awe. It was sharp, deadly. A gift of purpose. I looked up at the Akquarian leader, astounded by his change of heart. "Thank you."

He nodded graciously and motioned to Dybgo. "I'm sure Dybgoforiamnuk will find the time to show you how to use it effectively. I'm under the impression this will be far more effective than your automatic weapons."

Twisting the dagger carefully between my fingers, I nodded. "Yes, I'm pretty sure it will be."

"Base of the throat or between the eyes are the best places."

"I'll remember that."

Havav watched me for a moment. "I am also allowing yourself, Miss Zamya, and Miss Cora to visit your colleague, Mr Oz. But only one at a time and you must be escorted by a chaperon."

"Of course. Thank you."

"I'm afraid I cannot permit you free movement around the fortress. There have been a few outbreaks of Tektrasc recently, so I can't risk it."

"I understand."

"Good." Havav rose to his feet, and I sensed all five of his men straighten further. Clearly a stern, respected leader, but here he was, sympathising with me.

"I've never been your enemy, Eden." He looked at me solemnly. "And I never intend to be."

Standing slowly, I clutched the dagger in my hand. This meeting had been a revelation. Perhaps without Rooke here, it had taken any extra pressure away from both of us. But even though I understood more and felt a little less uneasy around the Akquarian leader, the main certitude I took from this interaction was Havav needed my alliance more than Rooke's.

I felt baffled.

Chapter Fifteen

Returning from the springs, Cora rushed in through the apartment door. "Eden, you'll never guess what?"

I was standing across the room holding the radio. Fully aware Rooke wasn't being monopolised by Havav's time, I'd tried contacting him to tell him about my unexpected visitor, but the radio appeared to be faulty. I glanced at Cora, the dampness in her hair caused her curls to tighten. Her young face was fresh and full of excitement.

"Sorry?"

"I found…"

Zamya walked in through the door behind Yuska, and I caught her eye, "Zam, do you know if this has been charged?"

"Yeah, I checked it yesterday. Is it not working?"

"I don't know." Rechecking the battery, it was fully charged. The radio light was on, but no static hiss confirmed it was functioning. Cora sighed with irritation, and I looked over at her. "Sorry, Cora. What were you saying?"

"I found some Akquarian children. There was a pool full of them at the springs. I hadn't heard or seen any since we arrived. I was starting to wonder if they existed."

Zamya yawned next to me. "I assumed they would be like giant tadpoles."

It wasn't hard to miss the disgusted look Yuska threw Zamya. I smirked discretely; aware Cora hadn't noticed. "They look like human children. Just paler."

"So, no mermaid tails?" Zamya quipped.

Yuska unexpectedly snapped, "I'll have you know; our children are the same as any human child! The only difference is they grow a lot faster."

Zamya folded her arms across her chest. "And how do you know that?"

Yuska's nostrils flared, and a hint of rose touched the skin around her cheekbones. "You already know we have libraries full of human books."

"Books. But have you actually seen any human children?"

"Of course not."

"Then, how can you be so certain?"

Yuska tutted and walked into the bedroom. Zamya shook her head. I caught her arm, aware of an underlying statement behind her question. "Zam, what is it?"

"I don't trust these people. Everything seems...off."

Havav held true to his word and granted us permission to see Oz, although restricted. We took it in turns to visit him. Zamya insisted she go first, pulling the doctor card, saying she wanted to give him a full medical examination. I graciously accepted. Then Cora jumped in on the chance and pleaded with me to allow her to go next. It wasn't until the third day that I got to leave the apartment.

As usual, Yuska dressed me in flowing Akquarian attire and led me to the end of the corridor, where the guards were usually stationed. My breath caught when I realised Dybgo was waiting by the stairwell. I hadn't spoken to him since that horrible, shameful day.

He inclined his head in greeting. An awkward smile painted my lips as a rush of heat rose to my cheeks. Nux, why did I feel so embarrassed around him?

Yuska swiftly took her leave, and Dybgo guided me down only two flights of spiral stairs completely in silence. He motioned for me to walk along another corridor, falling instep beside me.

"How are you feeling?" His voice bounced off the high ceiling, startling me. He continued to stare ahead as I glanced up at him.

"I'm feeling a lot better, thank you."

"Good. It pleases me to hear that."

I smiled. He was so polite. More gentlemanly than any man I'd met back at home. Perhaps this was how it once was for my people, when men and women evolved into the era between primal behaviour and modern equality. It shocked me to think I kinda liked it.

"Is everything...okay with you?" I asked. "I mean, you haven't received any further punishment from Havav?"

His lips twitched. I could've sworn I saw a hint of a smile there. "No. Havav is not an unreasonable leader. My punishment was swift and that was the end of it."

"A punishment that was unnecessary."

"To you, perhaps. But I get the impression you do not think highly of yourself."

I chuckled. "I'm not imitable, Dybgo. And I'm certainly not a queen."

Something unspoken flashed in his eyes and I watched his Adam's apple bob, swallowing down his thoughts. "Maybe not, but to us you are...special. All females are."

Yes, they were sacred. Even me, apparently.

The infirmary was an area on the eastern side of the fortress. A cluster of open rooms with made up beds ran along an array of large, slitted windows. The area appeared empty apart from a warrior standing guard outside a closed off room.

He opened the hefty, stone door, revealing a small, bright room. My eyes quickly found Oz laying on an oval shaped rock-bed to the right. On the opposite side of the room, a young Akquarian female stood over a table laden with glass bottles and clean bandages. A blue sash tied around her waist. *Another chaperon.*

I made a beeline for Oz, who winced a lopsided smile as I approached. He was propped up by a cluster of foam pillows. His chest was bare, his left shoulder dressed with a neat white gauze. There was no sign of yellowing pus or blood. The colour in his cheeks had returned, as well as growth on his usually shaven hairline and beard. And even though he looked tired, I caught a glint of a sparkle in his blue eyes.

"Hey, you," his voice was raw and raspy.

Smiling, I sat down on the edge of the bed. "You're looking better than the last time I saw you."

He chuckled. "I can't remember the last time I saw *you*."

"Do you remember anything?"

He shook his head, scrunching up his face. "I don't remember much after the day we landed. I stupidly asked Rooke where Sym was. He had to tell me what happened. I thought it had all been a bad dream." He glanced downwards, remorse flooding every line of his face. "We shouldn't have gone outside. I made him go outside."

I reached for his hand. "If you want to blame yourself, you better get in line." He looked up at me. "Kobe and Rooke blame themselves. I blame myself. I'm sure Zamya blames everyone."

He snorted, the grief leaving his features momentarily before he narrowed his eyes towards a movement behind me. Heavily sighing, I closed my eyes, remembering where I was and what I had just done. And as expected, Dybgo appeared beside us.

Before he could speak, I pulled my hand away from Oz's and held it up. "I apologise. Oz is my friend, and I was comforting him. Neither of us are remotely attracted to one another. I promise we won't start fornicating in front of you."

Glancing up at the towering, golden warrior, I saw a hint of surprise shimmer across his face. But he graciously gave me a curt nod and retreated to the table, where he resumed conversation with the Akquarian female.

Oz was frowning when I looked back at him. "Speak for yourself," he japed.

I rolled my eyes.

Twitching his head in Dybgo's direction, Oz lowered his voice. "Who's the big guy?"

"That's Dybgo. I'm pretty certain he's been appointed as my personal bodyguard."

"Ahh, that explains it. He looks at you a lot."

I frowned. "Probably paranoid I'll slip his net." Peering over my shoulder, I caught Dybgo's eye. In all seriousness, I couldn't understand why he was here. Yuska could've escorted me. She was a chaperon, and I was positive it had been her who'd escorted Zamya and Cora here over the past two days.

Dybgo broke eye contact and continued to speak with the pretty Akquarian nurse. He seemed relaxed in her company, lounging in one of the wooden, slated chairs, which looked far too small to accommodate him. Flicking my eyes over his acquaintance, I realised she was really pretty, stunning in fact. Large, glassy blue eyes, high cheek bones structuring a long, delicate face, with a set of full, defined, pink lips. Her white-blonde hair was pulled back into a practical bun, and her nose was dainty but pronounced.

"Is that your nurse?" I asked Oz, turning back to him.

"Yep." He gazed at her, smirking with adoration. "That's Oonla. She was the first person I saw when I woke up. I thought I'd died and gone to heaven."

I huffed a smile. "Don't get too attached, Oz. We're leaving as soon as it's possible to do so."

"Can I not smuggle her onboard? She can stay in my room."

I chuckled. I'd always known Oz was a roguish flirt, I'd been on nights out with him enough times, but I'd never seen him act so boyish before. "Not up to me."

The door opened and we all glanced towards it as Rooke entered. His face was as grey as the storm clouds looming outside. Looking back at Oz, I whispered, "Maybe avoid asking him about kidnapping her today."

Sweeping his eyes over our commander's dark presence, Oz said, "Nux, you don't have to tell me that twice."

Rooke scratched his head in irritation as he sat down on the opposite side of Oz's bed.

"You okay?" I asked him.

He glanced over to the two Akquarians. "Yeah." He clearly wasn't.

I continued to speak with Oz, trying to ignore the uninviting aura resonating from Rooke's presence. Thankfully Oonla interrupted, asking for a moment to redress Oz's wound. Pulling Rooke over to the corner of the room, furthest away from Dybgo, I asked as quietly as possible, "What is it?"

Rooke swallowed hard, flicking his eyes between Dybgo and Oonla, nervously. "I've lost contact with Troy."

My gut twisted. "Since when?"

"Three days ago. One of the probes he sent out to scan the active satellite was incapacitated. The next thing he knew, he was the one being scanned."

"By what?"

"A smaller probe. He couldn't tell where it had come from. He was planning on repositioning himself behind the moon for a few days to lay low, but then the radio connection suddenly dropped."

I cursed under my breath. "I've been trying to contact you for days. The radio seems faulty."

"They're not faulty. We're being jammed, Eden. Deliberately so."

"By whom?"

Rooke's scowl landed on Dybgo. "A bit of a coincidence, don't you think? Troy finds an active satellite days after Golden Boy boards the Parvos."

"You think he saw something on Kobe's computer?"

Rooke repositioned his hard gaze onto me. His jaw tightened, his expression cold and pointed. "Like I said, a bit of a coincidence."

If Rooke was correct, this was my fault. But why would the Akquarians do such a thing? If they had found out about Troy and The Orka, would they really jeopardise any chance of us returning home?

I felt Dybgo's eyes on me. I couldn't look at him. I couldn't trust myself not to ask him out right what he'd done to aid the situation. But deep down it didn't seem possible he could be so conniving. He was brash, yes, but genuine, sweet even.

Rooke glanced over at Oz, then turned his back on the room

entirely, quieting his voice to barely a whisper. "Promise me you won't mention this to anyone, especially Cora."

Nux, what if Troy was… "I won't." I sucked in a tight breath. "I hope Troy's okay."

"You and me, both."

An hour later, Dybgo walked me back to the apartment. I could sense him glancing at me. He knew something was amiss. My mood had outwardly changed as soon as Rooke and I finished our conversation.

I was finding it hard to think straight. I couldn't imagine the Akquarians being capable of conducting such a hostile act. I'd been led to believe Dybgo's presence was for my protection, to protect me with his life. He'd already proven that. And Havav's words—the ones he'd spoke not three days past—echoed around my mind, *I've never been your enemy, Eden. And I never intend to be.*

Why would he say that if his intention was to incapacitate our subspace ship? Had all this been said purely to fool me, to fool Rooke?

I barely registered that Dybgo had opened the door to the apartment. It was only when his fingers grazed against mine that I remembered he was there.

"Eden, is something wrong?"

I glanced down at my hand, at his fingers now dangling at his side. He'd touched me. Was he allowed to do that? My brain felt swamped with dense fog, and I fought the urge to look up into his hypnotic eyes. The tone of his voice was different. He genuinely sounded concerned, but why would he do that if his race was deceiving mine? Nux, was Troy dead? Was that the reason why Rooke couldn't contact him? No, no, it couldn't be. The radios were being compromised, nothing more…

"Eden?"

This time Dybgo's voice coerced my eyes upwards. His tone was soothing, mesmerising. Why was he looking at me like that?

"I…" I had to know if the Akquarians were lying, if he was

lying. "Dybgo, have the Akquarians ever been to space?"

He looked baffled; almost amused. "You mean into the sky and beyond? No, never."

"Why not?"

"We don't have the knowledge or the technology to do so."

"But you have libraries full of ancient human engineering books."

"Yes, we do, but my species are very much content with our feet firmly on the ground...or in the water." A frown formed on his brow. "Why do you ask?"

Damn, I shouldn't have said anything. Shaking my head, I tried to find the words to shut the conversation down, but instead my thoughts ran away with me, "Are there any other intelligent lifeforms on this planet?"

His eyes dilated; an aspect of surprise hidden there. "I'm...not certain. We are a small sea faring community. We don't venture far. Your questions are very...strange." He peered at me. "Is something worrying you?"

"No...no, it's just my mind and its crazy thoughts." I attempted a smile and walked into the room. Glancing back, I thanked him, prompting his departure. A sigh of relief escaped me when I heard the door shut behind me.

Ambling across the empty room, I headed to the open archway. I needed fresh air to clear my head. Thoughts of Troy, satellites, and technological Akquarians swirled around my head. I felt useless, I wanted to scream. It was all too much.

On the balcony, I took one, long, deep breath and turned back to the room, flinching at the sight of Cora slumped on one of the long chairs. I hadn't noticed her when I came in. I thought she'd gone to the springs with Zamya.

Walking over to her, I realised she was sprawled in a haphazard way. Her face was pressed into the cushions, her feet and knees at an odd angle on the floor.

I called her name. When she didn't respond, I knelt down beside her, nudging her shoulder. She groaned and flopped off the chair onto the floor. Pushing her onto her back, I noticed her cheeks were red and swollen. Multiple purple lesions had erupted across her forehead and down her neck. They were on her hands too.

I shook her harder. "Cora?!" Panic began to ignite inside me. She could barely open her eyes. Her skin was scorching to touch, a mist of sweat gathering at her temples. *Nux!*

I launched myself to the door. Heaving the heavy stone open, I entered the corridor, frantically searching for someone, anyone to help. No one was there.

Instinctively, I began to run towards where the guards were posted by the stairwell. As I neared, I spotted Dybgo speaking with them. He saw me before I howled his name. Sensing my panic, he was beside me in seconds. "What's wrong?"

"It's Cora. She's…"

I didn't need to say anymore, he was hurtling back towards the apartment with me in tow. Dybgo took one look at her condition and muttered a string of Akquarian words. He scooped her up into his arms and headed for the bedroom.

"What's wrong with her?" I asked.

Placing Cora on her bed, he replied, "Bluepox."

Chapter Sixteen

"What the hell is bluepox?" Zamya asked from Cora's bedside.

"A childhood illness," Yuska replied. "Most Akquarians catch it when they are two or three. It's called bluepox because of the blue sores that appear on the skin. It seems to be more of a purple colour in Cora's case."

"And how contagious is it?"

I glanced over my shoulder, noticing Yuska shift on her feet. She met my gaze and said solemnly, "Highly."

Zamya muttered a string of curses. This was her worst nightmare. This was why she wanted us to remain in atmospheric suits when we arrived, purely breathing sterile air.

I peered down at Cora, she was unconscious. Her freckled, creamy skin was now an obliteration of purple lumps and sores. More were forming as the hours passed. "She must have caught it when she interacted with the children at the springs."

I felt Yuska's cold hand squeeze my shoulder, compassionately. "You are probably right."

"So, when you say highly contagious," Zamya went on, "is it transmitted through air or touch?"

Yuska stared at her.

"You don't know, do you?" Zamya retorted.

"No, but I do know that whoever has been in close contact with Cora over the past couple of days, who hasn't already had the illness, will be infected and contagious themselves. There will be no symptoms for a couple of days."

I closed my eyes in horror. Cora had seen Oz yesterday. He was still recovering from his wounds. We'd all seen Rooke, and Rooke had seen Kobe. It was inevitable we'd all contracted it. "How ill will we get?"

"It's a mild illness for a child. It can be extremely unpleasant for an adult."

Zamya held her head. "Unpleasant! Be more specific, Yuska! Are we going to die?!"

"I doubt it. But," she sucked in a breath, "there have been cases with lingering effects."

"Such as?"

"Chronic fatigue, headaches…blindness."

It was me who swore this time. "We need to get word to Rooke."

"He's going to be overjoyed," Zamya groaned. Nux, he already had enough to worry about, what with Troy's disappearance.

Dybgo's voice rumbled from the corner of the room. "I'll get word to him."

I'd forgotten he was there. I stood up and looked over to him, my eyes full of gratitude. "If you could, please. Thank you for everything." He bowed his head and left the apartment.

Zamya appeared next to me. "This is going to be a tough few days."

Zamya and I spent that night trying to keep Cora's raging fever down. She was uncomfortable and delirious. Occasionally she ventured out of bed and wandered about the room searching or calling for people she'd left on Allura. She was clearly hallucinating, sometimes shouting and screaming. By morning I was exhausted.

That's when the illness took Zamya.

Thankfully Yuska and Bibska appeared and helped me with the patients. I felt Yuska's gaze on me, constantly observing—waiting.

It was late afternoon when the nausea and dizziness started. The skin on my face and the back of my hands tightened and started to itch. Then the swelling began and a throb in my head intensified.

The fever crept in rapidly, and I could no longer distinguish between what was reality and what was a dream. My vision became blurred and fuzzy. Faces distorted and words were noncoherent. I felt as though I was drowning in waves of water yet gasping with thirst at the same time. Images of Yuska, Zamya, and Rooke faded in and out. My mum made an appearance several times, pleading with me to leave the fortress and return home. I found myself running after her, but the door was always blocked or too heavy to open. In a frantic attempt to escape, I ran onto a veranda. The waves were crashing far below. The temptation to jump and swim was overwhelming. I needed to get away from this place, my mum was insisting. But the attempt was quickly shut down by a pair of strong hands and Dybgo's assessing eyes.

"You saved me."

A fresh breeze sizzled against my skin, cooling my senses, and visions of horses began to dominate my dreams. I'd been riding one through a dark, dense forest for days, searching the night sky for a sign, any sign of the way home. Paranoia had started seeping into every bone in my body. I wasn't alone. Something or someone was stalking my every move. Watching. Waiting.

Desperate for a drink of water, I dismounted my horse and made my way down the forest verge to a beautiful green lake. Its tempting waters shimmered in the twinkling moonlight, coercing me closer.

Thirsty, I was so thirsty.

Beyond delirious for that drink of water, I let my guard down and an Igknamai pounced, snapping its jaws at my legs, my feet. I tried to scamper away, but it sank its fangs deep into my calves, ripping at my flesh. My body thrashed violently with the pain. I tried to scream, tried to call for help…

Dark green eyes met mine, soothing me, sending me back into the void of oblivion where more confusing images and sensations battled against my subconscious.

Water. All I craved was water. It was everywhere, but I couldn't reach it.
Water.

A harsh brightness tried to penetrate my eyelids making my body squirm. After several torturous moments, I realised I was blinking, attempting to open my dry, sore eyes.

A soft groan escaped my lips, and I noted a figure move above me. A dark shadow. *Another dream, it must be another dream.*

"Hey you. Are you finally awake?" I knew that voice. The low grumble. The sensual purr he always used when he was consoling me.

"Rooke." A sharp pain nipped at my dry lips as I attempted a smile. Trying to focus on his handsome face, I reached for him, laboured by the effort. He took my hand between his and caressed the tender skin.

"Is this a dream?" I croaked.

"No. I'm definitely real. As are you."

I blinked several times, clearing the haze from my vision. I could make out Rooke smiling down at me, an array of emotions dancing in his eyes. It felt as though I hadn't seen him for years. A sight for sore eyes, to be sure. His golden skin shone in the soft sunlight. Eyebrows, the darkest shade of brown, framed those beautiful green eyes. His dark hair looked a little unruly, and a new growth of stubble was covering his jawline.

"You're real," I said, hoping this wasn't another dream, that he really was here with me.

"Yes. But now I'm interested to know how often you dream about me," he japed.

Too often. "Wouldn't you like to know." My throat felt so raw. "Can I...water?"

He was there in an instant, supporting the back of my neck as

I took a long sip from the glass he held to my lips. The water tasted like a tiny piece of heaven.

I coughed as he gently laid me back into the pillows. Nux, I felt like crap. I squeezed my eyes together, still trying to shake the fogginess. Opening them again, I recognised the high marble ceilings peering down on me. I was in my Akquarian bedroom.

"How…" I looked at Rooke. "How did you get permission to be here?"

"I practically begged. Then didn't take no for an answer." He glanced over his shoulder. "I had to bring Golden Boy along for the duration."

I peeped around his body and saw Dybgo pacing up and down on the far side of the room. Pacing, not standing solidly on one spot assessing like he usually did, but pacing. One of his hands sat on the hilt of his sword, the other opened and closed constantly making a fist. He looked drained, uncomfortable.

"He doesn't look happy," I said.

"I don't give a damn about him. He's not my responsibility."

"How are the others?"

"Cora and Zam are resting, but they're both pretty much back on their feet. Oz and Kobe are recovering." He gave me a gentle look. "It was you who caused us great concern. Your fever seemed to persist. We couldn't pull you out of it quite so easily."

I stared at him, bathing in the warmth of his compassionate gaze. "How long was I out?"

"Five days. I told Havav I had to be here with you."

My heart began to ache at his words. Why couldn't he be this attentive all the time? I squeezed his hand tenderly. "Thank you. It means a lot to me."

"Ah…" He shrugged the comment off. "You'd do the same."

"Probably." Smiling, I ran my eyes over his perfect skin. There were no signs of bluepox whatsoever. "How are you? Did you…"

He chuckled. "Yeah, I caught it. I had extremely mild symptoms." He showed me his arms where a small scattering of crusty purple spots sat around the insides of his elbow. "Yuska mentioned I had it milder than most children. Zamya pointed out it's probably because I am an immature bastard."

I laughed, which sent me into a coughing frenzy. Rooke offered me some more water, halting the hysteria for a moment. Licking my lips, I laid back in the bed again. He grinned. "I think it's more the case I'm just awesome."

"I prefer Zamya's diagnosis."

"That's what everyone else said."

"Mmm."

"Anyway, are you hungry?"

The thought of food made my stomach roil. "No. Just really thirsty."

"Okay. Give me a sec. I'll go and get you some more water." Unexpectedly, he leant forward and kissed my forehead. I sighed contentedly as I felt him stand and walk away.

Opening my eyes again, I spotted Zamya fast asleep in her bed. Her brown skin appeared sore where purple scabs covered her forehead and cheeks. I touched my face and grimaced at the roughness of the skin. Pulling my hands away, I noticed the swelling and spots on the backs of them too. How bad did I look? The itchy soreness encased my whole body. I could barely move.

I felt exhausted.

It was dark when I woke. The only sound was the lapping of the waves outside, and the only thing I could think of was water. I was so ridiculously thirsty.

Pushing the covers off, I dragged my feet over the edge of the bed. My legs felt wobbly, taking a while to find my balance, but I persevered to the doorway. Whilst holding the stone edges of the wall, I peered into the main room next door. The moonlight casted long, haunting shadows across the area and I started to wonder if I had fallen back into another one of my nightmares.

I blinked several times before I spotted a glass of water on the coffee table. I ambled towards the circle of chairs surrounding it. In a desperate frenzy, I lunged for the glass, dropping to my knees. I downed the tepid water, ignoring the pain in my body and the roughness of my hands as I wiped my mouth dry. Sitting back on my legs, I sighed. The water tasted amazing.

A soft snore disrupted my moment of euphoria, and I eyed Dybgo asleep in one of the chairs. Still dressed in his armour and blue cape, he was slumped to one side. An air of power and grace continued to resonate from him, but his skin looked ghostly white from the bright moonlight streaming in through the archway.

I glanced toward the brightness. The sky was as black as deep space, the large moon low on the horizon bleaching the stone balcony. And there, standing, looking at the view was Rooke. His figure was silhouetted against the harsh light, but I knew it was him. Strong shoulders, slim, toned—perfect.

I found myself wandering towards him, like a moth drawn to a flame. It had been the same for years now, and I doubted he even realised it, nor wanted to. The thought struck a sorrowful chord deep within me. Would I ever tell him how much I loved him? Especially after the Igknamai attack and the chilling thought that if I'd died, he'd be none the wiser.

Inwardly, I wilted at the realisation I could never tell him. How could I? It would be selfish to do so. What we had worked.

"Eden?"

Rooke's voice jolted me from my thoughts, discovering I had stopped halfway across the balcony terrace and was just staring at him.

"Eden? Are you okay?" He was casting me the oddest expression; his words and movements slow and cautious. I frowned, confused by the way he was acting. "Baby, are you awake?"

Baby? "Why are you looking at me like I've got two heads?"

He smirked. "Okay, you are awake."

I eyed him sceptically as he sauntered nearer.

"The last time we found you out here at night, you tried to jump the balcony wall. It was lucky Dybgo had noticed you and grabbed you before…well, before you jumped."

My eyes widened, vaguely recalling the dream. "That was

real?"

"You were hallucinating. You were trying to get to your mum, or something along those lines. But the risk was very real."

I cursed under my breath. There was at least a fifty-metre drop to the rock bed below. If I had jumped…Nux! "I thought Cora had been bad enough with her crying and screaming."

"Oh, you did that too."

Closing my eyes, I let loose an unstable breath, fighting against the flood of embarrassment. "I'm so sorry."

"Don't be." I heard him step closer. Opening my eyes, his arms latched around my waist and pulled me into his chest. "I'm glad you've come out the other side." He was gazing down at me dotingly. I liked this side to him, it never felt strained. But as usual, it was short lived. A sudden smirk twitched at his lips. "Your spots look grey in this light."

I shoved at his chest, almost depleting my reserve of strength. He stepped back, laughing. "You still look gorgeous, though."

"Ha ha! You're such an arsehole."

I followed him to the balcony wall and noticed one of our radios sitting on the edge. A feeling of guilt shot through me. I had forgotten about Troy. "Have you heard anything?"

He touched the dark box lying dormant on the stone ledge and a forlorn expression fell across his face. Shaking his head, he said, "No. Nothing. I'm getting the impression our chances of getting home have been diminished." He met my concerned gaze, his eyes glistening with regret. "I hate to think what's happened to him. He's so young…and to be left on his own. I…" He dropped his gaze. "I've failed you all."

"No, you haven't." I reached for his arm, clasping it tight. "Rooke, you haven't. By bringing us here you've kept us alive."

"Not Troy, though."

"We don't know for certain he's dead."

Rooke raked his fingers through his hair and lifted his gaze to the starlit sky. "What am I missing, Eden? I honestly can't believe the Akquarians could be so deceptive."

"Neither can I, but…" My mind shifted to my haunting

dreams from the past few days. "Rooke, I know this sounds crazy but hear me out."

Frowning, he turned his body fully towards me, giving me his full attention.

"Havav came to visit me before I was taken ill. Whilst he was here, he explained why he was so protective over the females. You see, he had a wife, a queen. She died when they returned from a colony visit years ago. He said they were riding home when they were ambushed by Igknamai, and she fell from her horse. But I can't figure out why they were riding horses. If their colonies are along the shore, wouldn't they have used a boat? It's been playing on my mind, and I kept having dreams about horses. *Horses.* Have you seen any here?"

"No."

"Neither have I. Apart from the figure on the hilltop. There must be a colony somewhere else. One with horses. Perhaps in th…"

"…In the forest."

"Yes. You said Troy found the location of the satellite signal in a wooded area. What if the Akquarians do have a colony there? It would make sense."

"You think they're capable of space technology?"

"I don't know what to think, but I am starting to wonder. Zamya thinks they're up to something."

"Zamya is a massive sceptic."

"Yes, okay, but what if she's right? They may not want us to leave. They may want something from us. Why else would they block our radio communication?"

Rooke stared pensively, remaining silent.

"Maybe I'm wrong…"

"No." He glanced towards the archway, lowering his voice further. "Why did Havav come to see you?"

"He wanted to tell me about the agreement he made with you regarding me."

"What agreement?"

"That I can leave the fortress as and when you feel it's

171

needed."

He stared at me. "I have no idea what you're talking about."

"He gave me a dagger as a gift. I tried to radio you to tell you, but…"

"It was jammed."

"Yes."

"Eden," he clutched at my shoulders, emphasising his next words, "you need to be careful."

"Wh…why?" I glanced to where Dybgo slept inside, making sure he was still unconscious.

"I don't think they want something from *us*. It sounds like they want something from *you*."

I'd had the same thought when Havav was leaving after his unexpected visit. I gulped, trying to fight the fear taking seed inside my fragile body. "But why? I'm not…I'm not important."

Rooke shook his head. A whirl of thoughts flooding his mind. "I'm not sure. But whatever you do, don't let your guard down. Promise me you'll stay in the fortress unless I personally ask you to join me on an excursion. Not through a messenger, but *in person*. I don't want to scare you, but they may be intending on taking you somewhere. Why else would Havav tell you, without my knowledge, you're allowed to leave the safety of the fortress? Promise me."

Returning his intense stare, I slowly nodded. A wave of fatigue suddenly fell over me and I slumped against Rooke's body. Wrapping me up in his arms, holding me against his chest protectively, Rooke mumbled, "I should take you back to bed."

A small part of me smiled at the prospect of that comment. *If only*. Instead, I told him not to. "I'd rather stay out here. It's nice and cool and I can see the stars."

He hummed against my hair. Briefly letting go, he sat down on the rock-foam lounger before pulling me back into his arms. I snuggled into his side and watched his mind tick over as he stared up at the night sky. He was beyond stressed, and it appeared I was only adding to that anxiety.

Did Havav have a purpose for me, and if so, what was it? I was beginning to question whether this was another crazy fever dream. The only part I welcomed was the sensation of being in Rooke's arms. I felt safe. I felt protected.

Chapter Seventeen

I woke to a sharp prod in my side. A rumble reverberated from beneath me and my eyes suddenly opened.

Yuska stood over me, her usual curt calmness replaced with vex. "This…" she snarled, pointing at me. Pointing at…Rooke. I was tucked in beside him, my head on his chest. His arm was around my shoulder, his body keeping me warm. "…is unacceptable!" She looked so angry. Her glower turned to Rooke. "You need to leave. Immediately!"

Rooke held up his hands. "We were only sleeping."

"It's unacceptable," she said again. "You know the rules. You are exploiting them. Havav has had the good grace to trust you, and this is how you treat his generosity!"

We both sat up, Rooke more graciously than I did. The world spun creating a brief moment of delirium. Where were we? It was dawn. We were on the balcony.

Rooke stood, still holding his hands up in the air, as if he was concerned Yuska would attack him at any moment. She pointed to the door. "Out! Now!"

"I'm going, I'm going." He glanced back at me before he made for the door. It was obvious he was reluctant to leave, especially after our conversation last night. To be honest, I didn't want him to go.

Still feeling the effects of fatigue, I struggled to my feet, ambling through the archway just in time to see Yuska closing the main door behind Rooke. She gave me a pointed look before she started puffing up the cushions of the chair Dybgo had slept on.

He was nowhere to be seen. I frowned at the concept. Wouldn't he have woken and found me and Rooke laying together? Wouldn't he have found great pleasure in demanding our removal from each other's arms? It seemed odd he had left Yuska to the task.

"Where did Dybgo go?"

Yuska punched a cushion firmly. I could have sworn the gesture was aimed at me. "He was needed elsewhere." She turned and scowled at me from under her fair eyebrows. She made me feel wretched, like a child being caught and scorned by an esteemed teacher.

"Yuska, we didn't do anything, I swear. Last night we were talking outside and must've fallen asleep."

"On top of each other."

"We weren't…."

Yuska tutted and walked towards the bedroom.

"It's the truth. Yuska, please. Rooke and I are good friends. He's like a brother…"

She turned abruptly and spat her words at me. "You know as well as I do that is a blatant lie." I frowned, bemused by her harsh tone. She tsked and shook her head. "You think I can't tell? Your scent gives it away. It changes when he's around." My breath caught. How was that possible? "You're attracted to him. You want him. Your mating scent is off the charts."

Yuska's expression pinned me in place. I felt breathless. If Yuska could smell it, so could they all. I didn't know what to say. She might as well have stripped me naked and scorned me for being in love with a man I had known half my life. What was wrong in that?

A whisper formed on my lips. "He doesn't know…and I'd prefer it if it stays that way."

"If he doesn't know, then he's more of a fool than I first took him for." Her flat nose scrunched up in disgust. "I find your human males reproachable. They don't deserve you. None of them do."

I swallowed down her comment, watching as she stalked into the bedroom. Why was she so angry?

*

After resting for the next few days, my mind felt less fogged, and the exhaustion began to dissipate. The spots on my skin began to scab over, some disappeared completely. Thankfully, those left on my face were few and far between. Several on my stomach continued to itch and ache but Yuska assured me they would heal.

Apart from the remnants of scabs on their arms and legs, Cora and Zamya were back to full health. Both fashioned dark circles around their eyes, but they seemed sprightly and, thankfully, far less argumentative.

I'd had no further communication from Rooke. The radio signal was still compromised, and he hadn't visited since the morning Yuska threw him out. I was certain Yuska had seen to it to end his prolonged visits. She still seemed angry with me.

Rooke's warning still echoed around my mind, but neither Cora, Zamya, nor myself had been requested to join Havav since the illness, since we were deemed no longer infectious. However, Havav's rules changed once again in our favour. Cora requested free reign of the library to pass the time, and Havav sent word of his approval, although limiting the number of visits to three times a week. He also extended the privilege to me and Zamya. Per standard rule, it was reiterated that a chaperon needed to escort us.

On the day I felt strong enough to leave the apartment, I accepted Cora's invitation to join her. Surprisingly, I felt a pang of disappointment when I found it wasn't Dybgo waiting for us outside our room. Another blue caped male, called Xandrak escorted us to the library instead. He was just as tall with a far icier demeanour than Dybgo. His armour was made of a rustic-red metal rather than the eye-catching gold, and the air about him lacked the grace and elegance I'd grown used to. Even his blonde hair was coarser, less managed.

The library was ridiculously large. Other than the thousands of books displayed in stacked shelves cut into metres upon metres of stone, it was empty. The walkways in between were narrow and dark, lit by the unusual blue lanterns.

Xandrak kept to himself, monitoring the main entrance for

the duration, while Cora scoured the stone racks for more material of interest. I glanced about, trying to find something with the semblance of an Akquarian Atlas, attempting to find some useful information regarding where that damn satellite signal was transmitting from. But everything was pre-Akquarian. I resorted to reading about the enormous interstellar ships the humans designed for use during the mass exodus. The book was decaying and the pages falling apart. It baffled me who the author was and when it had been written.

Cora's delicate footsteps came up behind me. I turned and found her staring at a small, withered looking book in her hands. The frown on her face was full of intrigue, but there was no sign of the usual excitement resonating from her.

Looking at me, she placed the open book on the window ledge I was using as a table. "I think you should see this."

She tapped the left page. The upper half was full of a strange, foreign, handwritten text. The other, was filled with a faded colour illustration of what I could only perceive as a pointed star with a dark centre, set against a complex and colourful nebula, forming into the shape of a swirl.

"Is this an Akquarian book?" I asked.

"Yes, but don't you see?"

"See what?"

Cora tapped the illustration again. "Does it not feel as though you're looking in a mirror?"

Full of bewilderment, I glanced up at her. What was she talking about?

She sighed and said, "Eden, this illustration is of your eye. Perhaps not as organic looking, but the resemblance is remarkable."

I ran my sceptical gaze over the picture. Yes, okay, it was an image of a multi-sided yellow star surrounded by browns, greens, and blues, but… "I don't see what you're getting at."

Huffing her exasperation, she hopped up, sitting on the stone ledge next to the book. "When I first met you," she said, "you know the time you conducted my induction in Torlan City. The

177

day before we left for Juno?" I nodded. "Well, I was fascinated by your eyes. So much so, I had to look into the genetics behind it."

A little concerned with where this was going, I said, "I thought you're an astrogeologist, not a geneticist."

"I like natural beauty. And your eyes definitely fall into that category. Anyway, I discovered it has occurred before. They call it a starburst iris, and only two other Allurans have ever had it. Both of whom were two of the original Nux warriors. At first, I thought you could be a direct descendant of them, but then I read something about neither of them being remotely related, and being born two hundred years apart. It seems both led our people to lifechanging liberations. They both were strong leaders, destined to prevail. And it is said that anyone who follows with the same eyes is destined for greatness."

I already knew this. The Nux priestess, who counselled me following my brother's funeral, had told me, trying to convince me that Jacob's death was a necessity to pave the direction of my greatness, and how I should embrace the fact he was sacrificed so I could succeed in my destiny.

I wasn't sure if it was because of guilt, shame, or anger, but I had never stepped foot inside a Nux temple since, not even when my mum died.

"It's nonsense, Cora," I forced my voice to sound uninterested, distant, attempting to disguise the pain of the memory pushing forward.

"That's what I thought," she replied. "Until I saw this." She patted the page, prompting my eyes to look at it again. "There must be something the Akquarians believe in, something similar."

I was starting to lose my patience. "That's a drawing of a star. It could symbolise anything."

"But what if there's truth in the connection? The ancient myth was true, why not this?" She mused to herself before saying, "You could be special, Eden. You could have a destiny that is…"

"The weirdness of my eyes is nothing but a genetic anomaly. It can't determine my fate nor my destiny, in the same way the colour of my skin can't."

178

"Yes, but…"

"We make our own destiny."

"I know, but…"

"It's complete nonsense!"

Cora fell silent, clearly stunned by my harsh, irritated tone. I gazed down at the book I was reading, the words blurring into a fuzzy grey as my mind ticked over with frightened intrigue and despair. My stupid eyes and the supposed destiny surrounding them was nothing more than a far-fetched, religious superstition; one most Allurans had no knowledge of. But seeing the image in that book, and Cora pouring her thoughts and conclusions at me; it left me feeling scared. What if this was an Akquarian belief as well? Was that why Havav was so interested in me? But what could I do for the Akquarians, what destiny could I provide for them?

"Eden, I didn't mean to upset you."

"You didn't." I peered up at Cora's young, concerned face. "I'm sorry, I…I'm feeling the pressure of everything right now."

Cora squeezed my hand, providing me with a gentle, affectionate smile. "We will laugh about all of this when we're back on The Orka."

I hoped she was right.

Chapter Eighteen

The following day, Havav's audience requests resumed. Zamya groaned profusely when it was announced she would be the first to be received. I was summoned the day after.

I walked down the spiral staircase and along the echoing corridors a step behind Yuska. We'd been in the fortress over four weeks now. I'd gotten used to the separation from Rooke, Kobe, and Oz. Even the flowing, elegant, sometimes revealing garments had grown on me, but my poor bare feet still ached against the harsh stone floors. I longed for warm socks and comfortable boots. I longed for woollen jumpers and brandy chasers, drinking them whilst sitting next to a glowing fire. Nux, I longed for home and its cooler climate. Would I ever see Allura again?

At the end of the wide, familiar corridor, adorned with ornate walls and glassless windows, two fortress guards opened the double doors. Yuska led me over the threshold, then pointed me in the direction of another familiar door. I let myself through and closed it gently behind me.

I recognised the pristine corridor, displaying several closed doors to the right, and the large, oval window at the far end. This was where I needed to wait until Rooke called me into see Havav. It reminded me of attending an appointment with my doctor or lawyer. I chuckled to myself. Havav seriously thought far too highly of himself.

Peering at the sea and distant cliffs through the oval window, I slowly ambled towards it, lost in the beauty of the view. But a figure emerged from around the corner up ahead, blocking it.

Walking towards me was an Akquarian male, dressed in bronze trousers clasped around the ankle. They hung off his slim hips, accentuating the series of muscles framing his abdomen. The broad shoulders and strong chest were familiar. The large, golden tattoo I recognised—Dybgo. His eyes were averted to the floor, his stance a little clumpy, but it was definitely him.

"Hey, you," I said amiably, "I haven't seen you for a while."

Halting his strides, he peered at me with an abruptness. The look on his face made me freeze. This male *was* Dybgo, but he was different. *Very* different. The look in his eyes was savage. A red swirl had been painted on his forehead, emphasising the rawness of the skin around his eyes. His fists were clenched so tight the whites of his knuckles shone through his pale skin. He appeared agitated, angry.

Everything about him felt off. He wasn't wearing his golden armour, nor the blue cape. There was something wrong with him, I could sense it. Was this…was this why he'd been absent?

Flaring his nostrils several times, his eyes raked the full length of my body. Then he began to stalk forward with such a ferocity, it scared me.

"Dybgo," my voice warbled. "Are you? Do you need?" Before I could finish my words, the air was stripped from my lungs as he forcefully pushed my back into the wall. Nux, he was strong.

Blinking back the shock, I realised he was standing over me, gripping my wrists against the cold, rugged stone, then raising them painfully slowly above my head. When my arms were at full stretch, he pushed his body against mine, pinning me in place. I stared at his powerful chest. He felt hot, abnormally so. And I could smell him. He smelt male. A strong, musky scent. Not despising but…strange. Was this…Nux, was this what Zamya had warned us about? Tek…Tektrasc? It had to be. He seemed possessed.

My breathing became erratic. What was he doing with me? I couldn't remember exactly what Zamya had told us about the extent of Tektrasc. It was primal, aggressive maybe? Nux, had she said it was highly sexual? I glanced up at Dybgo's face high above

181

mine. He was watching me with a fierce intensity, his nostrils still flaring.

Lowering his face to the crook of my neck, he pushed his full weight against my hips. Shit, I could feel his…this was definitely sexual.

I tried to push him away, but he was a monstrous weight, an immovable force.

He took one, long, deep inhale, breathing me in. The incredulous panic rising deep within caused my breath to catch several times as he traced his nose along the line of my neck, my jaw, before nuzzling at my ear. His voice grumbled, "You smell divine."

I tried to say something to deter him, but what could I say? He was drugged with testosterone. Drunk with desire.

Unable to stabilise my breaths, the panic reached a new peak, and I glanced down the corridor, praying someone would witness this and help pull him off before…

His hand clamped around my neck and my eyes widened. He turned my face to his and I met his blood shot eyes. The crystal blues were there, but diluted by red, primal lust.

"Dybgo,   please.   You're…you're   not   yourself."

He rumbled his disagreement and in one swift move, he turned me around. My cheekbone hit the wall as I was pressed into the uneven stone. With Dybgo's large body behind me, encasing me, I couldn't move.

Both my hands were clasped above my head in one of his, allowing his free hand to roam the fabric of my bodice and skirt. Dread flooded my body. I could feel the fresh air hitting my legs, then his hot hands were on the skin of my thighs, rising.

"Dybgo, please." I was trying to keep calm, but the tears were burning at the corner of my eyes. "You need to stop."

In response, he lent forward and nicked my earlobe with his sharp canine. I squeezed my eyes together. A wave of confusion drowned my thoughts. This was the male who saved me from the Igknamai, who protected me and made me feel safe. And now…

now it appeared he was going through the primal motions of unconsented mating. Every action was beginning to scream rape. He wasn't going to stop, I knew it.

That's when I began to shout. "Help! Help! Someone, please!"

In an attempt to silence me, Dybgo grabbed at my neck, ripping the neckline of my dress. I haphazardly stumbled backwards and found myself being launched, facedown, onto the chaise lounge. Now with Dybgo's large hand covering my mouth, I felt him kneel behind me, raising my skirt. I whimpered at the action. I didn't want this!

I fumbled to pull my skirt back into place, but he growled, pulling at my wrists painfully. A tear trickled down my cheek and for a moment I laid there like a rag doll, allowing his hands to rove my curves. I needed to calm down and think myself out of this situation. The thought of Rooke walking out into the corridor to find us like this, with my bare butt in the air, let alone try to intervene…Dybgo would rip him apart. No, I needed to get myself out of this. I still had time.

A chilled air touched the skin of my upper back and I realised Dybgo was unbuttoning the bodice of my dress. Why would he do that so attentively if he was possessed with primal lust? Hot lips traced the ridge of my spine as more buttons unfastened. My skin prickled, my muscles tensed. I felt sick, but it was clear this action was his attempt to seduce me, trying to pacify and entice me to come round to his advances. And in doing so, he seemed calm. I needed to act now.

"Dybgo?" The waver in my voice made the words sound pathetic, not quite as convincing as I'd hoped. "If you want me in this way, please, let me look on you. Let me see your face." The words felt wrong, so wrong, but I needed him to turn me over.

He raised himself over me and rumbled his approval in my ear. Before I could think, I was abruptly flipped over, and just as I'd presumed, he was now standing over me, straddling my legs. I met his gaze. There was so much heated desire pouring out of those eyes. A look I'd seen him give me before. A look I'd previously regarded as sympathy or concern. Nux, had he always wanted me? I needed to put an end to this.

With all the strength I could conjure, I swiftly flicked my knee into my chest and kicked him hard between the legs. Eyes wide, he groaned and stumbled back. The shock that lined his brow was quickly replaced by ruthless anger. His recovery was rapid, and he lunged for me, only to be met by my foot in his chest and my fist in his jaw.

The force jolted my bones, but I sprang to my feet, adrenaline surging through my tired legs as I accelerated down the corridor to Havav's study. Rattling the door handle, I cried out. It was locked and I could hear Dybgo's anger escalating. I hammered both my fists against the stone, trying to get Havav and Rooke's attention. "Let me in. Let me in. Please, I…"

Dybgo was upon me in seconds. This time, he was furious. He slammed my back into the wall sending a sharp pain rippling down my spine. His large hand wrapped around my neck, and I felt my windpipe crushing under the sheer strength. With his face up close, he bared his teeth, snarling animalistically. I clawed at his fingers, trying to dislodge his grip, but it was no use. I'd pissed him off. He wasn't going to let me go this time.

Another snarl escaped him, and he licked the edge of his elongated canine. "You're mine."

Clenching my eyes, I was unable to think straight. He was strangling me, and yet, he wanted to claim me as his own. I would've laughed if I wasn't being starved of oxygen right now.

The door to Havav's study opened, causing my heart to leap with relief, then fear. I heard Rooke's jovial voice echo around us. "Eden, are you that eager to see me…oh, shit."

I could see him in the corner of my eye. He was frozen to the spot at the sight of Dybgo pinning me against the wall. He didn't know what to do. "Uh, Havav? Your assistance is needed. Immediately!" The command in his voice noticeably cracked on the last word.

Dybgo turned his head slowly and glared in his direction. A warning made up of hisses and snarls was aimed at Rooke, but Rooke didn't falter. He held his palms up and said gently, "Hey, Dybgo, buddy. Um…I don't think she can breathe."

In response, Dybgo tightened his hold and hissed, "She's mine."

In the next instant, Havav was standing in the corridor barking commands at his general in his native tongue. Dybgo took a step back, dragging me with him. Possessively pulling me into his chest, his arm encircled my waist and arms, restraining me—strategically placing me as a barrier between them and him. I concentrated on Rooke, hoping his presence would calm me, but Rooke just stared. He looked petrified. Taking in Dybgo's possessive hold, he rested his eyes on my terrified face, holding my gaze. The terror building up inside of me reflected in his own eyes.

Dybgo tugged me closer as Havav's words intensified in pitch and demand. He growled something back in reply, but Havav's words seemed to have stumped him. His head snapped down at me, prompting every muscle in my body to tense—even more so than they were already. His looming presence was terrifying. I could smell him, feel him everywhere. He was so close, too close.

Ignoring the tear trickling down my cheek, Dybgo pressed his forehead against my temple, hard. I felt his rapid breaths change to a deep inhale as his hand moved across my hip, over my breast. Havav barked one final demand, and to my utter surprise, Dybgo thrust me forward, out of his grasp. Roaring at his leader, he turned and disappeared down the corridor, ignoring Havav's further commands.

Stunned by the sudden loss of warmth, goosebumps erupted across my arms, my chest, down my spine. I shivered, thankful for whatever Havav had said to deter Dybgo. Clutching at the soreness around my neck, I winced at the bruise forming there, and stumbled towards Rooke. But Havav stepped forward and intercepted me before I fell into Rooke's arms. He gestured to the open doorway and without physically touching me, guided me into his luxurious study.

"Here you go, Eden, my dear," Havav's sympathetic voice was genuine. "You're safe now."

Seating me on a long chair, the warmth of a used jacket was draped around my shoulders, covering my exposed back. I looked up and found Rooke standing over me, now in his shirtsleeves. He stalked across to the armchair opposite. Perching on the edge, he frowned at Havav. "Would you care to explain what just happened?"

"Indeed." Havav sighed, prolonging a tense silence before he spoke again. "That, unfortunately, was an example of Tektrasc. I was recently notified that Dybgo had entered the phase. The mating season begins in a week and it's common for more cases to arise just before the start. It's caused by the subconscious anticipation. But Dybgo..." He shook his head, drawing his eyebrows inwards. "It's unusual for him. He's a highly ranked chaperon because it doesn't affect him. Other than the standard Tektrasc that occurs when an Akquarian male finishes puberty, he has never entered another phase. It was a shock, to say the least."

"I thought males going through that are detained."

"They are."

Rooke's face flushed. "Then why was he in your corridor?"

"Dybgo...he resides in this area of the fortress. He must've let himself out of his room."

"Let. Himself. Out?!" Rooke growled. "To me, the word detained means unable to let himself out!"

"I can only apologise." Havav glanced at me. "In a normal case, Dybgo may have ignored Miss Eden's presence, but it appears the scent she is currently producing has allured him."

"What do you mean?" I asked.

"What scent?" Rooke snapped.

"Eden's ovulating."

I gaped at the Akquarian leader.

"I can smell it." Havav peered at me. "And Dybgo could also.

Did Miss Zamya not inform you of the risks of walking about the fortress during such a time?"

"Yes, she did, and we check our temperature every day to…" I gasped at the realisation. "My temperature has been up and down since the bluepox, I didn't…I didn't…" Tears stung at the back of my eyes. This was my fault. I coerced Dybgo…

"It's not your fault, Eden," Rooke said, reading my mind. "Dybgo shouldn't have been out of his room."

"And I will assure you, I'll look into how…"

"You already assured me there wouldn't be any chance of this happening. Any male suffering with Tektrasc will be locked away, you said. He clearly wasn't locked away!"

"Commander…"

"No, Havav. I'm not taking this bullshit. You demand the females here are protected but how can they be when he's walking around freely?"

"He can't leave this section of the fortress. The doors are heavily guarded."

"Nevertheless, you invited Eden here anyway, fully aware Dybgo is being detained in the same area?" Disgusted rage rippled across Rooke's face. "Did you intend for this to happen?"

"Of course not." Havav looked offended by the allegation. "It was a mistimed coincidence."

Rooke chuckled in disbelief. "I'm starting to wonder."

"Rooke. Don't." My eyes begged him to stop. He was making this far worse than it already was. His eyes softened when they met mine and his tone became gentler. "Havav, I don't intend to offend. We are overly appreciative of your generosity…"

"I understand," Havav replied. "You need not apologise. I take female protection seriously. This is my mistake. One I hope to rectify." He stood, and I glanced over at Rooke. I knew what he was thinking. He wanted to find a reason to leave this place, take us somewhere where he could keep his crew safe, but he had run out of options. He needed to remain on Havav's good side, so he would follow through on his promises. Our ship was sitting in

Havav's hands. Without his cooperation, fixing it would be a lost cause.

"I will call for Yuska to escort Eden back to her rooms," Havav said, ringing a small glass bell that sat on a stone table in the corner. "I assure you, she will be safe there."

"I will go with her," Rooke said.

"That is not necessary."

"I *want* to go with her."

"And that is completely against the rules."

"The rules?" Rooke huffed an incredulous laugh and looked to the ceiling. "Believe it or not, I can contain my urges around beautiful women."

"This is not a laughing matter, commander," Havav snarled.

"I'm not laughing!" Rooke glared at Havav. "Tell me, what exactly would Dybgo have done to Eden if we hadn't intervened?"

I didn't think it was possible, but Havav's pale complexion whitened further. "It does not need to be mentioned."

"I think it does!"

Havav mumbled something in Akquarian, then sighed. "Very well, if you wish to know. He would've forced himself upon her. And if she tried to stop him, he would have likely killed her…along with anyone else who tried to intervene."

Dybgo was one of the largest, most powerful Akquarians I had seen here. He was at least six-foot-nine. He would easily rip anyone apart. I couldn't bear to think about what would have happened. The pain around my neck was proof enough of what he was capable of.

"But you stopped him," Rooke said, scornfully. "How did you manage that?"

"I am his esteemed leader, and even though the sane, obedient male inside is being compromised, he is still in there. But to be honest with you I acted on instinct, and it was sheer luck he listened."

Rooke cursed, shaking his head. But it made me question why Havav would protect me against his prize warrior, potentially sacrificing himself. What did he want with us? With me?

Minutes later, with Yuska by my side, I was marched back to my apartment by three guards and Xandrak. When I entered the bright room, my heart sank to find it empty. I needed consoling, I needed a hug. Both Cora and Zamya must've been at the library.

I flinched when I heard the door screech shut behind me.

"You should get changed," Yuska said, coming to stand in front of me. She touched the ripped neckline of my dress. "He made a mess of this, didn't he?"

"Did you know?" My voice was softer than I intended. All the fight inside of me had been drained.

Yuska looked up at me, regret filling her eyes. She was so petite. "You mean about Dybgo?" She sighed, her brow knitting together. "Yes. It was I who detected the signs."

"Is it true it never usually happens to him?"

"Yes."

"Then why now?"

"I don't know."

"Is it because of our presence?"

"No…I don't know. I can only apologise for not correctly detecting your current scent. I mistook it for something else entirely. I would never have let you leave this room if I'd known."

It wasn't Yuska's fault, I knew that. "Is he going to be okay?"

As a comforting gesture, she touched the arm of Rooke's jacket I was still wearing. "Give it a few days, Dybgo will be back to his normal self."

I looked down at my right hand. My knuckles were red and sore from where they'd connected with his jaw. "Will he remember what happened?"

"Yes. I've been told Tektrasc is like having your mind trapped inside a body you can't control. He'll remember. And I know Dybgo, he will feel mortified."

The thought brought tears to my eyes. Before this had occurred, Dybgo and I had an understanding. It could've resembled an early form of friendship, but today's events flooded me with conflict. And that filled me with sorrow.

"I've left your native clothes on your bed. Why don't you go

189

and change?"

Half-heartedly, I nodded and dawdled towards the bedroom.

A tap at the main door halted my steps. I heard Yuska open it and a low, mumbled voice spoke with her. Turning, Yuska looked at me with her assessing eyes. She opened the door wider, allowing me to see Rooke hovering on the threshold.

"You have five minutes," Yuska said to him, and he half walked, half jogged towards me. Without prompt, I ran into his arms, burying my face into his neck. His citrusy, fresh scent hit my senses and I began to weep. I needed this. I needed him so much.

He accepted the barrage of tears, wrapping me up in his love, his warmth, his embrace. There was so much intensity in that hold, so much compassion. The perfect stature of a supportive figure. One of the reasons why I loved him.

Parting us slightly, he held my head tenderly in his hands and placed his forehead against mine. "We're getting out of here as soon as we can. I'm going to get us home."

His words were a solid promise. Whether or not he was convinced he could fulfil them was a question for another day, but in that moment, it was what I needed to hear.

He pulled me back into his chest, wrapped me up in his arms, and sank his face into my hair. We remained that way for the full five minutes Yuska allowed him to stay.

Chapter Nineteen

Looking in the mirror, I admired the dark green, flowing dress Yuska had found for me. The only issue was the square necked, long sleeve garment left the horrible purple-green area of my bruised neck exposed. I touched the tender area, wincing slightly. It was healing quickly but not quick enough. Every swallow, drink of water, and mouthful of food reminded me of how I acquired it.

"This should cover it." Yuska appeared next to me, holding a long, golden scarf. She wrapped it gently around my neck twice, both ends draping down my back, nearly touching the floor. I nodded my approval. It did the trick, covering the extent of the damaged skin.

I stood up, nerves tingling their way through my body. Another dinner with Havav awaited me. Another evening listening to him patronising and preaching. Thankfully, Cora and Zamya were invited this time.

Other than the trip to the springs earlier today, I hadn't left the apartment for three days. Strangely, and completely against my character, I'd preferred it that way. There wasn't any chance of running into sex crazed males, high on testosterone. The incident was eating away at me, more so than the Igknamai attack. I knew the Igknamai were savage beasts, but Dybgo…he was Dybgo.

"I assure you, there have been no further cases of Tektrasc." Yuska swept her eyes over my face, sensing my worry. "You will be safe."

Yuska had become gentler, more open with me over the past few days. She even asked me about my relationship with Rooke. The day of the incident had proven how close we were, how much I needed him. She seemed to accept that.

Peering at me through the mirror, she said carefully, "I should inform you, Dybgo has recovered. He will be back in his usual role. I presume he will be present this evening."

My gaze dropped to the floor, unsure how I felt about seeing him. I swallowed nervously, thanking Yuska for her honesty. She gave a small smile, then tilted her head towards voices coming from the bedroom. "Miss Cora and Miss Zamya seem to be bickering again."

I rolled my eyes. "They act like flipping teenagers."

Yuska tutted as I picked up my swishing skirts and opened the door. I found the pair of them standing on the threshold to the main room.

"What's going on?"

They fell awkwardly silent. Cora looked sheepish, eyeing Zamya warily, but it was Zamya who turned to me. "It's nothing. Can we just get this over with…please?"

From behind me, I heard Yuska sigh with irritation, although a subtle smirk played on her lips as she walked past. "Come along, then." She gestured to the main door. "Your escort is waiting."

We were marched to dinner by at least eight guards. I swore there had never been this many previously. Out of paranoia, I glanced at all the burly warriors, searching for the possessed, savage look that had been haunting my nightmares. Although, not dreaming about Rooke lying dead in a coffin or on the beach had become a relief. My nightmares were now about my own survival.

It was Oz whom I noticed first when we entered the dining room. His askew smirk and mocking expression confirmed his thoughts about his attire, which consisted of an embroidered, robed jacket and harem pants. The jacket covered the majority of his new scar on his shoulder, but the tattoos and toned muscles on his chest and abdomen were hard to miss.

I sauntered past him, exchanging an amused look. "Forget your shirt, did you?"

He chuckled as I sat down next to him. "They didn't give me one. I'm starting to think they want me to join their ranks." He nodded to Rooke and Kobe on the opposite side of the table. "Those two are obviously far too scrawny to make the cut."

"Maybe Havav simply likes admiring a large, toned torso."

He snorted.

To my surprise, Havav wasn't present. Thankfully, neither was Dybgo. I glanced at the guards lining the wall. Xandrak stood behind Rooke. He oozed precedence among the other guards, all of whom seemed less on edge and far more relaxed than usual.

I rested my eyes on Rooke across the table. He'd been watching me, trying to disguise a frown from creasing his brow. Did I really look that bad? I raised my eyebrows at him in question, and he slowly responded with a tight smile.

"So," Zamya said, sitting in the chair beside Rooke, "is it just us tonight or are we expecting the fish king?"

Rooke closed his eyes in despair. Oz and Cora, on the other hand, snorted in unison which sent the rest of us into a raucous bout of laughter.

"Fish king," Oz mused. "I like that."

"I have names for all of them." Zamya's eyes shone with delight.

"Which one do you think is the original Aquaman?"

I tried not to smirk when Rooke groaned. "I'm glad you're all feeling better." He glanced at Oz. "But...ugh...can you please keep those types of comments to yourself. If you haven't noticed, we aren't alone. They can understand us."

I glanced at Xandrak. He had shifted on his feet. He knew what had been said. It was inevitable he would relay it to Havav, just like Yuska always did.

"Oonla said the majority of them can't speak our language," Oz said, gesturing to the guards.

"Who's Oonla?" Zamya asked.

Before Oz could reply, I discretely tapped his leg with my foot under the table. He glanced at me, frowning. I shook my head, deterring him from announcing his attraction to the young Akquarian nurse. I doubted any Akquarian male here would accept Oz's opinion of one of their sacred females, and how he was considering kidnapping her when we left.

"Um…she was the nurse who healed my shoulder."

"Oh, her. I'm still shocked they allowed a female to tend to you."

Glancing along the line of guards, Oz said, "Why are there only men here?"

"They're not men," Zamya quipped, "they're males."

I leant towards Oz and whispered, "You have a lot to catch up on."

"Ha. Yeah. That figures."

The main door screeched open causing the line of guards to stiffen. Havav breezed in, an air of exasperation surrounding him. He smiled at us, but the sentiment didn't reach his eyes. "Welcome. Welcome. My apologies for my tardiness."

He reached the head of the table and glanced at our glasses. "I see you have yet to be served." He clicked his fingers and barked harsh commands in Akquarian at the staff before settling in his chair.

My eyes lit up as my glass was filled with the delicious peach-coloured wine. I reached for it, downing half the glass in one gulp. *Ouch!* Nux, my throat felt like it was on fire and being stabbed simultaneously. The thirst from the bluepox was more tolerable than this.

Touching the fabric around my throat, I heard the door open again, and a flash of gold and blue caught my eye. Instinctively, my gaze flicked in its direction and my breath caught. Dybgo was here.

I tried to avert my stare, but it was a poor attempt. He marched down the room, behind Kobe, Zamya, and Rooke's chairs, keeping his focus fully on his prestigious leader.

I forced my gaze to my place setting, aware Rooke's attention was on me. I could feel his discomfort. It matched my own.

When Dybgo reached the top of the table, he spoke discretely to Havav, resulting in the leader spitting harsh Akquarian words back at him. The words *red* and *wood* were comprehensible. The same two words I'd recognised during their discussion a few weeks ago in Havav's study. I glanced up at Rooke. He'd heard it too.

What exactly did red-wood mean?

Havav placed his hands on either side of his table setting and smiled around a deep sigh. "Shall we eat? I'm famished. After such a trying day, it is a relief to have such wonderful company this evening." Every word was forced. Underneath the calm exterior, he was seething with anger or frustration. The tension could be felt throughout the room, keeping us all uncomfortably alert.

Food began to be served and while we ate, the room remained silent—tense. Havav stared pensively at the table as he masticated. I glanced at the crew. No one felt comfortable enough to speak, not even Rooke. It was only when Oz spoke, the frigid atmosphere shifted but only slightly.

"This food is delicious."

"Nice to see you've got your appetite back." I smiled, watching him fill his plate for the third time.

"Indeed," Havav drawled, whilst sipping on his wine. "Do pray tell, how is your shoulder?" I smirked to myself, noticing Havav eyeing up Oz's exposed chest.

Oz held his shoulder and circled his arm around. "It's good. Glad it's not my right one."

"Why is that?"

"Um…" Oz glanced at Rooke awkwardly. "It's my stronger side. My fighting arm."

"My warriors are trained to use both arms equally."

"I can understand that. Your warriors fight enormous beasts. We don't have such things on Allura."

"Thankfully," Zamya muttered under her breath.

"Then what do you fight?"

There was a pause while Oz looked to Rooke for direction. Havav stared at Oz then Rooke, his nose scenting.

"We occasionally fight our neighbours," Rooke replied, still holding Oz's gaze.

"Oh, I see." Havav glanced over his shoulder at Dybgo. "Wars among humans." His tone was repugnant, judgemental. Nux, he was in a foul mood. What on earth had caused it?

I flicked my eyes to where Dybgo was standing in his usual position by the wall. Like the true soldier he was, his attention remained ahead, obedient. But I noticed his eyelids begin to flicker, as if he was dissuading himself from glancing at me. I quickly looked away, only to sense his gaze fall to me for a moment. Yuska was right. He felt humiliated. And for some reason, I felt a sympathetic pull towards him.

"Talk of war is not for the dinner table." The flapping of Havav's hand pulled my attention away from his general. "I have good news." He lounged back in his seat, swirling his wine about in his glass. "My ship builders have confirmed your raft will be ready in the next few days. Which means you can transport what remains of your ship back here for repairs."

I caught the optimism in Rooke's expression before he said, "That's fantastic news."

Havav inclined his head graciously. "But before your time is monopolised by such things, our season festivities begin tomorrow. We would be honoured if you all join us in celebrating. The Sparzak Ball is in two days, and we would very much like you to attend as our esteemed guests."

When he said season, I assumed he meant one of their three mating seasons. I hadn't imagined it being a public or elaborate affair. Adding to my scepticism as to why we would be invited to such an event, I noticed Zamya narrow her eyes at the prospect. Rooke threw an unusual look my way before accepting the invitation on behalf of us all. To which Kobe's complexion paled noticeably. Even Cora didn't voice an interest.

*

"Sparzak Ball," Zamya's hiss was an abrupt whisper as she perched on the end of her bed that evening, braiding her silky dark hair. "Fancy name for a mating orgy."

"Zam…."

"Why do we have to attend and witness that? I'm a biologist but I can't imagine finding a mating frenzy anything but…gross."

I nestled down in my bed, pulling the covers higher. "The Akquarians seem too prudish to condone such things."

"No, Havav is. The Akquarians, as a race, are barbaric."

"Zam, hopefully it's the last bit of Akquarian nonsense we'll have to endure. We get the ship back soon, and then we can return to The Orka and go home."

A heavy sigh escaped her. "I cannot wait to get out of this pompous piece of rock."

Chapter Twenty

"What time of year is it?" I stared out the window of the dressing room. It was evening, yet the sun was still hitting the horizon. The cloudless blue sky was filled with the promise of summer.

"It's Maskidow," Yuska replied. "The ancient humans called it May."

Nux, how long ago had I left Allura? I was certain it would be nearly October there now. Even though we used the same month names as the ancients, time felt different here. The days were shorter, the months longer. I had lost trace of what the Alluran date was.

Yuska appeared in front of me and placed a stiff, golden bracelet around my left wrist. It had multiple loops hanging around the circumference, as if charms were meant to be hung on each one. She noticed my frown and said, "This is your claiming bracelet."

"My what?"

"Claiming bracelet."

"I got that part. What does it mean?"

"During the Sparzak Ball, if a male is interested in a female, he will clip his claiming token to the female's bracelet. During the following weeks, she can choose which of those males she wants to mate with."

My frown deepened. "I thought you said a female can take any mate she chooses."

"Yes."

"But he has to stake a claim to her first?"

"Yes."

"Well, that's not an open choice, is it? What if she doesn't like any of the males who have claimed her." Claimed; what a horrible word.

"A female must always choose at least one of her claimers. It's a written law."

"Hold on. Why are you giving me a bracelet? I'm not Akquarian."

"Havav wants you to feel involved."

"Involved?" I scoffed. "I think I've had enough involvement with Akquarian rules and behaviour to last a lifetime."

Yuska scowled as if I had offended her. She walked over to the dressing table and gestured for me to stand in front of the mirror.

"Am I no longer required to cover my arms and legs?" I asked, glancing at myself in the mirror. I wasn't wearing very much at all considering I had been draped in long, flowing skirts and heavy sleeves for the past month. I now wore a light green, heart shaped top that exposed my midriff. My long, dark blue skirt was wrapped around my waist and held in place by a small topaz broach clipped to one side. It looked nice but there wasn't a slightest chance of modesty, especially as in standard Akquarian dress, I wasn't wearing any underwear.

"Not during the season," she replied, placing a thick choker of dainty pearls and blue gems around my neck. "Akquarian females don't need to cover their branchia at such a time."

"Branchia?"

"The slashes of skin on our arms and legs. The obsolete gills."

"Ah, I see." I had forgotten about the strange flaps of skin I'd seen on the males' arms. The fortress guards tended to cover them with their metal vambraces.

"There." Yuska stepped back, her eyes surveying me. "You look perfect." Pride danced in her eyes, like a doting mother on the day of a daughter's wedding. I frowned at the concept.

Touching the choker, I took another long look at myself in the mirror. The beautiful piece of jewellery covered the bruise on

199

my neck, yet still looked dainty enough to not overwhelm the outfit. My dark hair was decoratively pulled away from my face with braids and gems, allowing long, thick waves to cascade down my back.

Smiling back at her, a blush touched my cheeks. "Thank you, Yuska. You certainly know how to make a woman look attractive."

She hummed her approval and opened the door to the bedroom. Zamya stood with her hands on her hips in the middle of the room. She took one look at me and said, "This is not fair." She turned to Bibska who was on her knees, bustling with Zamya's skirt. "Even Eden gets more clothes than I do."

"Barely," I replied, noticing my legs poking out between the moving fold of my skirt.

"I'm basically wearing a bikini."

I stopped and studied her orange-gold outfit. Yes, okay, the top looked like a halter neck bikini, but it complimented her petite figure. And her long skirt was made of a sheer material, showing glimpses of her slim legs and an extremely short skirt underneath.

"You look fantastic, Zam."

She whispered, "I have no underwear on."

"Neither do I." I pulled my skirt slightly open, exposing my legs.

"Why aren't we allowed underwear?" Zamya peered down at Bibska.

"Underwear is an unnecessary human antic," Yuska voiced her opinion from behind me.

"I don't think unnecessary is the correct term," Zamya's tone pitched, using both hands to gesture towards her groin.

Yuska rolled her eyes. "The underskirt isn't that short."

I laughed. "I've told you before, Zam, no dancing on the tables and you'll be fine." I heard Zamya growl as I continued through to the main room.

Cora sat quietly in an armchair, her gaze distant and perturbed. She was dressed in a neon turquoise two piece, fashioning thin straps and a straight neckline. The skirt was flowing and fell to the floor, but the colour didn't suit her. It made her skin look ghostly white. And her blonde hair was pulled back so tightly it made her face look older, harsher.

As I approached, her gaze shifted, and she gave me a small, laboured smile.

"Is everything okay?" I asked, sitting down next to her.

She dropped her eyes and said, "I miss Troy. I haven't spoken to him for weeks. Rooke says I'm still not allowed to."

My heart pained at the lie we'd fed her. Other than Kobe, the rest of the crew still didn't know about Troy's loss of contact. We still didn't know if Troy was dead or alive. I reached for her hand and squeezed her delicate fingers. "I'm sorry."

"I don't suppose you'd ask Rooke if there's a chance I could…"

"Cora…"

"Please. I really need to speak to him." There was an intense pain in her eyes. One that shouldn't be possessed by someone so young. Nux, I felt terrible for lying to her. But what could I say?

Stupidly, I nodded and said, "I'll see what I can do."

In response, she gave me a genuine smile that lit up her face.

"Come along," Yuska's curt voice cut through the moment. "Only Havav is allowed to be late, and myself and Bibska still need to get ready."

As we followed her out of the door, Zamya fell in step with me, shaking her golden bracelet. "I'm not sure about this thing," she said in an undertone.

"It's for decoration."

"Then why do I feel like we're going to be placed on display? A meat market or slave auction comes to mind."

I huffed a laugh. "You and your dramatic thoughts."

She groaned. "Why are you so calm?"

"I have to be, Zam. Doesn't mean I am inside." And I certainly wasn't.

There were no guards stationed at the entrance of the stairwell today. It looked as though everyone would be joining in with the season festivities. As Zamya presumed, this truly could be a

201

mating frenzy. I prayed the ball itself was as innocent as it sounded. But the whole situation had me thinking. With so few females, and for it to be the females' choice of who they mate with, it was no wonder the males went crazy outside of the mating season. Especially those rejected during the season. Tektrasc? I wouldn't be surprised if it translated to sexually deprived.

We emerged from the stairwell in the main part of the fortress. As we neared the western side, a distant sound of tranquil music filled the air, and the hubbub of voices began to grow louder. The corridor led to a huge open doorway, flanked by two towering pillars, decorated with vines of blue and pink flowers. Passing over the threshold, a wide staircase of shallow steps stood before us. At the bottom, a crowd of Akquarians thronged, filling the vast area. From where I stood, the crowd consisted of only males. All were fully clothed in a wide variety of Akquarian-coloured jackets. All laughing and speaking with their neighbour, drinking, and toasting. It was uncanny how humanly civilised this felt.

Dominating the far side of the room loomed three large, decorated arches leading to an outdoor veranda. The gentile music seemed to be filtering in from out there.

Yuska led us down the steps. I kept my eyes averted, avoiding the occasional stare. We must've looked an oddity to any normal Akquarian. Strange human females gate-crashing their sacred mating festival.

As we reached the bottom, the Akquarians parted for us, and I noted a few females standing in amongst the males. They were so petite in comparison, and stunningly elegant. Dressed in flowing fabrics, accentuating their slim, attractive bodies, their blonde hair intricately braided with an array of pearls, gems, or shells. They were dressed to impress. Dressed to allure the mates they intended to be claimed by.

We walked through one of the arches into the evening sun. It was beginning to set on the horizon, softening the colour of the rustic stone making up the walls, floor, and balcony. The veranda itself was as vast as the room we'd just exited. Both areas were large enough to hold a party of hundreds, perhaps thousands. To the left, a quartet sat to one side of a stone staircase, which accessed another veranda twenty metres up. More Akquarians ambled about up there behind a balcony wall of flowers.

Several clusters of small, white barked, blossoming trees encircled the middle of the vast area before us. The tree roots were growing out of circular holes in the stone floor, their pink flowers glowing in the evening sun. Yuska stopped and gestured towards one of the tree clusters, to where a burly male with a shaven head, and two slightly smaller, dark-haired males stood. I smiled to myself. All three of them looked smart in high collared, dark tailored jackets and matching trousers. All clean and freshly shaven.

They turned towards us as we approached. Oz's grin was unmissable. "Hey Zam, I can see your belly button."

"Zip it, Akquarian wannabe."

He laughed. "In a good mood today, yeah?"

She groaned her opinion, and I caught Rooke rolling his eyes. He stepped forward, ushering us in closer and said, "Okay, as we're all here together, I should lay down some rules."

"More rules?" Zamya folded her arms across her chest.

"It's necessary given the occasion."

Zamya muttered a response under her breath. I tried to hide my smirk, but Rooke caught it. His eyes sparkled when he began, the first rule clearly aimed at me. "Rule number one; don't drink too much. Two; stay on your guard and don't wander off anywhere alone. And three; strictly no intimate contact with any Akquarian whatsoever. This may be some kind of mating ceremony but it won't involve us. Understand? Oz?"

"Hey, why specifically me?"

"It's not aimed specifically at you, but I can see you scanning the crowd. You're searching for Oonla, aren't you?" All five of us looked at Oz. The old battle scar running down the left side of his jaw stretched as he ground those muscles tightly. "She's off limits, Oz."

He held up his left hand and flicked at a small, dark gem

dangling from the cuff. "Then, what is the purpose of this token thing?"

"It's for decoration," Zamya chided, repeating my own words.

"That token," Rooke pointed, "is not to be removed. We're here as guests, nothing more. I will not condone you performing an act that can potentially kill you."

Oz scoffed. "Not sure about you, boss, but sex never killed me before."

"No, but a strange, alien STD could."

"I'd also like to mention," Zamya added, "that we're trapped in this shithole because you were dying in the first place, so be a good boy and keep it in your pants."

Oz stared at her, contemplating her words. He straightened his broad shoulders and mumbled, "Fair point."

"Nice to see not all your brains are in your dick. I'm going to get a drink." Zamya grabbed Cora's arm, pulling her over to where two elaborately decorated rock-tables stood on the far side of the veranda. Oz and Kobe followed.

While Rooke watched them go, I closed the gap between the two of us, taking in the sight of him. His jacket and trousers were a dark green, matching the colour of his eyes. The high collar and cuffs fashioned an intricate golden pattern, giving him a look of refined stature. The outfit suited him. Nux, he looked so damn handsome. I smiled and his eyes shifted to me.

"What are you smiling about?"

My smile widened and I said, "You look rather dapper this evening."

He smirked, stepping forward to peck my cheek. The sensation of his breath tickling the skin of my neck made me tense as he whispered, "You look beautiful." He pulled back, holding my gaze. His eyes didn't contain the amusement they usually held when he mocked me. Was he being authentic?

"Starting to appreciate my elegant side, are you?"

"Elegant?" He chuckled, flashing his teeth. "I was thinking it was more…flaunty?"

Ah, there it was. It baffled me why he could never pass a compliment and let it settle nicely. He always made a joke out of everything between us. I sucked in a deep inhale, trying not to take the bait. "You're a rat, Rooke Maddox. Let's get a drink."

He chuckled and followed me through the ever-increasing crowd. Several females turned to look in our direction as we passed. At first, I thought they were admiring Rooke, but then I realised they were looking at me. One took in the jewellery I wore around my neck, meeting my eye with a look of distaste. It unnerved me. What did they have to worry about? I wasn't going to steal their males from them. The only one I longed for was the dark-haired commander walking behind me.

The two drinks tables were situated in front of a section of balcony wall on the furthest side of the veranda. Potted plants were strategically placed, sectioning the area off from the main party. Small groups of Akquarians lingered, helping themselves to the array of brightly tinted pink and blue drinks covering the expanse of each long table. We stopped next to the pink ones displayed in odd bowl-like glasses without handles.

"These look interesting," I said, wondering what was in them to give the liquid such a vibrant colour. Picking one up, I took a sip. It had a smooth yet bittersweet taste, but it settled nicely on my tongue, and the after taste was extremely morish.

Rooke sipped one. I watched his nose crease up, making an effort to swallow down the beverage. His mouth instantly flew open, trying not to gag. "What the hell is it? It's vile."

"I thought it tasted nice."

He peered into his drink and grimaced. "I think I'll pass this time." He went to place his unfinished glass on the table when an Akquarian female snatched the glass out of his hand. The shock on Rooke's face was quickly replaced with intrigue when she said in a strong accent, "Neb, neb. Not yours."

I watched her grab a blue drink from further up the table. Returning, she offered it to Rooke. She pointed to him and the drink. Then pointed at herself, to me, and the pink drink I was holding.

Rooke nodded in understanding and sipped the blue concoction, albeit sceptically. He raised his eyebrows in surprise, sending a charming smile her way. "That's much better. Thank you."

Fluttering her eyelashes, she gave Rooke a dashing smile, before she graciously bowed her head and walked away. Sipping on his new beverage, Rooke tracked her sensual movement as she glided towards the crowd. I frowned, watching him soak up the sight of her enchanting body, draped in thin turquoise chiffon, leaving barely anything to the imagination.

"Hey." I clicked my fingers at him, failing to keep the green-eyed monster at bay. "You can't chastise Oz if you're gonna drool after pretty Akquarians yourself."

He snapped his head to me. "I was simply admiring."

"Drooling."

"Admiring."

"So, tell me," the spite in my tone was a little too obvious, "is she beautiful or just flaunting it?"

He stared in her wake. I assumed he was conjuring up some kind of witty response, but instead he downed the rest of his drink, gave me a hard look, and placed his glass on the table behind me. "What's up with you?" his voice was quiet, intimate. "Can you not take my jokes anymore?"

I shrugged, glancing around the vicinity. Rooke leant back against the table next to me. "I'm sorry," he said, leaning closer. "I've always bantered with you. I forget you've been through a lot recently." His eyes flicked to my neck, regret filling them. I knew what he was thinking. He blamed himself for everything.

I bumped his shoulder with mine. "I'd be worried if you didn't banter with me."

He bumped mine back. "So would I." His smile was genuine but unwontedly distant.

A low, grumbling buzz ripped through the air, sending everyone into a hushed silence. All heads turned towards the stone staircase. There, at the very top, standing on the edge of the upper balcony, was Havav dressed in an elaborate white suit and turquoise cape, with an entourage of pristinely dressed Akquarians behind him. A female, dressed in a flowing white and gold gown held onto his arm as they began to descend the steps. Havav waved his hand towards the musicians, commanding them to play on.

"Damn it," Rooke said to himself. I glanced at him. He was scanning the crowd.

"What is it?"

"The female with Havav." He nodded in her direction. "That's Oonla. I'm worried what Oz is going to do." He walked forward, trying to find a better viewpoint. I remained at his side, also scouring the crowd for our friend and colleague.

"Is he really that smitten with her?"

"He's like a lovesick puppy. I haven't seen him like this since…well, in all the years I've known him, I've never seen him like this. He's usually so calm and cool with the ladies."

Glancing at the steps, I watched Havav give Oonla a doting smile, placing his hand over hers on his arm. "Why is Oonla on Havav's arm?"

"She must be his daughter. Havav told me yesterday, he'll be arriving this evening with his children."

Running my eye over those following behind them, I realised she was the only female in Havav's entourage.

If Oonla was Havav's daughter, she was most likely seen as a sacred princess—cherished and admired. But what I couldn't understand was why she'd been Oz's nurse? A faint recollection of what Yuska had told me whirled around my mind. She had said the Akquarian females could choose whatever occupation they wanted to follow, whereas the males were assigned to theirs. Did that apply to Oonla as well? It must have. It seemed she was the daughter of their esteemed leader, a chaperon, and a healer.

"There you are, you big oaf." I followed Rooke's line of sight to the top of the upper balcony. Oz was perched on the balcony wall, watching the Akquarian leader escort his stunning daughter down the steps into the thick of the congregation.

"Perhaps Oz should have the rules reiterated to him," I suggested.

"Oh definitely. Especially now. I doubt Havav would welcome Oz's attention towards his blessed daughter." He looked at me, squeezing my hand. "I'll be back in a bit."

I gave him a small smile and watched him disappear amongst the mass of towering Akquarians. I glanced back to Oonla and Havav as they finished their descent, submerging into the sea of bodies.

The musicians resumed playing. Their melody had altered to a less tranquil tune. It was still soothing, perhaps slightly haunting, but it held a more rhythmic sound. A primal sound, if such existed.

The large floor space within the circle of blossoming trees had emptied, and a few Akquarians were venturing into the area to dance. Some as a couple, some in small groups of females, some on their own. And as I watched the Akquarians twirl and sway in unison, a figure on the opposite side caught my attention…

Dybgo.

Dressed in a suit similar to the one Rooke was wearing but made of a golden lustre material, he looked the part of a glorious general. I watched him walk to the edge of the dance floor, elegant and powerful. His long white-blonde hair was pulled away from his face by a single braid. The light accentuated the sharp planes of his cheekbones and jaw, making him look savagely attractive.

I tried to focus my eyes on something else, anything, but they kept finding their way back to him. He smiled at a lone female, whose face reddened at the interaction. Another cluster of females stopped by him. He spoke to them attentively, albeit briefly, before moving on, inclining his head at several males in greeting. Stopping to survey the dance floor for several moments, a female stepped in front of him, stroking his arm in a coquettish manner while they spoke. Given this was some kind of courtship ball, a part of their mating season, he seemed uninterested in her. Eventually he smiled, bowed, and walked on, leaving her gazing in his wake. I realised she had been the female who gave me the look of disdain when I passed her earlier.

Flicking my eyes back to Dybgo, I found he'd stopped at the

edge of the dance floor again, but this time his eyes were locked on me.

Nux!

I hadn't spoken to him since…

Suddenly, I felt hot—my mouth dry. I quickly turned and scurried back towards the potted plants next to the drink's tables. Concealing myself behind one, I found Cora. She was humming happily to herself, nursing a glass of pink tipple.

She grinned when she noticed me. "This drink is delicious," she said raising her glass. "The blue ones, not so much."

"I think the blue ones are for the males."

"Oh, really?"

I peered through the green leaves of the plant next to me. I couldn't see Dybgo anymore. He was on the move again.

Zamya's voice sounded behind me. "Cora, I told you to stop drinking those."

Snapping my attention back, I eyed Zamya sceptically. "Why can't she drink it?"

In an aggressive manner she pointed at the pink liquid. "That is not a standard drink."

"It's alcohol, Zamya," Cora tittered. Was she drunk already?

"I think it's more than that." She looked at me. "The females aren't drinking the blue ones and vice versa."

"Yeah, we got that."

"But why?"

"I don't know, Zam." I took in her frown, the anxiety eating away behind her eyes. "It's a party. It's the most human thing we've witnessed here. Try and enjoy it. Is it really as bad as you thought?"

"I'm worried about the drink." She shot Cora an odd look.

"Oh Zam." I reached for her arm. "There's a dancefloor. You love dancing. Go and dance."

She sighed and looked towards where the music was coming from. "I'm not sure. I'd rather not be on show."

"Ahh, come on." Cora emptied her glass, grabbed Zamya's

hand, and pulled her towards the dancefloor. Given she was highly sceptical about the whole situation, Zamya didn't put up much of a fight.

"Let's go shake our booties!" Cora's voice carried over to me and I laughed, watching her force Zamya onto the dancefloor. Zamya stood rigid for a few moments, glancing over her shoulder to find me, but Cora pulled her further in.

Rotating her hips to the strange music, Cora mimicked the females dancing a few paces from them, causing Zamya to laugh and the cobwebs of doubt to flutter away.

I smiled to myself, enjoying the moment. Content we were safe.

"Are you not intending on joining them?" The Akquarian accent directly behind me made my entire body freeze. Goosebumps trailed down my arms and across my stomach. I stared ahead for a moment, hoping he was a figment of my imagination.

Where had he come from?

Peering over my shoulder, I met the gold material of his jacket. Studying the intricate, swirling stitching, I felt my eyes strain against the pull to look up. "No. Not until I've had more of these." I gestured to my drink and looked back towards the dancers.

A glimmer of gold appeared in my peripheral and I downed the rest of my drink. The nerves tingled up and down my legs, anticipating what was to come. He remained silent for several moments, pretending to watch the dance unfold. Eventually, he turned to me, grazing his fingers against my elbow. "Can we talk?" His tone was gentle, but expectant. "Somewhere a little less…distracting." Sensing my apprehension, he added, "We don't have to go far. The balcony edge is usually quieter."

Still watching Zamya and Cora, I nodded. "Okay." I'd always felt safe with him. He was no longer under the influence of Tektrasc, so I should be safe with him once again, right?

He held his arm out and I took it, shocked by the bulk of muscle laying beneath the material, reminding me how strong he was. My throat ached at the memory of his hands around it, squeezing. Suddenly preferring to create a tiny amount of distance between us, I dropped my hold on his arm. But he snatched my hand up in his and held it there.

He led me around the edge of the crowd, over to the middle section of the balcony wall. I hadn't realised this part was segregated off by a couple of shallow steps and a line of more giant, potted plants. It created a space to sit and talk. And judging by the couple in the corner getting rather familiar with each other, it was a place to be intimate.

As we crossed the space, I glanced at the couple, who clearly hadn't noticed us. Their lips devouring each other's, their hands roaming freely. I noticed the female's wrist. Her claiming bracelet was already glistening with at least a dozen gems. All different shades and sizes. She was obviously quite a catch.

As we reached the opposite side, Dybgo took a seat on the low balcony wall. I remained standing, flicking my eyes behind me. The sun had almost disappeared beyond the horizon casting dark shadows across the veranda. Blue lanterns hanging from the trees, plants, and walls were illuminated, but it was difficult to make out faces. I'd lost sight of Zamya completely. I wondered if she'd seen me leave with Dybgo. The distance I'd just put between me and my crewmates was unnerving, maybe a little irresponsible. Rooke had said not to wander off alone.

"Please sit with me?"

I looked back at Dybgo. His large form silhouetted against the nearly extinguished sun, yet I could see the planes of his face, the gleam of the lanterns in his eye. He tapped the wall next to him and I reluctantly stepped forward, obeying him.

Whilst adjusting my skirt modestly around my legs, I waited for Dybgo to talk. I could feel his eyes on me, assessing. Nux, he was making me nervous. "Dybgo, I'm here, please say something…"

"Why won't you look at me?"

His comment was not what I expected. I swallowed hard, fighting the urge.

211

I felt him shift in his seat. "Eden? Please look at me."

I forced my eyes to meet his. I could barely make out the colour, but I knew they were crystal blue. I'd seen them enough times haunting my dreams. His gaze trailed down my face, landing on the choker around my neck. I saw it then, the remorse flooding his thoughts; the mortification Yuska had assured me he'd feel. That was why he wanted to talk. I owed him that.

I touched my neck. "It's healing. I'm fine."

"It's not *fine*. I hurt you." He dropped his gaze and mumbled a string of words in Akquarian. "It doesn't happen to me. Since my adolescence, it's never happened."

"Dybgo, you really don't have to explain."

"I do." He leant forward, resting his elbows on his knees. "Sorry isn't a strong enough word. Nothing can erase what I did to you. What I could've done to you."

I didn't know what to say. Had I forgiven him already? It wasn't him who haunted my thoughts, but the male with his face consumed by Tektrasc.

"I know why it happened," he said. "My episode of Tektrasc. It came…it came about because…of my attraction for you." His sudden spout of words were soft as a whisper, laced with what sounded like shame and suffering. For some reason I didn't feel shocked by his confession. He'd always been attentive. Subconsciously, I'd always known there was a deeper meaning hidden in his gaze. But it didn't stop a dreaded revelation from dawning on me whilst I listened on.

"It's unusual for my kind to feel so drawn to one person. I suppose we're kept away from the females to ensure that remains the case. But with you…" he glanced back at me, "I was assigned to be your protector." He looked down at his hands, now clasped together. "I tried to push any thoughts of you away. Tried to deny the impact you were having on me, mentally and physically. I thought I was in control. But then you caught bluepox. You were struggling. Your body wasn't fighting it, and I felt useless. The next thing I knew, I was chaperoning your commander while he tended to you. Watching him openly show his affection while you lay there writhing and screaming, lost in fever driven dreams, I…I started to feel the pull of insanity, the rise of jealousy and possessiveness. It was when I woke and found you both laying on the outdoor lounger, entwined in each other's arms that tipped me over the edge. Visions of breaking every bone in his body consumed my every thought. I was grateful Yuska appeared before I'd lost the resistance to move."

I sucked in a breath, replaying that morning in my mind. That was why Yuska had been angry at me. She'd sent Dybgo away because she'd sensed the change in him. I had caused Dybgo to fall into the insanity of Tektrasc. Me! What would've happened if Yuska hadn't appeared in time? I'd put Rooke at risk without the slightest notion.

"I thought I was hallucinating when I saw you in the corridor that day. I wasn't supposed to be out of my room. The detainment was driving me mad. I went for a walk. It was only supposed to be a solitary walk…" He held his head and shook it several times, as if trying to shake the memory away.

I shifted forward, aiming to reach for his hand in a comforting gesture, but I stopped myself. What if my touch was something he resented? I'd caused this. I didn't want to make things worse.

"I didn't mean to hurt you."

"I know that much." I gently placed my hand in between his board shoulders. He looked back at me with something that symbolised hope. "I'll be gone soon," I said. "I think this situation has proven the sooner the better."

He sat back, scrunching his eyebrows together. His large body suddenly felt imposingly close, so I stood, creating some distance. "I should get back to the others."

"No." He grabbed my hand, pulling me closer as he stood up. The pace of my heart increased tenfold, and for a moment I felt scared. Dybgo must have sensed it. Releasing my hand, he created a small space between us. "I need to give you something."

His intense gaze did not leave my face as he reached for the left cuff of his jacket. Before I could react, he took my left hand and clipped a yellow-gold stone onto my claiming bracelet. Anxiety filled me, uncertain of what this action truly meant.

"You can't do that. I'm…I'm not Akquarian."

"You and I are not very different."

"We're a different species, Dybgo. I don't even know if what you're suggesting is possible."

"It is." How did he know that? "But that's not why I'm claiming you."

"Take it off!" I thrust my wrist at him.

"It's done. It cannot be removed."

"You can't waste your claiming token on me. Take it off!"

"I'm not wasting it." His voice was ridiculously calm compared to my erratic tone. "There's no other female I want."

"Dybgo, I'm not here to be had." I stepped away, noticing the heated gaze he was smothering me with. This couldn't be happening. I needed Rooke, Zamya, anyone. "I'm not here to find a mate. Humans don't do that." He raised his eyebrows, questioning my comment. "I'm here as a guest. To enjoy the party. Nothing more."

He looked to his feet and smiled to himself. "Eden." He stepped closer. "I'm fully aware of that. I'm not intending on taking you to my bed tonight. I offer you my token as a symbol of my devotion. A promise that I will continue to hold you in high regard." He stepped even closer. "Sometime in the future, maybe you'll start returning my favour. And when that happens, I will be waiting for you."

I realised I'd been holding my breath, trapped in his intense gaze. He certainly knew how to woo a female with his presence. A part of me wanted to melt into his words, but another found them arrogant and presumptuous.

"I will be gone soon."

A hint of sadness warped his face for the briefest of moments. "And until that day comes, I will be waiting."

Thankfully, the gap between us had remained comfortable. He had not encroached on me, nor forced me in anyway. He was a gentleman; I knew that much already. But the situation left me feeling confused and unsettled…

"Is this because of my eyes?" I blurted out, suddenly remembering Cora's comments about the illustration she found in an Aquarian book; that the Aquarians could believe in a ridiculous prophecy like the Alluran Nux priestess had. "My eyes do not make me special."

Dybgo's baffled expression confirmed he had no idea what I was referring to. "Your eyes truly are stunning, but that is not the reason why I offer myself to you."

Nux, how was this possible? He wanted me. Me, Eden Riley. A pilot in the Alluran Solarfleet. I was nothing special, not overly sociable. I'd lived my younger life in the shadow of my outgoing friends, who no longer held that title. Yes, I'd dated before. I had three ex-boyfriends. One who had been a fleeting teenage crush. Another who had cheated on me profusely. Rooke insisted I should've left him on several occasions, but my previously mentioned friends kept telling me he would change. He never did. I dumped him the week after my mum's death.

The third one had started out with potential. Ben Otley was his name. We had been good together. But as the months dragged on, my work had taken me away for longer spates, and it became more of a casual affair. Eventually it turned into something non-existent. I'd stopped calling him when I realised my thoughts were consumed by Rooke and not him.

Lost in the memory, I realised I missed Ben and the non-complexity of our relationship. It had been easy. What Rooke and I had wasn't even physical but it was complicated. But comparing it to what Dybgo was suggesting made it all look comfortable and acceptable.

I chuckled inwardly. After so many years of living in the shadows of the crowd, who would've thought I'd be here, standing on mythical Earth, essentially being asked to date an alien male in a rather nonconventional way? This was beyond comprehensible. If the scenario had played out on Allura, Dybgo would be seen as the ideal man. He was kind, loyal, strong, protective. And to

215

compliment it all, he had an amazing body. One my own seemed to be calling to.

Wait…what?

I squeezed my eyes together, trying to shift a strange sensation from settling over my senses. Placidity seemed to be replacing my rational concern towards what was happening here. I felt alive, contented.

A long, deep, soothing breath escaped me, and I looked at the stone dangling from my bracelet, then back to Dybgo. Nux, he was handsome. "Okay, so…are you allowed to give me this?"

"Havav has given me his approval, yes."

Has he now? "Well then…I guess…I'll let you know if I change my mind."

He subtly bowed his head, accepting my answer. I took that as my cue to leave.

It appeared the couple in the corner had been watching our interaction unfold. As I passed them, the female glared at me, at my wrist, which confirmed my thoughts of how other Akquarians would view this union—not that I was going to allow it to happen.

Nux, I needed a drink.

I scurried to the drinks table. Snatching up a glass, I downed the pink liquid. Wow, that tasted good. After slamming it on the table, I threw back another one.

"Eden." My head whipped round, and I found Zamya hurrying towards me. The anxious worry had returned to her face. "I've lost Cora. Have you seen her?"

Chapter Twenty—One

We found Cora bending over a plant pot, vomiting. Yuska stood behind her rubbing her back. Her look of disapproval pinned us as we approached. "She told me she's drunk both pink and blue drinks."

Zamya looked at me and I shrugged. I had no idea how much Cora had drunk.

Yuska tutted. "To be honest, she shouldn't be drinking anything in her condition."

"Her condition?" I asked. Cora groaned from below. I didn't miss the look Yuska and Zamya exchanged.

"She's still suffering from the aftereffects of the bluepox," Zamya said. "It's her stomach."

"Why didn't you say something?" Eyeing Zamya with scepticism, I walked forward and squeezed Cora's shoulder. "Shall we get you back to the apartment?" I asked her. She nodded and attempted to stand.

"I'll take her," Yuska insisted, literally pushing me out of the way. "You two stay and enjoy the ball."

"I don't mind…." Yuska shot me a hard look. I swallowed down the words. "Very well. You may take her."

Speaking softly to Cora, Yuska coerced her to stand. We watched them amble towards the archway into the fortress. She'd be safe with Yuska. I had no doubt about that.

"Why didn't you tell me?" Slowly removing my eyes from Cora, I turned to Zamya. Her face told a thousand stories as she shrugged. "You've had a lot on your plate."

"We all have."

"Not all of us have nearly died…twice. Plus, the attempted rape thing."

"I…" I tried to deny her comment, but I couldn't. I had been through a lot. If the shoe was on the other foot, I would've kept Cora's condition to myself as well. I huffed a sigh and glanced about the area. Akquarians were everywhere. I felt out of my comfort zone again. "I'm gonna get a drink."

How long I stood by the drinks table, I didn't know. My thoughts drowned out everything around me.

Dybgo—what did he want with me? The more I thought about the token clipped to my bracelet, the more prickles of uneasiness cascaded down my body. Was it simply an act of affection, perhaps an obsession? What if him claiming me in this way caused a lawful bond, one I wouldn't be able to break? Rules. Havav loved rules. Was this one of them? One, I hadn't realised I'd become tangled up in. Rooke was already concerned Havav had a plan for me. What if Dybgo claiming me was the first task setting the wheels in motion? What if…

I drank another morish pink drink. I needed to speak to Rooke, but I hadn't seen him since he went to speak to Oz.

Under the peculiar ambience of the blue lights shining through the darkness, I continued to watch the dancers twirl and sway. It was only when I noticed Zamya speaking with Bibska that I was pulled out of my trance. The sight of Zamya's attendant shocked me. I couldn't believe how stunning she looked now she was exposing a little more flesh and her silky blonde hair was removed from the usual stark bun. Several tokens dangled from her wrist. I smirked to myself. She was going to have fun over the next few days. Yuska had mentioned the females weren't restricted to only one mate. I wondered how many Bibska would entertain?

Lost in that vision, I looked back at the dancers, entranced by their movements once more.

*

I didn't know how many drinks I'd consumed, but I knew they were taking effect. Unlike the alcohol I was used to, my vision hadn't become fuzzy. In fact, it felt sharper, more focused. And instead of feeling numb, my body and mind felt alive, tantalised. All my senses felt energised and aroused.

The longer I watched the dancers sway to the sensual music, the more I saw, the more I felt. The closer I listened to the continuous, enchanting rhythm, the stronger it called to me. There was a confidence growing inside me, making me feel invincible. I wanted to dance. I wanted to let go and show them all how captivating I could really be.

As if I was floating on a soft breeze, I entered the dancefloor through the threshold of blossom trees. My skirt flowed behind me, gaping at the thigh, exposing my long, slim legs. The confidence oozed out of every pore as I glided through the dancers, taking in the connections between the couples. Several male and female hands reached out to touch me as I floated past, some meeting my eye with a hazed pleasure surrounding them. They were lustfully drunk on the music, so close to taking the final step in completing the reason why they were here.

Closing my eyes, the music flowed through my body, coercing the primitive part to move in time to the slow, sensual rhythm. My hips rotated. My hands skimmed the outline of my hips, waist, rising along my neck and through my hair. Nux, I felt sexy, and I didn't care why. I enjoyed the freedom, the poise stirring within.

I opened my eyes and took in the Akquarians standing around. Several males had already noticed me. I didn't care what they thought. I wanted the attention. I felt amazing.

The slow hip movements and accentuated twirls came naturally, sending me into a spiral of insatiability. Under heavy, lustful eyelids, I noticed Dybgo watching from the balcony wall. To my surprise, I wasn't repulsed by his attention. I liked him watching. I liked the way his eyes roamed my body. He desired me. I smiled at the thought. If I could attract a powerful male like him, I could attract anyone. But I didn't want anyone. There was only one person I craved.

Like following a homing beacon, my eyes clocked Rooke in an instant. He wasn't hard to find. The only dark-haired person standing among a court of blondes. He looked small compared to the Akquarians, but he was far from small. He was strong and clever, every part the commander.

Standing by the balcony, he spoke with Havav and two other Akquarians. He looked relaxed, confident, perfect.

As I continued to dance, my eyes devoured every inch of him. Raking them over his handsome, shaven face, down the lean, toned body hiding under the Akquarian suit. I pictured the tattoo on his left arm. I'd always wanted to trace my fingers along the intricate detail from his collarbone to mid-bicep. Nux, the thought of his body was driving me crazy. I wanted him to see me, to find me as attractive as I did him. I wanted him to be drawn to me, to come to me.

My breath hitched when his eyes flicked in my direction. By the way he was smirking, he'd already seen me dancing. I ignored it, continuing to let the music guide my movements, attempting to allure him in. Closing my eyes, I turned my back on him, slowly losing all awareness of where I was. My mind was only focused on one thing—the man I cherished, adored. Needed.

I was unsure how many minutes passed before I opened my eyes again. But as if it was perfectly timed, warm hands rounded my hips from behind, and a familiar rumble was in my ear, low and seductive.

"What are you doing to me?"

I smiled at the implication, rotating my hips backwards into him. "I'm trying to get you to dance." My voice matched his sensuality.

Rooke's breath tickled my neck as his chuckled. "You know I don't dance."

"Yet here you are on the dancefloor with me."

He turned me around, so he could see my face. His dark eyes

searched my own, never once glancing down at my curves. "I couldn't leave you on your own, looking all promiscuous."

"Promiscuous?" I laughed. "That's a new one."

"Your sexy dancing is causing quite a stir with the onlookers."

"Let them look."

He smirked, glancing at our spectators. I started dancing again. "So, you have come to dance with me."

Rooke adjusted his hold on my hips, halting their movement. "I told you; I don't dance."

"Maybe you should." I leaned into him, attempting to loosen his solid stance. But he was having none of it. I straightened up and said in a sultry voice, "Think how many of your lady friends back home would be impressed if you did."

He continued to dive deep into my eyes, and I returned his gaze with confidence. "How many lady friends do you think I have?"

"You have queues of them, waiting for you to get bored of the current one."

He looked shocked. "Should I take that as an insult, Miss Riley?"

"No. It's not your fault you're so damn fine."

He grinned widely at that, and I found myself staring at his heavy lower lip. *So damn kissable.*

"One question..." He tilted his head. "I've never really asked you this before, but why haven't there been any men in Eden's life over the past couple of years?"

"Hmm...I don't get time. My boss is a slave driver."

"That's complete nonsense. I pretty much baby sit my crew and I still find the time for the ladies."

"Ha." I pointed at him. "See, you even admit you're a Casanova."

He threw his head back and laughed. "No, I don't. And you haven't answered my question."

I shrugged, dropping his gaze. "You know me. I'm quiet. I'm certainly not a head turner."

221

"You're gorgeous. Why are you avoiding the question?"

Every motion in my body paused. For a moment I forgot to breathe. Even my heart felt like it had stopped for several surreal seconds. Was this my chance to tell him what he meant to me? Was I brave enough to admit the truth? My newly acclaimed confidence convinced me I was. I searched his handsome face, diving back into his mesmerising green eyes. My voice didn't waver when I said, "Isn't it obvious?"

I didn't falter. I remained assured, pouring the emphasis of my words out through my gaze. The obsession to get closer to this man was reaching a new peak. His stare turned solemn, unreadable, and a vulnerability attempted to take root, trying to crush my confidence.

A cheer erupted from the upper veranda, causing us to finally break eye contact. I realised the sound was the Akquarians' most human attribute yet. I grabbed Rooke's hand and smiled. "Let's go see what's happening."

Walking to the stone stairs, Rooke adjusted his grip on my hand, intertwining our fingers, palm flush with palm. A new smile swept across my lips. Maybe he'd caught onto what I was implying.

At the top of the stairs, we found a congregation of male Akquarians dominating the balcony space. One was walking towards an entrance to the fortress. He was carrying an unconscious female draped in his arms. A sinister grin danced across his face. Another Akquarian male hurled aggressive words at his back whilst being detained by two other males. There was a sheer rage roiling within him. The grinning male seemed to ignore the abuse and disappeared inside. The angry Akquarian lunged forward, thrashing and snarling. He was clearly disturbed by the action.

Before I could ask Rooke if he knew what was going on, the angry male freed one arm, sending his fist into one of the males holding him back. Within seconds a brawl broke out.

I stepped back, avoiding the impact of a burly Akquarian's

elbow. Rooke instantly grabbed my arm and pulled me across the veranda, away from the stairs and the fight.

"I don't think this is a place for us." He steered me towards a narrower terrace on the far side. It curved around to the left beyond the fortress wall.

I looked back at the ongoing brawl. "I guess they're not so different from humans after all."

Rooke raised an eyebrow. "I certainly wouldn't want to get in the middle of that."

"Did you find Oz?" I chuckled. "He may have started it."

Rooke hummed a distant response. I looked back at him. He was lost in thought, glancing around the bend in the path before us. Pulling me along with him, he continued around the curve. It was secluded around here, empty. A three-metre-wide promenade stretched out before us. To the right, the wide, stone balcony wall was topped by wooden trellises, edged with green foliage. The wooden beams continued overhead, where bunches of purple and red grapes hung. To the left, blue lanterns intermittently lined the fortress walls, brightening the long expanse.

"This is pretty," I mused to myself.

The sound of the fight faded behind us the further we walked. Rooke eventually stopped and perched on the edge of the balcony wall. He checked we were alone and said, "I need to talk to you."

"I'm listening." Standing square on to him, I smiled softly. He was still looking back the way we came, checking no one was following. "Is something wrong?"

"No...no." He looked up at me. "I saw you with Dybgo earlier. Are you okay? What did he want?"

I groaned, loudly, causing Rooke to chuckle.

"That bad, huh?"

"Yes." I shuffled on my feet. "He apologised...I think. He also gave me this." I raised my left wrist to him, allowing the yellow token to swing freely.

Touching the stone to take a better look, Rooke cursed.

"I told him to take it back, but he refused. Apparently, it

can't be removed."

Rooke cursed again. "He can't have you."

"I told him that as well…but…Rooke, I'm worried this is a trap. Yuska said females can refuse all but one of their claimers."

Rooke frowned. "What else did Yuska say?"

I shook my head. "I can't remember everything. I'm pretty sure she said any male to get in the way of a female's choice will be executed. But what if a female only has one choice? And do those rules apply to me?" I felt a sense of panic rise inside me. Not as much as I expected, but it was there, unsettling the equilibrium currently falling over my senses. "I assumed we were guests, not partakers."

"We are…but just in case." He detached the token hanging from his left cuff. I hadn't noticed it beforehand hiding under the gold embroidered edging of his sleeve. I watched him clip it onto the opposite side of my bracelet to where Dybgo's far larger token hung. "If they force you to make a choice, you now have two. And you'll choose me."

He stood up and wandered a few paces along. I looked down at his token. It was a small black sphere with a jagged white line circling the middle. *"I'll always chose you."*

"Huh, what was that?"

I whipped my head round to see him reaching up, trying to pick a handful of plump grapes from the trellis above. *Had I said that aloud?* "Um…nothing." My confidence seemed to be faltering. "It's a good ploy."

Watching Rooke jump and pull down a whole section of grape vine, I laughed.

"Whoops," he chimed. "I know I'm not the tallest, but my height really doesn't seem to be sufficient here. I actually feel small." He popped a couple of grapes in his mouth, then smirked before forcing one into mine. Wow, they tasted good. I frowned, ripping a bunch from the vine dangling from Rooke's hand. Everything seemed to taste good this evening. Everything smelt and looked good too.

"Havav's kept his word," Rooke said as I ambled along the

promenade, noticing the half-moon looming above the clifftops in the distance.

"Are you talking about the raft?" I leant back on the stone balcony wall, concentrating on eating the grapes.

"Yes. It's ready."

Looking up at Rooke, my heart skipped with purpose. Not at the news of being one step closer to fixing the ship, but because of where Rooke's gaze was resting...

He was the ladies' man who never, *ever*, looked at me inappropriately. Yes, he said things, but that was simply banter or to mock me. To my despair, never once had I seen him appreciate or admire my subtle womanly curves. But, to my utter surprise, he was currently tracing the length of my leg with his eyes—my bare leg, where the fabric of my skirt had fallen away due to the angle I was sitting.

I smirked to myself when he realised I'd caught him looking. He cleared his throat and refocused on his grapes again. "Are you feeling up to joining us in retrieving the ship tomorrow?"

"Of course I am."

"Are you sure?" He peered at me, clearly concerned I wasn't ready after everything that had happened the last time we ventured there.

The breeze shifted and strains of the music from the party wafted over us. I gave him my most dashing smile and said, "Yes, I'm sure." Closing my eyes, I savoured how captivating the music made me feel, swaying in time with it.

An empty grape vine tapped the floor, followed by the sound of Rooke's huffing.

"Come on, then," he said. On opening my eyes, I found him extending his hand out to me. "I'll dance with you."

"Really?"

"Yes, come on. Get off your ass before I change my mind."

With a wide, triumphant grin, I stood up and took his hand. He twirled me in and out before pulling me into a promenade position, swaying us gently. The movement was nothing like the Akquarian primal dance, it was more in line with an old fashioned,

Alluran ballroom style. There was an innocence and grace to the movement.

Smiling up at him, I said, "I guess you'll be asking Solarfleet for a pay rise when we get home."

"For having to dance with my lieutenant to keep her happy? Definitely."

I laughed, watching Rooke's facial expression change into something a little more earnest.

"Do you think we'll get home?" he asked.

"I hope so."

"What do you miss the most?"

"Freedom. And underwear." We laughed and I pondered the subject for a moment. "But what I really miss is the fresh smell that comes down from the hills every morning, along with the sound of the milk bike jangling over the cobbles outside. I miss quiz nights and pizza at the pub. And you bringing me coffee and pastries on Saturday mornings. Especially that."

He smiled at the latter. "It's funny, really." He gazed down at me, a new tenderness settling in his eyes. "When I think of all the people and places I miss back home, I realise there's one person who's always in those memories. And she's here with me now."

Holding his gaze, I regarded his words, savouring the truth behind their meaning. A gentle breath escaped me as he tenderly brushed my cheek with the back of his fingers, then his thumb. Unable to fight the urge to close my eyes, I pressed into the warmth of his touch, smiling at the gesture, at the closeness this moment had given us.

Rooke's position shifted under my hands. I wasn't expecting the feel of his breath on my cheek, nor a feather like touch brushing against the top of my lip, circling back across the bottom one. I half opened my eyes and found his lips hovering, anticipating my reaction. Glimpsing at those sultry lips, I met his gaze. His actions were an invitation, one he seemed unsure of, but one I had no trouble in answering.

I lifted my head, bringing his lips closer. His breath fluttered against my skin. The scent of him filling every inch of me with excitement. Heat flooded my body and the whole world fell silent as I closed the final gap bridging us.

His lips were warm and soft against my own. They felt like heaven.

We barely moved for the first few seconds, not until his lips took command and began to caress, torturing my senses. He gently coerced my mouth open, flicking his tongue against mine, and a small moan escaped me. Nux, I had wanted this for so long. I was worried I'd wake up and discover it was just another one of my dreams.

His fingers traced the outline of my curves, his hands settling on my waist before pulling me closer. The muscles of his body felt solid as I arched into them. I swept my hands up over his shoulders, into his hair, and the kiss intensified. Every waking part of me tingled; my head whirling in triumphant pleasure.

My back hit the wood of a trellis beam and Rooke pushed himself against me. So caught up in how passionate this was becoming, my confidence took root again. Subconsciously, I traced the toes of my right foot up the length of his trousered leg. Gravity pulled on the fabric of my skirt, exposing my leg the higher I lifted my knee. When it grazed against his waist, he grabbed my thigh, holding me in place. The warmth of his hand began to travel higher, cupping my buttock firmly, pulling me in even harder against him. It was his turn to moan into my mouth and I felt the unrelenting urge to get closer. Nux, I wanted him. I needed him. My whole body felt aroused, expectant.

The warmth of his hand trailed back up to my knee, and our lips parted. My eyelids slowly opened, and I found Rooke gazing down at me with hooded eyes. I saw it then, the lust spilling out from within. The wanting. He wanted me.

"Eden," he whispered as if it was a question, expecting me to respond. But I didn't want to talk, I wanted to play. Placing my forefinger vertically across his lips, hushing him, I pushed him backwards with my other hand. At first, he seemed shocked by my reaction, but after reading my playful expression as I shoved him back again, a rakish smirk danced across his lips.

The backs of his legs hit the balcony wall, forcing him to sit back on the wide, stone ledge. The desire grew in his eyes as I climbed onto his lap, instantly reclaiming his lips. With my legs straddling his thighs, I didn't care the pieces of my skirt had fallen to the side, baring my sex to him. I wanted to feel him against me. And as in response to my silent plea, he grabbed my hips, pulling me forward onto his hard, covered groin. We both gasped in unison as my weight pushed down onto him. Our panting breaths clashed against each other's, becoming fervid as I began to grind my pelvis up and down his length.

"I want you," I whispered against his lips, reaching down to the drawstrings of his trousers. The adrenaline surged within, exciting my body further. After all these years of dreaming, I'd finally…

The last thing I expected was his hand to force mine to stop, stunting me further when he whispered, "Eden, I can't…we can't do this."

An invisible force slammed into my chest, removing the haze around my conscious. I searched his face, realising the desire I'd seen not minutes ago had now changed into something agonising. He didn't want this. Why had I believed he did? This was me, not one of his gorgeous, stunning, beautiful lovers. This was me…Eden.

Scrambling off his lap, wave after relentless wave of humiliation struck me hard.

Rooke reached for me. "Eden, it's not that I…" I retracted from his touch, stumbling backwards. "Eden, please." I couldn't look at him. I didn't want to see the shame and remorse rising in his eyes.

My feet scuttled away, back along the promenade towards the party. My head spun with the pain of rejection. What had I done? Why had I gone against every previous instinct? What we had worked! And it was always meant to stay that way.

I could hear Rooke's padded footsteps behind, his voice calling my name. I didn't want to talk to him. I wouldn't put us both through the embarrassment. Everything felt overwhelming. Why was he following me?

As I rounded the corner, I hardly registered the Akquarians ambling about. I needed to get away from here, away from this party. Keeping my eyes averted, I stumbled into the fortress. My vision began to feel cloudy, my head pounded with every irrational heartbeat. Nux, I felt dizzy. I felt sick.

The ground beneath me seemed to distort and disappear. And in the next instant…

Darkness.

Chapter Twenty—Two

The pounding in my head woke me. On opening my clammy eyes, I strained against the harsh brightness. My stomach roiled. Hell, I needed to be sick.

I launched myself out of bed, scurrying to the weird toilet-cupboard with my hand pressed against my mouth. Pushing my head through the hole in the rock wall, I vomited, violently. The smell of those pink drinks hit me, and my stomach roiled again.

I gripped the jagged rock surrounding the opening. My body scraped against the rough surface, while the cold wall dug into my knees. This was so uncomfortable. *What I'd give for a porcelain toilet pan and a heated floor right now.*

After a few minutes of expelling the contents of my stomach, I collapsed onto my heels, wiping my mouth with the back of my hand. A vague recollection of images of last night started to jumble about in my mind. Visions of sexy dancing in front of Dybgo. Rooke and I dancing. My eyes widened recalling his lips caressing mine. Nux, did I grind myself against his…?

"Shit."

It had all been real. And Rooke had rejected my advances.

"Shit."

I held my face in my palms and silently screamed. What the hell was wrong with me last night? I didn't do those types of things. That wasn't me.

"Both the cursing and sicking ones guts up is neither acceptable nor femalelike."

Finding Yuska standing in the doorway, I scowled at her. "What the hell was in those drinks yesterday?"

She tutted and turned on her heel. Struggling to stand against the dizziness, I staggered after her.

"You'll feel better once you've had something to eat. A late breakfast is ready on the table for you." She stopped halfway across the bedroom and turned to look at me. "You'll need to tidy yourself up. Your commander has asked you to be ready the first hour after noon."

"What for?"

Yuska glared, taking in the physical state of me. I was still wearing my clothes from the party. "To retrieve your ship, I believe."

Nux, how was I going to face Rooke after what happened? "Shit."

She raised her eyebrows and tutted. "Your language is appalling today. Come. Eat."

I trudged behind her into the main room of the apartment. My head pounded with every footstep I took. What the hell was I going to say to Rooke? If my memory served me correctly, I had tried to have sex with him, and he'd stopped me. Nux, this was humiliation nightmares were made of. I wanted the ground to swallow me up and never spit me out.

Amusement danced in Zamya's eyes as I seated myself at the table opposite her. "You look like hell," she said.

"Thanks." I slumped a little, eyeing all the food in front of me. My stomach began to gripe again.

"Where did you go last night?"

"I, um…" I squeezed my eyes together. "I don't know. I was drunk."

"No, you weren't drunk. You were drugged."

I looked over at her as she casually cut up pieces of fruit. "What do you mean, drugged?"

Zamya pointed her coral knife at me, then Cora, who sat to my right, and said, "I told both of you not to drink that stuff, and I was right."

Cora and I glanced at each other before returning our gaze to our resident biologist and *know it all*.

"Don't leave us in suspense, Zam," I grumbled.

"Those drinks were infused with hormone enhancers. Which is the reason why they were labelled by colour. Among other things, the pink ones heighten oestrogen to encourage the females to feel confident, sexy, more susceptible to…you know."

Holy souls, that explained a lot.

"The blue ones had been laced with a mild sedative to calm the males' predominantly primitive behaviour. I wouldn't be surprised if they were incapable of making rational decisions. It's all in the attempt to make sure every female mates without alpha dominance getting in the way. It widens the gene pool, apparently."

My head found the palm of my hand and I groaned inwardly. That explained why Rooke seemed interested in me. He hadn't been thinking straight.

"You make it sound like a farce, Miss Zamya," Yuska said from behind me.

"Isn't it?"

Yuska appeared in my peripheral. "Of course not," she snapped. "It encourages the success of a natural and essential process."

Zamya scoffed. "You think drugging people is encouraging?"

"Why do you always make my cultural traditions sound outrageous? Just because it is different to yours, does not make it wrong."

Zamya laughed, and I turned to look at Yuska. Her cheeks were red, proving her fluster.

"Why didn't you warn us…about the drinks?" My tone was quiet but pointed. When she didn't answer I glared at her. After everything that had been communicated between us over the past few weeks, I'd hoped I could trust this older, wiser female. Clearly, I was wrong. "Why, Yuska?"

"I must've forgotten." She was blatantly lying. "Besides, I would've thought one of you would've worked it out, as you are such an intelligent species." The sarcasm laced in her final words were sneered at Zamya.

Zamya sniggered around a mouthful of food. "Are you going to tell her the rest?"

Glancing at me for a brief second, Yuska swallowed nervously before replying. "And stop you from telling her in your own delightful words? Here." Yuska brashly placed a glass of red, cloudy juice in front of me. "Drink this and you'll feel better."

As I stared at the strange drink, I heard the door screech open and shut, announcing Yuska's departure. Peering across the table at Zamya, she seemed amused with the effect she had on our Akquarian attendant.

"Tell me what?" I asked.

Zamya pouted her lips, swallowing her mouthful of food. "You know we were informed the females here choose their mates, blahdy blahdy blah. Well, it's nonsense. Bibska told me that if Havav or any of his royal spawn offer a female their claiming token, she is obligated to choose in their favour. So, those females have no choice. The royal takes precedence. And if you think that's bad," she made a face before shaking her head, "I was told, if a female faints within a few minutes of kissing a male, it's deemed they are soul mates. I mean, come on, *soul mates*? But the Akquarians apparently believe in that crap."

"Which means?"

"It means, even if she had decided who she wants to mate with, the soul bond supersedes any of her choices. Even Havav would have to stand aside. They class the bond as sacred. A type of destiny. No one can interfere with it."

"So, she has absolutely no choice in the matter?"

"No. Her soul mate scoops her up in her unconscious state, takes her back to his room, and is, basically, allowed to take advantage of her for the duration of the season."

I stared at Zamya. I felt appalled. It was no wonder Yuska hadn't told me this. She knew I'd be disgusted. I already held reservations about how the females were treated here. Then a vague recollection appeared in my mind. The male carrying the unconscious female into the fortress last night, the male with the snarky expression. Had that been an example of the soul bond? *Yes, probably.* I assumed the male being restrained had been her first choice, but she'd foolishly kissed another male and wham! She was unconscious and had become soul bonded, stripping herself of any independent decision.

"She probably had too much to drink," I murmured to myself.

Zamya mused. "I'm interested to see if there's a truth in the fainting aspect. There must be something in the two drinks that causes a chemical reaction. I'd love to get my hands on a sample."

"It sounds like nonsense to me," Cora said. I glanced at her. She had been so quiet and still, I'd almost forgotten she was sitting there. She looked exhausted, picking at the food on her plate. I frowned, remembering what Zamya told me yesterday about her stomach. But her face was bright and full of glow as she smiled at me. "Eden passed out."

"Eden drank too much." Zamya chuckled.

"So, it is nonsense," Cora said. "It was a good job Rooke was with you when you did," a grimace spread across her face, "otherwise a random Akquarian could've picked you up, claiming you were his soul bonded."

I couldn't remember getting back to my bed last night. I couldn't remember anything after…

My eyes widened. Did I pass out? Just after Rooke kissed me? My breath hitched. We'd both been drinking those drinks. My mind whirled in contemplation. No. No, the soul mate phenomenon was absolute nonsense. It wasn't possible. Just another Akquarian ruse to detriment a female's integrity. Surely…

"Rooke was with you?" I heard Zamya ask, forcing myself away from my ridiculous thoughts. I found her narrowing her eyes at me. Nux, did she know?

"Um…yeah. Like Cora said, good job he was."

Zamya wasn't convinced. As I drank the red juice, she continued to watch me with a questionable look in her eyes. To my relief, the liquid soothed my roiling stomach, and I began to feel better within minutes. I suppose Yuska did have her uses.

Dressed in the comfort of my Solarfleet uniform, I sat onboard a small rowing boat, heading for the cave mouth and out to sea. As we exited the darkness, daylight hit my face and I glanced down at the golden bracelet locked around my left wrist. I had tried to remove it while I dressed, only to be chastised by Yuska for doing so. I couldn't help but think she was keeping more information from me regarding the politics behind the claiming tokens.

Dybgo's yellow stone weighed one side down, but it was the opposite side I was focusing on. The small black stone with a jagged white line running around the middle; Rooke's claiming token. He had given it to me in case the Akquarians forced me to choose a mate. I was still unsure if their rules included me, but with Rooke's token hanging there too, if I was forced to make a decision, I'd have a choice between him and Dybgo, and I'd obviously choose Rooke. No strings attached.

But I couldn't remove the memory of the passionate kiss we shared last night, and the direction in which it was leading. Nux, what would've happened if he hadn't stopped me? Would I be sitting here, panicking about speaking to him? Would an awkwardness have fallen over us, more so than what I was expecting now? Would we have woken up in each other's arm, relishing in the fact we loved each other?

I shook my head. Whatever happened last night was instigated purely because we were drugged. Nothing more. But it didn't help the heaviness dwelling in my heart.

What we had worked.

The small rowing boat approached a large Akquarian sailing ship, anchored half a mile from shore. It was far larger than any I'd previously boarded; too wide to access the harbour in the cavern under the fortress.

Three turquoise scalene sails locked onto wooden masts towered above the deck. Its beautifully crafted hull was bulbous, the bow lower than the stern. To the rear, connected to the ship via thick, durable rope, sat a large, wooden raft, wide enough to load the Parvos onto. Compared to the sailing ship, its deck was far closer to sea level, bobbing and crashing against the waves, drenching the expanse of the flat surface.

The air was cooler today, the sea choppier. A dark cloud loomed on the horizon threatening to storm. I tucked my bracelet under the cuff of my fleeced jacket, hiding it from view.

To my surprise, and relief, Dybgo hadn't escorted me this afternoon. Two of his warriors, who I recognised from our previous trip, were given the task. But I knew he would be onboard the main ship. I knew he'd be waiting for me.

As the small boat pulled alongside the ship, I sized up the height of the ladder fixed to the hull. Following one of the warriors up the wooden slates to the gunnel, I swung my legs over the ridge at the very top and found Dybgo holding his hand out for me. I ignored it, jumping down onto the deck with ease.

Returning his hand to the hilt of his sword, I looked at the bare chested general, discovering he had no blue sash tied around the waist of his trousers.

"Chaperons aren't needed during the season."

I glanced up at his face. It was scary how well he could read me. His warm, attentive gaze made me feel uneasy. I forced a small smile, attempting to ease whatever this was between us. "Nice to know."

Spotting Oz standing on the raised helm, I began to meander my way around the deck towards the back of the ship. Bare chested Akquarian males with turquoise swirled tattoos were everywhere, hauling the sails and rigging, loading supplies. Others, with golden tattoos, similar to, but far smaller than Dybgo's, sharpened their weapons. It hadn't occurred to me how much manpower was needed to manoeuvre the Parvos onto the raft. There must have been at least two hundred warriors and seaman on board.

A number of them nodded their head in my direction as I passed. Aware Dybgo and my two bodyguards were following me like an unwanted shadow mass, I assumed the acknowledgment was aimed at their general. But when I approached the steps leading up to the helm, two Akquarians stopped, stood aside, and literally bowed to me. I frowned, peering over my shoulder at Dybgo, who didn't seem fazed by their reaction.

Weird.

At the top of the steps, Oz approached me. His face was stern, scanning the three Akquarians hovering behind with scrutiny. I was surprised to see a large Alluran laser rifle hanging over his shoulder. "Is that thing still charged?" I asked.

Oz looked at the black machine and said, "Yeah. Kobe somehow supplied it with an additional boost." Lowering his voice, he gestured towards the stern of the ship. "Rooke's over there. He wants to speak with you."

Rooke was standing with his back to us, leaning against the rear railing. The thought of speaking with him made me pause. What did he want to talk to me about? Today's excursion or what happened last night? Nux, what was I going to say to him?

Sensing Oz's confusion at my reluctance to move, I took a deep breath and marched towards the stern. I only made it two steps when I realised Dybgo was following me. I swiftly turned and gave him a pointed look. "You don't need to follow me everywhere."

"I believe I do."

I huffed an incredulous laugh. "I'm only going to speak with my commander. I do not need you accompanying me…making me feel uncomfortable."

Dybgo frowned. "I make you feel uncomfortable?"

"Right now, you are, yes."

He stared at me, analysing my words and the way I glared at him. If I hadn't felt scared and uncertain about what he had started last night, I would probably have found his confusion endearing. Eventually, he inclined his head and said, "I will be standing over there, if you need me."

I mumbled, "If you have to," and began to march away, eyeing Dybgo's position, happy he was far enough away not to eavesdrop. The captain of the ship appeared in front of me, making me jump. He was an older Akquarian. Built just as large and

237

sturdy, but the skin around his eyes, neck, and turquoise tattoo sagged slightly, showing age and experience.

Wide eyed, I watched as he smiled, inclined his head, and said a string of soft Akquarian words to me. I copied his gestures, baffled by everyone's response to me today. Last time I boarded an Akquarian boat, I was certain I was completely ignored.

I resumed walking and found Rooke smirking at me, amused by the captain's reaction. As I neared, he said, "He seems to like you."

I chuckled, glancing back at the amiable male. "They all seem to today."

Rooke gave me a careful look, concern filling his expression. "How are you feeling?"

I stopped next to him by the wooden railing, overlooking the sea and the raft floating behind. "A hangover threatened to persist earlier, but Yuska's disgusting breakfast juice seemed to do the trick."

A brief smile pulled at his lips, before returning his gaze to the ocean. It was obvious he was trowelling with a series of thoughts, so I spoke. I had to get this off my chest.

"Rooke…last night…I'm…I'm beyond sorry if I did anything stupid. I was…"

"You didn't." His eyes locked with mine and I felt my stomach flip. "We were both high on atmosphere. And after speaking with Kobe this morning, it appears we were acting under the influence of drugs."

"Zamya said the same."

"Hmm. So, you have nothing to apologise for." He returned his gaze to the ocean again. "If that had been a party back on Allura, I doubt either one of us would have paid that type of attention to the other."

I stared at his profile, trying to ignore the pain of rejection striking through my heart with every beat. I forced myself to smile, but I couldn't prevent the frown forming as I replied, "Yeah, I guess you're right."

He nodded his head impassively and gestured to the raft.

"Looks good, doesn't it?"

"Yeah." I refocused my attention to the task at hand. "How easy will this be?"

"By the sounds of it, fairly easy. We have enough manpower. Dybgo has assured me we should be back in time for dinner."

"Good. Any news of Troy?"

Avoiding my eyes, he shook his head. "Once we get the Parvos back, Kobe's going to construct a laser signal which should penetrate the jamming signal. If Troy's there, hopefully he'll reply. If he's not…we attempt to send a signal home."

If Troy wasn't there, it was inevitable we'd have to endure another six, seven, perhaps eight months of Akquarian rule and hospitality. How long would I be able to avoid Dybgo's subtle advances without being forced to abide? I didn't warm to the thought.

The boat was fast. It only took us twenty minutes to reach the cove where the scouting ship sat decaying against the harsh rockface. The two piles of stones covering the sand graves of Captain Lewisham and her lieutenant were visible from where I stood at the stern of the ship. The harrowing thought of how that could have been our fate, if we hadn't discovered the Akquarians, was unsettling. We owed them more than I was reluctant to accept.

We rounded a familiar headland; fully aware our ship was positioned up the beach a mile or two. A strange excitement tingled through my body. We could be going home in the next week if repairs went to plan.

Before the ship came into view, the sun behind me was blotted out by Dybgo's towering shadow. He lightly touched my arm and I huffed at his persistent attention.

"Tell me." I snapped my head towards him. "Does the touching stop when the season is over?"

I could've sworn he looked offended, but he chose to ignore my question and the tone I addressed him in. Instead, he said, "When the raft is taken to shore, you are to remain on the ship."

"Um…no, I don't think so."

"You have no say in the matter."

"Like hell I don't! My commander asked for me to accompany him…"

"Which I can't understand why."

I stared at him, registering his tone was the sharpest I'd ever heard him address me with. "Havav said if Rooke deemed my presence necessary, I could leave the fortress. I am Rooke's second in command."

"Yes, but you're also female."

"Don't start that bullshit again!"

"Eden," he snarled; a deep, authoritative rumble emanating from his chest. "You are to remain on the ship. That is my order, and that is what you abide by. I don't care what your commander says. He isn't in charge here. I am!"

A commotion consisting of a solitude voice stopped me from retaliating. Behind Dybgo, with Oz in tow, I saw Rooke storming towards us. His face was angry but as pale as the sun casted moon.

"Where is it?" Rooke shouted at Dybgo. "Where's my ship?"

I frowned, wondering what he was talking about. Turning, I scoured the coastline for the sleek, albeit decaying Solarfleet vessel—our lifeline. I found nothing but sand and rock.

I rushed over to the railing. My eyes strained against the distance, but I recognised the stretch of beach. It was where I had landed the Parvos weeks ago. Even Sym's grave sat near the cliff face, confirming the area's identity. But the ship wasn't there. Neither was the mass of metal and cables littering the sand.

I glanced back at Dybgo. His eyes were as wide with confusion as mine.

"Where is it?" Rooke hollered.

"Are you sure these are the correct coordinates?" Dybgo asked.

"Yes!"

Dybgo looked to the ship's captain, who also seemed in agreement.

"I…" Dybgo stammered, an obvious panic building within.

"I don't know." He met Rooke's raging stare. "I don't know."

The Akquarians ambling nearby began to stir, exchanging whispered comments and disconcerting looks.

Rooke lowered his voice and stepped closer. "Is this part of Havav's plan?"

"What plan?" Dybgo snapped.

"You tell me?"

Marching over to me by the railing, Dybgo continued to scan the beach and cliff horizon. He genuinely looked baffled. When it was apparent he wasn't going to answer Rooke's snide question, Rooke exploded.

"Where's my damn ship, Dybgo?!"

Through gritted teeth Dybgo replied, "I. Don't. Know!"

"I doubt an Igknamai, with its small animalistic brain could move it. Your people are the only ones intelligent enough around here, so stop lying and tell me where…"

"That's not entirely true."

Rooke paused, narrowing his eyes. "Which part?"

I watched Dybgo carefully. He continued to watch the horizon, clearly analysing his options. "I don't know how much Havav has told you."

"Uh, you know exactly what we've been told. You're always present. Always guarding, chaperoning. Whatever the hell you do. No doubt listening."

"There have been times I was not present."

Laced with anger, Rooke chuckled. "You mean the time you were banished to your room because you couldn't restrain yourself around the opposite sex. Around the same time you savagely assaulted my lieutenant? *Don't look at her*!"

Dybgo's eyes drifted to me for a brief second before removing them at Rooke's demand. "That was an accident."

"An accident?" Rooke snarled. "Do you think I haven't noticed your eyes wander every time she's present? Do you not think I see your lingering gaze? I'm well aware you put your disgusting claiming token on her last night…"

"Rooke," I pleaded gently, trying to stop him from making a scene. I didn't like the way this conversation was going. But Oz pulled me a few steps away and softly said, "Let him."

It seemed Rooke had every intention of putting Dybgo in his place. I grimaced as he continued, Rooke pinning Dybgo with a vengeful stare.

"Let me tell you, buddy, if this situation hadn't been forced upon me, and I wasn't obligated to abide by Havav's rules of conduct, I would've gouged your eyes out for what you did and tried to do to her. I don't care how much you are respected here, or how tall and powerful you are, if you ever touch her again, I swear, I will inflict so much pain upon you, you'll wish you were dead."

Surprisingly, a small smirk graced Dybgo's lips. "So, you humans do protect your females?"

"Of course we do! We protect them! Not lock them away, then drug them every few months when they're needed for sexual pleasure and breeding. It's absolutely sickening!"

Dybgo's smirk vanished. He shook his head and glanced at me.

"I said, *don't look at her!*"

In a heartbeat Rooke was aiming his handgun at Dybgo, prompting a platoon of Akquarian warriors to appear out of nowhere, swords drawn. Two had their curving blades touching either side of Rooke's throat, but he didn't flinch. His stare remained defiant, formidable.

"Stop it!" I demanded, stepping forward. "This isn't helping!" I turned to Dybgo. "If you don't know where our ship is, who will?"

Still staring aggressively at one another, Dybgo gave the nod to his warriors to disengage, prompting Rooke to lower his gun.

"We'll head back to the fortress," Dybgo said calmly, avoiding me entirely. "Havav may have an explanation."

Rooke growled. "You mean he *will* have an explanation."

Dybgo ignored him and ordered the crew to turn the ship around.

I looked back at the deserted beach, at Oz, who was scowling behind me, back to Rooke, who was holding his head in his hands. He growled, cursing several times. "Are we ever gonna get off this rock?"

Chapter Twenty—Three

Havav was waiting for us in the throne room, leisurely lounging in his large rock and sharded glass throne. Armed guards lined the walls, but their presence didn't deter Rooke. Before the ground to ceiling doors had closed behind us, he started shouting.

"You need to tell me what the hell is going on? Dybgo has implied you aren't the only intelligent species in these parts, so start talking!"

Havav exchanged a look with Dybgo before laying his eyes on my raging commander. "I assure you, your ship was seen in its original position, by my scouts, not two evenings past."

"So, where is it now? If you don't have it, who does? I'm under the assumption you've been keeping important information from me. Information I have asked you about several times!"

Havav held his palm up. "Calm down, commander." He looked at Dybgo again and said, "Fetch Llexzus."

I watched Dybgo pause for a moment before passing the message onto a guard standing near the doors. Dybgo's eye caught mine and I saw a flash of shame hiding there. I realised, he had purposely lied to me when I asked him, weeks ago, if any other forms of intelligent life existed here. My esteem for him was slowly dwindling. Nux, I'd been foolish to believe I could trust any of these people.

Rooke stepped closer to the dais. "Are you going to tell me, or are you going to make me stand here and guess?"

Havav's nonchalant expression infuriated me, so it wasn't surprising to see Rooke's shoulders tighten. The tendons in his arms bulged as he squeezed his fists together. I could sense the steam fuming out of his ears from the rage and exasperation boiling up within.

"I believe the Igknamai have your ship," Havav replied with a sigh.

Rooke laughed, glancing back at me and Oz. "The Igknamai? You mean the horror beetles can move a spaceship?"

"Not the Igknamai you have encountered, no." All three of us stared, wide eyed at the pious leader. Havav began picking at invisible pieces of dust on his coral jacket, holding his reserve. "There are creatures who control them. Highly intelligent beasts with a savage, murderous nature. I didn't inform you of them because I didn't think it necessary. You were safe here. They never venture this far. They send their beetles to do their dirty work. But to move your ship…" He glanced up at us, scanning each of our faces, letting us conclude his statement.

"Why didn't you tell me?" Rooke asked, his tone deep and full of frustration.

"Like I said, you are safe here. We have our own…protection." Havav must've noticed Rooke and I glance towards Dybgo. "Among other things, Dybgo maybe my best warrior, but even he cannot fend off hordes of Igknamai alone."

"Havav, please stop talking around the subject!"

"If you can call upon some patience," Dybgo growled from behind us, "you'll see what he means any moment now."

Rooke snapped at the general, "I believe I have been patient enough!"

Dybgo glared back, and Havav hushed them, trying to ease the tension.

The double doors shrilled open and a grumbling, obnoxious voice reverberated around the room. "You called, your regalness? This better be important, I was about to be in the middle of something tender and wet."

We turned towards the voice, and I stiffened at the sight. A tall male, with a physique identical to Dybgo's, strutted into the room, an air of arrogance and unrighteousness surrounding him.

His long hair was as black as night, far darker than Rooke's, with an almost bluish hue to it. It was braided back in the same way the Akquarian males wore theirs, exposing small, strange, pointed ears. He was dressed in dark leather armour, stark against his pale skin. His smirk was devious, wicked, as his eyes scanned the room, exchanging a few snarling Akquarian words with Dybgo, before landing those eyes on me, sending razor sharp chills down my spine. His eyes were black, rounded, and unusual. A shimmer of turquoise pulsed through the dark iris, circling the pupil. They were odd, nonhuman, reminding me of the Igknamai who had eyed me up for dinner a few weeks ago.

He closed the distance between us, and the air suddenly felt heavy, unbreathable. I backed up into Oz, who placed a comforting hand on my shoulder, stabilising me.

"You have guests," the new male said, turning to Havav, who was descending the shallow steps of the dais.

"I do. So behave," Havav replied sternly. He turned to Rooke. "Commander, may I introduce you to Llexzus. He is our valued means of protection from the Igknamai."

Under sceptically drawn eyebrows, Rooke said, "What is he?"

"He is an Akquarian-Igknamai hybrid."

More chills of concern and repugnance shivered through me simulating cold electricity. I watched Llexzus agilely climb the dais in one swift step, taking the seat Havav had just abandoned. He intermittently grumbled sentences at Dybgo, who snarled back short, one-word answers. I couldn't help thinking they were bickering, like brothers or friends, but Dybgo's face expressed a true distaste for the creature lounging in Havav's throne.

"How? Why?" Rooke asked abruptly. "Is he dangerous?"

"On the contrary. He protects my farmers and hunters, my people who need to venture near or into the forest. He has the ability to calm and control any Igknamai who come into close proximity. The same command as the devils themselves."

"So, there are more like him?"

"No, he is unique. He's half Akquarian. The others are

246

monsters."

And he isn't?

"Does he have any interaction with the others?" Rooke went on.

"No."

"But he can control the beetles?"

"Yes."

Rooke continued to ask questions, but my attention kept drawing to Dybgo and Llexzus' conversation. Llexzus lounged in Havav's throne, an ankle laying across the opposite knee. Both wrists dangled over the arm rests, as if he was bored by everything that was occurring. He continued to smirk, occasionally exposing his elongated canines, which were far longer than the standard Akquarians. His evil, dark eyes taunted me as he flicked his attention from Dybgo to Rooke, to me, and back again.

"I need my ship, Havav!" Rooke's comment pulled me back to his and Havav's conversation. "If you believe they have it, where can I find these Igknamai leaders?"

Havav chuckled. "Commander, you have too many questions."

"Where are they located?"

The bickering between Dybgo and Llexzus continued, and an irritable expression crossed Havav's face as he clocked it. He shot a harsh glance towards them. "Will you two stop it!" he barked, followed by more words voiced in Akquarian. Both fell silent, and Havav turned back to Rooke. "We do not know where they are located. Their lair has never been discovered, but we presume it's in the forest."

"The forest?" I mumbled, and Rooke looked over his shoulder at me. Following my train of thought, Rooke asked, "Are they intelligent enough to use subspace technology?"

Havav shrugged, shaking his head. "Unfortunately, that is something I certainly do not know."

Rooke turned around, lowering his voice so only Oz and I could hear. "If these Igknamai controllers are as intelligent as we fear, they must have been the ones who lured the scouting ship here. We need to warn Allura."

"How? We have no ship, no radio."

We all looked back towards Havav, who was shooing Llexzus out of his throne. Rooke stepped forward. "If our ship is in the forest, we require a guide, some warriors," he pointed towards Llexzus standing beside Havav, "and him."

Relaxing back into his throne, Havav shook his head. "No. We have done all we can for you. I will continue to provide you with the hospitality you've been receiving. You can stay here as long as you wish. We enjoy your company. But I cannot offer you anymore."

"We'd only need…"

"It's suicide!"

"You said Llexzus can control the Igknamai."

"The beetles, not the devils."

I watched Rooke's head hang to the floor, his hands resting on his hips. He was distraught, his hope of getting home depleted. Havav seemed content in allowing us to stay here, but to what cost? We wanted to go home.

"I'll take them," Dybgo's voice echoed around the room. I peered up, witnessing the pointed look Havav threw his way.

A brief, complex discussion in Akquarian was exchanged between the two, resulting in Havav huffing, Dybgo frowning, and Llexzus chuckling to himself.

"Very well." Havav stood up, releasing an irritated sigh. "You have your wish, commander. I suggest you leave tomorrow after sunrise."

Chapter Twenty-Four

"And when, exactly, were you gonna tell us you've lost all contact with Troy?" Zamya folded her arms across her chest, her tone of voice both angry and distraught. I noticed Cora's face pale as she took in the statement. My heart pained for her.

Rooke pushed his fingers through his short hair and sighed. He felt ashamed, as did I. "When I thought it was necessary."

"Which is now?"

"Yes."

"Because you want to justify why we're leaving the safety of the fortress to find our ship somewhere in the wilderness?"

"If we want to get home, we need the ship, Zam. Without it we can't communicate with anyone who can help us."

"When did you last have contact?" Oz asked, clutching his laser rifle. It was apparent he had been kept in the dark as well.

"Twenty-one days ago."

Zamya cursed. "So, we only have eleven days before Troy returns to Allura. If he's there at all."

Rooke nodded.

"Great!"

"We have time."

Zamya thrusted her arms in the air. "To find the ship in the depths of a giant forest!"

"Before Troy went dark, he supplied information of an area where an unknown satellite signal is transmitting from. And that's where we're aiming to look."

Zamya cursed again. "The dropship option really seemed like the better choice right now."

"The dropship was not an option!" snapped Kobe. Adjusting his backpack, he stalked ahead, through the iron gate, down the windswept corridor leading to the springs.

"He's right, Zam," Rooke said, a frown forming across his brow.

Zamya held her palms up and began to walk after Kobe. "Just don't talk to me right now." Oz and Cora followed, and I heard Rooke's huff of despair beside me.

Swinging my large backpack over my shoulders, I clipped the harness together across my stomach. "We're all behind you, Rooke. Even Zamya." I squeezed his arm and marched along the stone walkway, glancing through the open arches at the rocks and waves hundreds of metres below. I was scared. The whole situation felt out of control. But I had to support Rooke and his choices. Choices that couldn't have been easy to make.

Waiting for us in the gloom at the opposite end of the walkway was Dybgo, fully dressed in dark armour and shin-high boots. He stood next to an open doorway to the left. I'd been to the springs several times during my stay. Never once had I noticed this door merged into the shadows of the rockface.

Ducking under the jagged rock ceiling, I stepped through the opening. A couple of metres ahead, an iron gate stood open, currently flanked by two Akquarian warriors, dressed in the same attire as their general. A set of worn, stone steps, moulded into grass and soil, ascended to a pale blue sky full of white swirling clouds.

I rounded the top step and discovered an expanse of green fields rolling down towards a dense, succulent forest. The trees spread for miles, sweeping the hills and mountain peaks beyond. Behind me, the edge of the sheer cliff face dropped to the rocks below, sectioning the enormous fortress off from the mainland. Only the slither of rock, forming the covered walkway to and from the springs, connected the two.

As the wind whipped at my skin, stinging my cheeks, I heard the iron gate being hauled shut at the bottom of the steps. Rooke and Dybgo emerged from the ground, exchanging a few words, while the two Akquarian warriors followed behind.

I began to trudge down the dew-covered hill, noting how many Akquarians were with us. I counted ten, including Dybgo and Llexzus. All armed with long spears, curving swords, and an array of daggers. Created by layers of leather which imitated fish scales, they were dressed in pristine, dark green armour, protecting the full extent of their torso. Thicker flaps protected their shoulders and pelvis. Their legs were covered with leather trousers and boots.

In poor comparison, the crew wore our light blue Solarfleet uniforms, consisting of a T-shirt, combat pants, a navy-blue jacket, and black boots. It gave us protection against the elements, but not against any weapons or fangs we may potentially face.

I tapped the gun wedged into the back of my belt, then clutched at the golden dagger hanging at my hip. I had a feeling I would be using these over the next few days. And I wasn't convinced it would be solely because of the Igknamai.

After walking for most of the day, we retired on a narrow verge, jutting out the side of one of the towering rockfaces in the depths of the forest. The area was high enough to be used as a viable lookout point, but low enough for our small campfires not to cause unwanted attention.

The Akquarians provided us with a fish dinner. The sun had set a while ago, and as we sat in groups around three small fires, we ate in silence. The whole crew had been unusually quiet all day. Zamya was still fuming from the information Rooke and I kept from her regarding Troy. Cora, too, had kept her distance, absorbed in her own thoughts. I'd noticed her cheeks drenched with tears on a couple of occasions, her eyes red and puffy. I didn't know what to say or do. I couldn't erase the fact I'd lied to her.

Kobe remained focused, concentrating on tracking our

location with Rooke, who had stayed close to Llexzus and our guide at the front of the party all day. But even Oz kept his quips to himself, resorting to a brooding silence.

For the duration of the day, Dybgo remained at the back of our group, guarding our rear with his warriors. They'd spoken amongst themselves, but I sensed their aversion to the task at hand. I, myself, was doubting if anything good would come out of this, but Rooke was adamant we had to find the ship.

After devouring my portion of food, I licked at my fingers, eyeing Llexzus. He stood to the left, balancing on a large piece of protruding stone several metres higher. Although his presence was essential to our safety, he made me feel uneasy. The arrogance surrounding him was filled with a dark, unnatural essence; something I couldn't fathom but subconsciously shuddered away from. It didn't help his devious smirk continued to torment me. What was he thinking? Did he think like a human? Was he more Igknamai than Akquarian? Every conclusion unnerved me.

A shifting figure to my right caught my attention and I found Dybgo taking a seat next to me. My muscles instantly tensed. Stretching his feet and legs out in front of him, he made a soft humming noise. "I don't wear these often. I forget how uncomfortable they are."

It was a contrast to my own thoughts regarding footwear. "Do you not come into the forest often?"

"No. My feet prefer the sand, stone, or sea. Not the dirt and tree roots, nor being restricted in these." He pointed to his boots.

"So why did you offer to bring us here?"

He paused and peered across the fires at Rooke, who was staring at the lapping flames, completely lost in himself. Nux, what was he thinking? He appeared so lost.

"I sensed your commander's despair. I would feel the same if I were in his position."

Nodding my head in understanding, I glanced up at Llexzus still standing defiantly on the stone ledge. "What is he doing?"

"Llexzus? He's keeping watch. Listening. Scenting the air.

He's protecting us."

"Doesn't he need sleep?"

"He can go several days with none or very little sleep."

"How is that possible?"

Dybgo chuckled. "I've been asking myself that for years."

When I looked back at Dybgo, he had shifted into an alpine position, resting his head on a piece of rolled fabric, which looked like his cape.

"Sleep," he said. "You are safe."

Maybe we were, but sleep continued to evade me. I watched the stars move across the clear sky. I listened to the buzzing of the insects and howls of creatures within the forest. I studied the sleeping faces of Dybgo and Oz lying next to me, envious of their easy slumber. I swear the fires had died out and the sky had begun to brighten before I dozed off.

A heaviness deep inside my head was the first thing I noticed when I woke. The second, was that someone was standing over me, taunting me from my sleep. A foot nudged at my hip and a grumbling, sardonic voice said, "Come on, Queenie, time to wake up!"

I forced one eye open, and to my horror, I found Llexzus standing with a foot either side of my body, bending over at the waist with his face inches from mine. I must've flinched at the sight of his haunting black eyes, jolting my body awake. An obnoxious laugh rumbled from him before he straightened up. "What's wrong? Were you expecting someone else?"

I froze at the sight of his devilish grin. Those long canines were insanely sharp. If it hadn't been for Oz stepping closer and telling Llexzus to leave me alone, I was certain he would have remained there, toying with me.

Rubbing my eyes, I noticed the rest of the group were up and about, readying themselves for another hike. I untangled my legs from the Solarfleet travel blanket and stood up, straightening my clothes. Cora caught my eye on the opposite side of our fire embers. She was holding her stomach as if she were in discomfort.

I frowned, starting to wonder if this excursion was too much for her. I hadn't asked her how much pain she was in; too ashamed to ask her if she was okay.

Before I could pack my belongings and go to her, Dybgo appeared, pushing a handful of berries and leftover fish at me.

"Eat. We are leaving imminently."

With unnerving attentiveness, he watched me swallow down the unusual breakfast, before ushering me to the edge of the rock verge. I was guided down the rockface by three Akquarians. All of them nodding their greeting courteously as I passed.

As I reached the forest floor, I secured my backpack, checking my weapons were in place. Standing to one side, conversing with Kobe, Rooke looked at me. He raised his hand in greeting and I approached.

"Are you okay?" he asked quietly. "Did Dybgo make a beeline for you when we arrived yesterday? I didn't realise he'd slept next to you all night."

"It was fine. With Oz next to me, he wouldn't have dared touch me."

Kobe eyed me suspiciously and I frowned at him. His sharp brown eyes spilled with disapproval, or was it exasperation? He rarely had time for chit chat but recently he hardly spoke to me at all.

"We're getting closer to the river," Rooke said to me, pulling my attention away from Kobe and his digital maps. "The guide said we should reach it before nightfall. Then, it may take a couple of days to locate the area we've pinpointed."

"Rooke," I pulled him away from Kobe, lowering my voice, "are you sure about this?"

The vulnerability in his eyes instantly resurfaced. He was doubting himself. "What else can I do? I don't know for certain if Solarfleet has been alerted to our situation. We could be trapped here."

I nodded my fragile head. Nux, how much sleep had I actually got last night? The feeling of fatigue was causing my head and eyes to ache. Glancing down at the golden dagger hanging at my side, a sense of uncontrollable fear overwhelmed me. "You know this could be dangerous, really dangerous. I'm concerned Cora's not strong enough. She's not a soldier, Rooke. She appears to be struggling."

Rooke scanned the group, resting his eyes on Cora, who was propped up against a tree, rubbing her stomach. Her cheeks were flushed, her hair a tangled mess of tight curls. She didn't portray the pretty, happy go lucky girl she'd been when we arrived over a month ago.

"I don't think the announcement about Troy has helped," I said.

Rooke watched her for another moment before looking back at me. "Stay to the rear of the group with Oz today. Keep an eye on her."

"Sure."

With gratitude, Rooke squeezed my hand before returning to Kobe to resume their conversation.

With the freshness of the sea breeze far behind us, the air had become sticky and uncomfortable. The only advantage was the Igknamai were less likely to be active when the day was so hot.

We stopped for food around midday but didn't linger. We were back, trudging the red soil before our stomachs had time to settle.

As Rooke requested, I kept to the back of the group with Oz at my side, Dybgo and five of his men behind us. Sweat beaded my forehead, across my chest, and down my back. I'd removed my jacket earlier that morning, tying it around my waist, but without its protection, my heavy backpack had begun to chafe against my shoulders. I sighed, shifting the weight of my luggage, glancing up at the green, towering canopy overhead. I could've sworn the trees were getting bigger. Thicker as well as taller.

It appeared we were in the depths of Igknamai territory now. The majority of green foliage, lower than two metres high, was missing or damaged. The forest floor was littered with dead animals, shredded in ways I wouldn't let myself contemplate. Only the red, mottled tree bark remained untouched.

We climbed a tiered ridge where the earth and trees fell away to the right, exposing a large, twinkling lake far below. The water was a stunning blue, entering the lake by a cascade of trickling channels through the trees. Surrounding the large pool were rocks and lush green grass, dwarfed by the towering trees and rockfaces. If I hadn't known better, it looked the perfect spot to take a swim. With the sweat soaking most parts of my body, the thought was tempting.

Voices ahead caught my attention, and I realised I had stopped walking, lost in the stunning sight calling to me. Oz was now walking with Zamya. Cora ambled behind them, completely oblivious to her beautiful surroundings. My worry for her was growing by the hour. Earlier, I witnessed her trying to discretely vomit behind a tree. Throughout the day, she continually wiped at her face, drying the tears that seemed to fall in abundance.

A gentle hand touched my elbow and Dybgo's voice rumbled, "You need to keep moving."

Continuing to watch Cora, I sighed and slipped back into a steady pace. Dybgo fell in step with me, and I adjusted my backpack again, only soothing my sore shoulders for a fragment of a second.

"If it's becoming an irritant, one of my warriors can carry your bag."

I frowned up at Dybgo. "That won't be necessary."

"You barely slept last night. You must be exhausted."

Why was I not surprised he knew every detail about my restless night? "I'm fine."

I increased my pace, but to my dismay, he matched it. His eyes continued to flick towards me, eventually resting on my exposed left wrist where the golden bracelet remained locked around it. I quickly shifted my hand, snatching Rooke's token up in my palm, obscuring it from view.

"Have you thought anymore about my proposal?"

With his eyes on his claiming token dangling from my wrist, it was obvious what he was referring to. My gaze remained ahead. "Yes. And the answer is still no."

There was a short pause before he said, "Is there a reason behind your stubborn reluctance?"

I huffed a laugh. "Do I really need to explain?" I gave him an incredulous look, only to feel baffled at why he appeared so confused. "Dybgo, I'm not Akquarian. And I have no inclination in becoming someone you can copulate with for a few weeks. It's not going to happen."

"That's not what I want." He pulled me to a stop, and I glanced at his hand gently cupping my elbow. He stepped closer, lowering his voice. "Eden, I'm different. I'm not looking for a mate to last a season. I want something more. I crave a connection, a belonging."

"And you believe I can give you that?"

"Yes."

I craned my neck back to look at his face. He was either an accomplished actor or he sincerely meant every word. The hunger in his crystal blue eyes was suffocating, but there was something more lingering there—hope.

"Dybgo, I'm not the one you seek."

Noticing the warriors at our rear gaining ground, I marched away forcing his hand to fall from my arm. But he appeared at my side in a heartbeat. "Come back to the fortress with me."

"No."

"You must."

"No!"

"Eden, this is ridiculous. If you continue to follow your commander, you *will* die."

A plume of dust rose from the ground as I jolted to a stop. Looking up at him, moisture prickled at the back of my eyes. A part of me knew he was right. But what choice did we have? We were grounded on an alien planet. We wanted to go home. Was that not worth fighting for?

Dybgo's tone softened to a whisper, "I am begging you…come back with me."

"What, so you can make me your wife?"

"Wife is a dull, human term."

I groaned in exasperation, aiming to continue walking, but he pulled me back, prompting me to witness the sincerity in his eyes. "If you come back with me, I will treat you like a goddess. I will worship you. Honour every choice you make. Protect you. Love you."

Completely lost in the romanticism of his words, I stared at him. How was this possible? What was it about me he found so enticing? Yes, we were similar, but we were different species with different principles and values. But I couldn't deny his words felt guileless, his expression full of sincerity. I had no doubt he would love me fiercely, but for how long? I didn't know his agenda. For all I knew we were pawns in a game Havav was playing.

Slowly, I shook my head. "I said no." Dropping my gaze, I marched away.

"Why?"

I ignored the growl of command in his voice, picking up my pace.

"Eden, why? Tell me why!"

Concerned Rooke may somehow hear him from up ahead, I swung round, halting Dybgo's outburst. "Because I don't trust you!"

He looked taken aback. "Is…is this about the Tektrasc incident?"

"No!"

"Then explain!"

"Explain?" I looked him square in the face. "I. Stupidly. Trusted. You! Believing you were my friend, a man of honour. But you lied to me about everything! If you had told me about the full extent of the Igknamai's capabilities when I asked, when I was literally pleading for knowledge, we wouldn't be here right now, acting on desperation and hope, rather than practicality."

258

"I never intended to lie to you. I had my orders."

I huffed, pitying how shackled he was to Havav. "Even you have a choice, Dybgo. Even you."

He seemed to accept my outburst, allowing me to finally place some distance between us. But as my feet stamped across the baren soil, I drowned in the realisation I was a hypocrite. I had withheld information from the crew about Troy because I, too, was following orders. Perhaps Dybgo and I were as similar as he had implied.

Glancing over my shoulder, he was back walking amongst his warriors again. From under his eyebrows, he silently pleaded with me. My place wasn't with him. My family was the crew…and Rooke. They were *my* choice.

Sickened by the feeling of disrepute gnawing away at my conscious, I caught up with Cora. Catching her hand, I cocooned it in my own. She looked up at me with puffy eyes and gave me a forlorn, yet grateful smile.

"Are you okay?" I asked, shamefully for the first time since we left the fortress.

She gently shrugged her shoulders. "I just…I just hope…Troy's alright."

I felt myself frown intensely. "So do I."

We continued up the incline, leaving the sparkling lake far below us. I could sense Cora overthinking, occasionally fighting the urge to cry. I asked her geology questions, hoping it would take her mind off the situation. It worked for a time, until she said, shifting her eyes skywards, "I don't know about you, but I feel like we're being watched."

I peered up at the enormous trees surrounding us and her comment sent a cold shiver down my spine. The red-brown bark contrasted against the green leaves fluttering high above. The trees were far taller than I'd realised. Far bigger than any I'd ever seen before. The trunks were as wide as some of the Akquarian boats, at least five metres in diameter. The thickness of the foliage high overhead was dense. Any creature, big or small, could be propped on one of those branches, in amongst the leaves, spying on us. The thought made my body go rigid and I tightened my hold on Cora's hand. "Come on, let's catch up with the others."

At the top of the vast incline, a towering face of yellow rock protruded from the ground, creating a natural fork in the path. To the left, the ground began to descend deeper into the forest, following the line of the rockface. To the right, the ground rounded down a couple of metres before levelling out to a flat plain of yellow and red soil.

Following Zamya and Oz through the trees, we headed down the bank to the right. An opening appeared, and as we stepped into the late afternoon sunshine, I realised we were in a wide ravine. The ground beneath us was cracked and rippled, as if it had once been the bed of a fast-flowing river. The area was sparce expect for the odd lone tree. Either side, tall trees loomed at the very top of the rockface high above. The rockface itself was at least ten metres high, stretching along the area for miles. For some reason, I didn't feel safe down here. It was too open, too exposed.

The ground crunched under foot as we followed Rooke and Kobe. They were a fair distance ahead. The two Akquarian warriors, who had been heading the group with Llexzus and the guide, passed us, heading back to Dybgo, rotating their position as they constantly did.

A cool breeze whipped through the ravine, cooling my sweaty forehead. Oz stopped to take a swig of water, whilst Zamya and Cora bent down over a cluster of plants. Vaguely registering their conversation about the flower being an unknown species, and why it had been left uneaten when everything else had been devoured, I noticed Rooke and Kobe standing up ahead, peering up at the rockface in front of them.

"Where's Llexzus and the guide?" I called to Rooke.

"Up there," he gestured to the top. "He must've sensed something. They told us to wait here while they check the area."

"We're going up there?" I shouted, eyeing the looming rockface. The surface wasn't completely vertical but there was a lack of obvious footholds and areas to easily climb, especially near the bottom.

"The river is a few miles on the other side."

I glanced along the dried-out riverbed, wondering if it led to the river we were looking for. Surely, that would be the easier option. But before I questioned it, a hissing yelp caught my attention. Zamya was peering at her finger as if she had pricked it on the flower stem.

"I told you to put gloves on," Cora said, kneeling on the floor with her backpack open. "It could be poisonous. I thought you were the one who's overly paranoid about those types of things."

"Ha ha." Zamya stuck out her tongue. "I've got antiseptic cream somewhere. I'm sure I'll be fine."

Amused by their behaviour, I walked back to them. Watching Cora pull thick gloves over her hands, then delicately placing the strange purple flower into a glass pot, I noticed movement from where we'd emerged from the forest. I frowned, realising Dybgo and the Akquarians were nowhere to be seen. Flicking my eyes back to the top of the rockface, I scoured the trees wondering where Llexzus was.

Paranoia struck me hard. This didn't feel right.

"Where are the Akquarians?" I said to nobody in particular. I glanced back to the forest opening and could've sworn blind I caught a glimpse of Llexzus and his scheming grin, disappearing moments before two large, yellow scaled-backed Igknamai stalked down the bank towards us.

I froze, trying to find my breath. "Cora. Get up. Now!" My tight tone caught her attention more than my words did. Following my gaze, I heard her curse on a sob.

"Rooke!" I shouted, aware Oz was now aiming his large gun in the direction of the beasts, taking slow, steady steps backwards.

"What do we do?" Oz called back to Rooke.

We all paused in suspense, watching the beasts slowly amble their way onto the flat plain. More appeared behind them.

We did not hesitate when Rooke told us to run.

Reacting to our sudden movement, the Igknamai roared. I grabbed Cora's arm and launched into a sprint, but Cora's small body seemed to drag.

"My bag," she cried.

"Leave it!"

Oz shot a cluster of lasers towards the monsters gaining on us, turning to run as soon as we made it past him. Rooke, Kobe, and Zamya had reached the same rockface Llexzus had climbed minutes prior. Giving her height to access the ragged, overhung area of rock, I watched Rooke lift Zamya up, but she struggled to climb any higher. The yellow stone was brittle underfoot, showering fragments of dust and sand down onto Rooke and Kobe.

The ground thundered beneath my feet. I didn't dare look back to see how many Igknamai were chasing us down. But Cora did. She whined a sob at the sight, moments before she tripped, taking me down with her.

Hitting the floor with a jolting thud, I flipped my body over, placing myself between Cora and the approaching monsters. Dislodging my gun from my belt, I shot several bullets at them, trying to halt their approach long enough for Cora to get back on her feet. Thankfully she righted herself quickly. I heard her boots accelerating away from me, leaving clouds of dust in her wake.

I smelt the stench of Igknamai breath as one came too close for comfort. I only just made it back onto my feet when its jaws snapped at my backpack. It forcefully tugged at the fabric and for a split second, I was moving backwards instead of forwards.

Fighting the panic overcoming my rationale, my fingers fumbled for the harness around my waist. Unclipping the fastening, I released my arms from the straps and sprinted for my life, leaving my bag in the jaws of the Igknamai.

As I ran, strange wisps of wind passed by my ears, causing me to flinch. I could've sworn something was being hurled at me from the sky. But I didn't look up. It would only slow me down, and I could hear another Igknamai hot on my heels.

Relief jabbed at me as Rooke and Oz pulled Cora up onto the rockface. She was safe. But from the look Rooke threw me, I knew the Igknamai behind me was too close to outrun. He pulled out his gun, but the reluctance to use it was evident, not wanting to hit me in the attempt to stop it. Not that guns seemed to be of any use against these beasts anyway.

Remembering my gift from Havav, my hand reached down to the dagger at my side. As I ripped it from my belt, I heard the beast's galloping feet leave the floor. Projecting onto the sparce ground beneath me, its shadow engulfed mine. I tried to ignore how colossal it looked in comparison; how close it was.

With the dagger grasped tightly in my hand, I drove deep within for every ounce of courage I could conjure up. I swung round, facing the four eyed demon beetle as it flew through the air. Its skeleton fingers reached for my shoulders; its saliva filled mouth open wide. A small whimper escaped me at the sight of its huge, sharp fangs angling for the side of my neck.

Within a fraction of a second before it collided with me, I thrusted the blade between the two middle eyes—the same place Dybgo's spear had perforated, ending the attack on the Parvos weeks ago—and twisted it, hard. Crumbling under its weight, I fell to the ground. The Igknamai thrashed and spasmed on top of me, and I grimaced, watching the light in its haunting black eyes flicker out, as thick, red blood poured out of its wound onto my face, neck, and chest.

As I tried to catch my breath, the sound of laser fire echoed around the area. A scuff of hurried boots, followed by warm hands grabbing at my shoulders, was the only thing I was aware of before I was hauled out from beneath the large, motionless beast. Once my legs were free, I pounced to my feet and sprinted to the rockface, with Rooke close behind.

Oz hauled us both up the side of the craggy wall, barely moments before two more Igknamai snapped and roared at our heels. Standing on a slither of rocks, I leant my forehead against the wall, panting, trying to calm my ragged breathing. Glancing behind me, a dozen Igknamai of various sizes monopolised the ravine floor. Smaller ones ambled at the back, whilst others ripped into Cora and my backpacks, littering the ground with our belongings. The majority of the larger ones reared and roared up at us, pacing along the base of the rockface immediately below.

263

The beast I'd killed sprawled on the floor, blood soaking the area surrounding its head, still with the golden dagger jutting out of its face. Sticks protruded from the scales at the back of its head. A smaller Igknamai lay dead further back, and another appeared wounded, hobbling around. Both had half a dozen of the same objects sticking out of their bodies. I frowned. They looked like arrows.

I glanced up the hazardous rockface. Oz and Cora were halfway up. Kobe was nearing the top, while Zamya crouched on the edge in safety, peering up at the trees, proving the ascend was possible.

"Where the hell is Llexzus?" Rooke mumbled.

"He was back in the forest," I snapped at his naivety.

With wide eyes, Rooke looked up at me. His forehead and cheeks glistening with sweat, his complexion unusually pale. Confusion flashed in his eyes. I pointed to the ravine. "This was a trap, Rooke. Llexzus asked us to wait here while he called them to us."

Trying to convince himself otherwise, he mumbled, "No. No, that's not…"

"Think about it? Where are the Akquarians? They left us here. They left us to die."

"The Akquarians were helping. They were shooting arrows."

"Arrows? The Akquarians don't use arrows! They have swords and spears, never arrows."

He frowned at me, trying to piece everything together.

Without another thought, I began to climb the rockface. The surface was no more than hard clumps of sand and brittle stone. It fell away from my grasp in several places, making the task even harder than I originally anticipated.

A desperate cry echoed around us, followed by an avalanche of sand and stone cascading down from the rockface above. Protecting my eyes, I heard Oz shout Cora's name as a body slid down the uneven surface nearby.

I peered up through the dust. Oz was holding onto the wall, reaching down as if Cora had slipped through his fingers. Now positioned lower than I was, Cora was struggling to place her feet, swinging on her hands whilst sheer panic filled her eyes. Her dangling feet were causing a rise in excitement from the Igknamai directly below.

"Hold on, Cora," I said, attempting to move across the fragile rockface towards her.

"No, let me." Rooke was closer to her than I was, but as he moved, the sand and rock disappeared from beneath his feet. Grabbing the wall, he pulled himself up, securing himself against it.

"Stay there. I'll go. I'm lighter," I said, and began to scale the wall sideways. I made it two steps before the rubble under my feet disintegrated. I scratched at the rock, bruising my fingertips as I slid down. A hand grabbed my wrist, pausing the falling momentum long enough for me to find my footing again.

I peered up and found Rooke holding me in place. His face filled with uncontrollable trepidation.

"Help! Please!" Cora whimpered. "I can't get up."

I glanced down at her. I could see her strength faltering. The sheer look of fear overwhelmed her dainty features. The fight in her body beginning to weaken.

"Rope," Rooke shouted up to Kobe and Zamya at the top. "Get some frigging rope!"

The sound of scurried movement from above trickled down to us, but how much longer could Cora hold? It was taking too long.

I began to move again. Rooke reached for me, objecting to my attempt, but I ignored him. This time I double tapped my chosen footholds before I placed my weight fully onto them. I could hear Cora sobbing—eating away at my nerves.

"Hang in there, Cora, I'm coming."

I cursed as my foot slipped again, but I held my position, searching for an alternative route.

"Eden!" I flinched at the sound of Cora's petrified wail as she slid lower.

I looked down, grasping how much further I needed to go to

get to her. But the sight of an Igknamai pouncing up towards her forced me to freeze. Her scream rippled through the ravine. Frantic, helpless cries from the crew followed as Rooke attempted to move again, but the weakening wall prevented him from going anywhere at speed.

Cora screamed, "Eden! It's got my leg! It's got my leg!"

The rope dappled the surface beside me as Kobe and Oz lowered it towards Cora.

"Grab the rope, Cora! Grab the rope!"

Her hand raised to catch the knotted end, grabbing and grasping to snatch it up. But in a desperate fumble, her fingers continued to miss, suddenly slipping entirely from view. Her haunting scream ripped through me as she fell…

Reaching for her, I felt myself screech her name. But my voice was drowned out by the Igknamais' snarling growls and Cora's harrowing shrieks of pain. Hands grabbed me, holding me still. Subconsciously, I was trying to get to her. Trying to save her.

We all hopelessly watched as she was hauled away by two Igknamai, biting down on a leg each. She screamed, reaching back to us in desperation. Her face was an image I knew would haunt my dreams for years to come.

"Boss?" Oz's tone was tight, full of anguish. "What are your orders?"

With glassy eyes, I looked up at him. He now stood at the very top, holding his rifle in a sniper position. My heart jolted in pain at the situation. We couldn't get to her. We couldn't save her.

"Do it." Next to me, Rooke's voice of command quavered, and I closed my eyes tight.

The sound of a single laser shot shuddered through the air.

Cora's screams fell silent, filling the void with a haunting echo. I whimpered a sob and reluctantly opened my eyes. She was motionless, being dragged across the ravine floor. Her arms and hair sprawled out behind her with a small laser hole sitting in her temple.

The silence was deafening, gut wrenching. I pushed Rooke's hands off me and began to climb the rockface, jolting every so

266

often when the surface shifted beneath me. I felt so angry, so agonisingly useless. I'd failed her. I'd failed my dear, intelligent, beautiful friend. Her stay with the Akquarians had taken its toll on her both mentally and physically. She'd been struggling. She didn't deserve this; didn't deserve to die at the hands of those demons. I blamed the Akquarians. I blamed Rooke for trusting them. I blamed myself for not getting to her in time.

My body weakened as Oz pulled me up the final metre, tears filling my eyes. Finding my feet, a whimper escaped me. I couldn't hold the emotions back anymore. She was gone. Cora was gone!

I rushed into the first set of arms I found—Kobe. He allowed me to sob into his shoulder. His body stiffened but his arms slowly encased my blood drenched body, rubbing my back in a comforting gesture.

Everything other than my thoughts seemed to go quiet.

Kobe tapped my arms, prompting me to lift my head. Peering up at him, I realised his focus was on the wooded area around us. Rooke must have rounded the top of the rockface. I heard him and Oz curse behind me.

Pulling myself free from Kobe's embrace, I met the sharp point of a steel arrowhead. My eyes flicked along the wooden shaft, discovering it was nocked onto a bow, being held by a tall, hooded figure.

Using the arrowhead, the archer gestured for me to step away from Kobe. Slowly, I obeyed. I turned towards them, raising my hands, as another hooded figure pulled my gun from my belt. There were at least eight figures surrounding us, either pointing their hostile weapons at us, or removing ours.

One stepped forward, lowering his bow. Pulling his hood back, I met a pair of sapphire blue eyes, encased in a striking face. Two bright eyes, a nose, mouth, rounded ears, and no pointy canines. His sun kissed skin was dirty and a mass of stubble framed his square jaw. His dark hair was greasy, some hanging over his forehead, resting just below those stunning eyes. The leather armour he wore was brown and worn. His dark cloak and boots were splattered with dried mud.

The realisation hit me hard. He was human. *They* were human. And once again, the Akquarians had kept their existence from us.

To be continued...

Are these people friend or foe?
Will Eden, Rooke, and the crew find their ship? Will they ever get home?

Find out what happens in the conclusion of this story; where opinions collide, morals are shaken, and hearts begin to break.

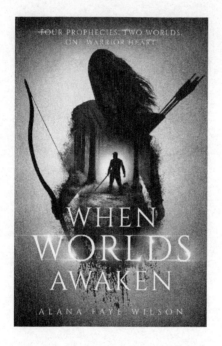

Due for publication early 2024

If you have enjoyed this book, you can leave a review at:

Amazon and/or Goodreads

Acknowledgements

A massive thank you to my husband for putting up with my farfetched, crazy, creative ambitions and for allowing me to be me. I love you—always.

To my darling daughter, who is my biggest fan. Thank you for showing interest and asking questions about my story and my characters. My love for you goes beyond the stars. My biggest hope is that I am as supportive and encouraging to you as you have been to me.

Carly, you are my amazing friend who has continually pushed and motivated me to keep going. You have been my backbone when the self-doubt crippled me; my anchor when I started to lose myself. You are the most encouraging person I'll ever know, and I am so grateful you were the extravert who found this introvert and befriended her.

Thank you to my sister and brother who took the time to read my book (pre-edit) and convinced me to publish. Even though I know you are a tad bias, I still believe we have a sibling relationship where you'd tell me if it was crap. So, thanks for saying it was good.

And lastly, a huge thank you to Jess Runyard, my editor, for spending so many hours helping me polish my work. You are fantastic, your comments are uplifting, and you have the patience of a saint.

And thank you to you, my reader, for taking a chance on reading this book. I hope you have enjoyed it as much as I have writing it.

About The Author

Alana is a Sci-Fi Fantasy writer who has a massive fascination with the universe. When she's not writing, she is trying to be a professional office administrator, although the dream is to become a full-time writer. She loves spending time with her family, going for long walks with the dog, and can usually be found in a coffee lounge. Reading and writing are her escape from the stresses of life. Her other creative passions include music, art, and photography.

Website:
www.alanafayewilson.com

Instagram:
https://instagram.com/alanafayewilsonauthor

TikTok:
https://tiktok.com/@alanafayewilsonauthor

Printed in Great Britain
by Amazon

41472269R00159